I'll Be the One

LYLA LEE

I'll Be the One

KT KATHERINE TEGEN BOOKS

An Imprint of HarperCollins Publishers

Katherine Tegen Books is an imprint of HarperCollins Publishers.

Library of Congress Control Number: 2020930399
ISBN 978-0-06-293692-9

Typography by Molly Fehr
21 22 23 24   PC/LSCH   10 9 8 7 6 5 4 3 2
❖
First Edition

TO MY FRIENDS. I COULDN'T BE
LIVING THIS DREAM WITHOUT YOU.

Chapter One

FAT GIRLS CAN'T DANCE.

It's something my mom said after one of my ballet recitals when I was a little kid. I'd already felt out of place. Even though we were all five, the other girls had somehow already lost their baby fat and had slender, angelic legs and arms while I had a jiggling cherub belly that could be seen from the balcony seats.

I guess a normal kid would have cried. Or gotten discouraged. Or maybe even quit ballet there and then. But instead, I stomped my foot on the ground with as much force as my five-year-old self could muster and yelled at my mom's face, "OH YEAH? THEN I'LL PROVE YOU WRONG!" and stuck with ballet for several years before the snobby prima-donna types irked me enough to switch to hip-hop and modern dance.

I suppose the whole dance thing is a pretty good representation of the relationship I have with Mom. Which is why, instead of telling her about *You're My Shining Star*, the new K-pop competition survival show in LA, I skipped school and rode the train to the audition. Sorry not sorry.

Thankfully, Dad came with me to the preliminary auditions when he was in town last week. He waited in line with me and signed all the parental permission forms, something Mom would never do.

While the open-call preliminary auditions were casual and quick, today's audition line is moving at a snail's pace—probably because everyone is being recorded with the potential of appearing on TV. It's my least favorite time of year—late August, when LA is humid and hot, like the fiery pits of hell. After standing for several hours in the soul-crushingly long line that snakes down Wilshire Boulevard, I'm a panting, sweaty mess by the time I enter the fancy office building where auditions are being held.

"Hi," I say to the lady at the front desk as I wipe away the sweat from my brow. "I'm here to audition for *You're My Shining Star*. My name is Shin Haneul, but my American name is Skye."

For my Korean name, I make sure to say my last name first, like my parents taught me to do. I've always loved both my names, since haneul literally means "sky" in Korean. Skye was just a cool variant of Sky that Dad chose for me when I said I wanted an American name for school. And the name stuck.

The lady at the desk, a fortysomething middle-aged Korean woman who looks as if she could be one of my mom's friends (really, she's dressed *exactly* like them . . . the same black blouse and everything) glances up at me . . . and does a double take. She doesn't even bother to hide the utter shock—and even disgust—in her eyes as she gapes at me.

"Y-you're auditioning?" she asks in Korean-accented English.

I switch to Korean. "Yes, I already got in at the preliminary auditions. Here are my papers, signed by my dad and fully notarized."

"Ah . . . okay."

Still looking doubtful, the lady takes my papers. As I wait for her to check me in, I take off my white-framed heart-shaped sunglasses so I can see the inside of the building better.

Without the rosy tint of my glasses, everything looks a bit stark. The building itself looks pretty old, like it was built in the 1920s. But nearly every inch of the lobby is decorated with brightly colored posters of the celebrity judges and Samsung LED HDTVs looping the promo video for *You're My Shining Star*. The judges are the usual bunch: Jang Bora, a now-retired member of Lovey Dovey, one of those OG K-pop groups from the nineties; Park Tae-Suk, the creator of *You're My Shining Star* and the founder of a top entertainment company in Korea; and Gary Kim, a Korean American rapper who's big in the LA Koreatown scene.

My skin practically buzzes with excitement over the fact that I'm about to see the three celebrities in person. During my audition in just a few minutes, I'm going to be so close to the judges that I'll be able to see their pores—if they even have any pores. My mom always says that Korean celebrities pay extra attention to their skin because HD screens show everything. I don't watch enough Korean TV to know this, but I make a mental note to see if she's right when I walk into the audition room.

Although *You're My Shining Star* definitely isn't the first K-pop competition to have global auditions, it's the first to hold auditions exclusively in America. I can never get over how big K-pop is now. Only eight years ago, people only knew about Psy and the memeable moments of humor in "Gangnam Style." Now, BTS is everywhere, and people from all sorts of different backgrounds are lined up to audition.

On the TV screens, the judges' faces fade to black, and suddenly I'm watching a nervous little kid standing on the stage. Her hair is up in curly pigtails, and she's wearing a bright yellow SpongeBob SquarePants T-shirt. The crowd laughs and says "aww" at her, until she opens her mouth and bursts into a soul-crushingly good rendition of Adele's "Hello."

"Holy crap!" says someone standing in line behind me.

"You've got to be kidding me. We have to compete with *that*?" says someone else.

I shudder. No one mentioned that we'd have to watch the other auditions as we waited in line, but I guess I shouldn't be surprised. This is a competition, after all. And what better way to raise the competitive spirit than to make everyone watch what they're up against?

"You're all set," says the check-in lady in English, bringing my attention back to the front. "Please go stand in line in front of Door Three. The current wait time is twenty minutes. You can also go sit in the audience before or after your audition, just please let a staff member know where you're going first."

I'm confused as to why she's speaking to me like I'm a foreigner—I already responded to her in Korean, which I speak without an accent. But then I notice the way she's looking at me. Eyes drawn together in a slight wince, lips pursed together in a worried pout. There's real fear and distrust in her eyes, like she's afraid that I'll somehow ruin the entire competition by just *being* here. If a bunch of wild animals suddenly burst into the room, she'd probably give them the same look as the one she's giving me now.

For a moment, I wonder if it's worth it to call her out for being rude. Normally, I would, especially since if we were in an American social context, complaining would actually do something. But we're smack-dab in the middle of Koreatown, where all the signs, restaurants, and even banks are Korean. At most, I'd probably get an evil eye from the lady for being a "rude American teenager." It just isn't worth it.

In the end, I try my best to ignore the lady and get in line, opting to stand and wait instead of going into the auditorium. Although it's still annoying, strangers' opinions about my weight are nothing compared to a lifetime of my mom's disapproving comments.

At that moment, the doors swing open and two girls walk in. They're both Asian, and one of them has dyed strawberry-blond hair while the other has a chic blue bob. Their winged eyeliner and lipstick are on point, and they have colored contact lenses that make their eyes varying shades of amber and mahogany.

I stare at them. Everyone else is staring too. Every inch of them is perfect, and their clothes are bright and colorful without being flashy, somehow managing not to cross that fine line between tacky and stylish. Like they've just come from shooting a K-pop music video, the two girls strut toward the check-in counter, their heels clicking in eerie unison on the marble floor.

"Welcome!" exclaims the lady at the desk in bright, chipper Korean. "Right this way! I just need your papers and IDs so I can get you two situated."

Surprise, surprise. I roll my eyes so hard that it's a miracle I don't catch sight of my brain. These girls are the type that my mom—and the front desk lady—would shave Satan's body hair for. If Satan even has body hair.

After they check in, the girls separate so the blue-haired one goes to stand in line at Door Two—the dance line—and the strawberry blonde goes to the line for Door One—the vocals line. I'm auditioning for both, which is why I'm standing in front of Door Three. It seems overly complicated, but after watching people go in to audition, I realize they're alternating between the lines in a neat and orderly fashion.

The strawberry-blond girl turns around and stares at me.

I unflinchingly meet her gaze. That usually does the trick when people rudely stare.

But instead of looking away, she cocks her head to the side, smacking her violet-colored bubble gum between her blue-painted lips. She doesn't look appalled like the lady had, just . . . curious.

"Hi," I say with a pointed eyebrow raise. "I'm Skye. Can I help you?"

Without missing a beat, the girl gives me a bright smile and extends a perfectly manicured hand in my direction.

"Hi," she says. "I'm Lana. What are you auditioning to do: sing or dance?"

Her voice is bright and clear, almost bell-like in a way that human voices shouldn't sound. It reminds me of all those announcers on the Korean news programs that my parents regularly watch. If it weren't for her Valley girl accent, I'd think she was from Seoul.

"Both," I say.

"Ooh, a double talent." Her shiny blue lips widen into a grin. "How interesting. Is that what the third line is for?"

I nod. "How about you?" I already know the answer, but I ask anyway, just to be polite.

"I'm mainly vocals," she says. "I *can* dance . . . just not well enough that I'd want to compete with dancers like *her*."

She gestures at the girl she entered the building with. The other girl shoots a wary look at me before she grins and waves at Lana. If Lana notices the look, she doesn't say anything as she waves back.

"I'm the other way around," I say. "I've been dancing all my life, so I'm honestly better at that. But I sing, too. I've been in choir since I was in elementary school."

"Ooh, nice!" She looks genuinely impressed.

Slowly, I let my guard down and give her a small smile. I'm relieved that this conversation is going better than I expected. I hate to admit it, but some part of me was waiting for her to make a comment about my weight like people often do. It's usually only a matter of time before someone like my mom asks, "How is it that you don't lose any weight even though you're so active?" or "Shouldn't you quit dance and focus on singing? You can't honestly expect to be a dancer with your body type."

Okay, so it's mostly Mom. But as long as I can remember, there've been at least a handful of people per year who ask me similar things. When I was younger, I tried my best to answer these questions, telling people about how everyone was big on Dad's side and how genetics determine body shape more than anything. I told them how my doctor said I was healthy. But no matter what I said, people didn't believe me. Then, I stopped trying to explain myself. It simply wasn't worth my time and energy. And honestly? It shouldn't matter why I'm a certain weight. Being fat doesn't make me any less of a person.

Lana and I watch the TV as some guy gets totally wrecked by the judges for singing off-key. I feel really sorry for him, because it's clear that they only let him through preliminaries so he could be a laughingstock on camera. I'm still thinking about how badly that must suck when I notice that Lana's not looking up at the TV anymore.

Instead, she's staring at *me*.

"Okay, so," she says. "Sorry if this is, like, totally rude, but . . ."

I hold my breath. *Don't ask me about my weight. Please don't ask about my weight.* Things were going so well between us, and I really don't want them to go south now. I brace myself, expecting the worst.

But then she asks, "Isn't auditioning for both things kind of a big risk? I heard that for people who audition for both, the judges won't let you move on to the next round if you're not good at either one of the things. Or they might make you choose one or the other on the spot. No offense, but I could never do that. Too scary."

"Well," I say, trying to relax again, "it's double the risk, but it's also double the reward. If you *do* get in for both vocals and dance, you get one more chance later on when you're eliminated from one category. Yeah, it sucks that they can eliminate me altogether during auditions if I'm only good at one, but if I do get in for both and were to get eliminated from one category during the competition, I can still stay for the other."

Again, Lana doesn't question me. She just stares at me with a curious, wide-eyed look. "Wow, you're really brave," she says. "Best of luck!"

I smile. "Thanks, you too."

Lana turns back to the other line to chat with her friend,

and I face my own line. Someone must have gone in, because there's only one person ahead of me now.

Although I rarely get stage fright, I can feel my hands tremble just a tiny bit. I didn't mention this to Lana, but the biggest gamble I have to make at this competition is whether or not they'll even take me seriously in the first place. Thanks to Hollywood, body standards are already bad enough in LA, but they're even worse in the world of K-pop, where even already-straw-thin girls are regularly asked to "cut a bit off their chin" or "get double-eyelid surgery." I'm neither straw-thin nor do I have double eyelids, so I can only imagine the long list of "suggestions" I'll probably get from the industry professionals.

Lose one hundred pounds! they'd probably say. *Get a nose job! Run up five thousand flights of steps every morning! Feed yourself to the sharks!*

Okay, they probably wouldn't include the last one. But I'd rather do the last one over any of the others on that list.

The thing is, I'm perfectly fine with the way I am. For the longest time, I wanted to be the "perfect" skinny daughter that Mom always wanted. I endured years of diets, strict exercise regimens, juice cleanses, and whatever other health-nut mumbo jumbo she discovered every week. I grew up in Orange County. That sort of thing wasn't really hard to come by.

But now, I'm over it. *All* of it. And if my mom couldn't change me for the last several years, no one can.

Just then, the outside doors burst open again. Screams erupt from outside, and I half expect some bizarre tornado to come rushing into the building. But instead, a massive, almost-seven-foot-tall bodyguard dressed in a full suit and shades steps in, holding the door for someone.

"Ugh," groans Lana. "It's *him*."

The blue-haired girl, whose name I realize I still don't know, also groans.

Whoever this "him" is, he's apparently bad news.

I'm about to ask who he is when it turns out I don't have to. I *know* who he is. In fact, it's really hard to *not* know who he is, because almost every Korean person in LA and most definitely in Korea knows the boy who walks through the doors.

In a way, it's kind of ridiculous how famous Henry Cho is. Unlike other celebrities, he isn't a member of a boy band and he hasn't appeared in a single Korean drama.

I vaguely remember reading an article on a Korean news site about how Henry comes from a really powerful jaebol family, like the ones that appear in K-dramas. Jaebols are basically huge family-led companies that do business across multiple industries like tech, food, and hospitality. That, plus the fact that Henry's mom is a famous actress, definitely explains why people know who he is in Korea.

But it's weird how well known he is here, where most people don't know who his parents are. In the States, the only notable things about Henry himself are that he's rich and ridiculously good-looking. And somehow, this is enough for him to get hired as a model for luxury brands, and his Instagram has over five million followers from all over the world.

Heck, even *I* follow him on Instagram (in my defense, his white Siberian husky is really cute) and just *know* about him, like everyone in the United States just *knows* about the Kardashians.

Let's be real. People probably only follow him because he's hot.

Easily six feet tall, with broad shoulders and high cheekbones softened by doe-like eyes, Henry Cho is just as attractive as he looks in his photos. He was blond in the last selfie he posted, but he's—in my opinion, anyway—impossibly more attractive now with his natural brownish-black hair. Everything from his casually swept-back hair to his pastel-pink button-down and white chino pants exudes "effortlessly cool," while the navy-blue blazer slung over one shoulder makes him look like he just walked out of a shoot for a fashion magazine.

It's close to a hundred degrees outside. Why does he have a freakin' blazer?

The lady at the check-in counter squawks—yes, *squawks*— and nearly trips over her own feet as she rushes to greet Henry at the door.

"Welcome, Mr. Cho!" she exclaims in Korean, bowing deep and low so her head is at the level of her waist. "Thank you for coming to audition."

"God," says Lana, rolling her eyes. "He gets *thanked* for just *showing up* at an audition. Can Henry even sing? Or dance? I really hate how this industry worships guys like him for no reason. Double standards much?"

She has a good point. I can't remember hearing anything about Henry's musical talents, or lack thereof. And to make things even weirder, he didn't even announce that he was going to audition in the first place. You'd think that someone as famous as Henry would make some flashy announcement about this sort of thing. But his last Instagram post, from around three days ago, was a photo of his dog lounging in the sun.

As soon as I think that, I want to slap myself on the forehead. *How and why do I even know that?* Social media really scares me sometimes.

A sudden crash sounds behind us, and a camera crew from SBC, the official broadcasting channel for *You're My Shining Star*, comes running into the lobby, along with Davey Kim, the show's emcee.

Lana and her friend perk up and smile, getting ready for the incoming crew. But the cameras rush right past us, like we're ghosts. From the way they barrel toward Henry, it's a miracle that none of them crash into us.

Davey ambushes Henry with a barrage of questions in Korean. To his credit, Henry answers in a calm, collected manner that makes it hard to believe he's seventeen, only a year older than me. As he speaks, he runs a hand through his hair, flashing the cameras an easy grin.

I can't hear him over the excited yells and squeals of the crowd around him, but whatever he says makes everyone laugh and visibly warm up to him. This guy is a class act.

"Skye Shin?"

I whirl back around to the front of the room, where a lady with a Samsung tablet waits for me outside Door Three.

"Please stand by," she adds, frowning at my puzzled expression.

Right. The audition.

I shudder. It's downright disturbing how my brain completely emptied itself of all other thoughts the moment Henry walked into the room. How could I let myself be so distracted?

He may be a celebrity, but he's just a boy, I tell myself. *You have to focus.*

I shake out my arms and legs, an old habit I kept from when I first started dancing. Everyone else is also busy warming up, so I didn't think I'd be eye-catching until I notice that *Henry Cho* is staring at me from across the room with an amused look on his face.

Heat rushes into my cheeks, but I ignore it and quickly turn away as I continue to warm up. I can't let some cute BTS wannabe distract me from the real reason why I'm here. I practiced countless months for this. I sang and danced every moment I could get in between homework and school.

Taking a deep breath, I follow the lady through the door.

Chapter Two

BACKSTAGE IS A CHAOTIC MESS. WORD OF HENRY'S arrival must have spread, because people rush back to where I came from to get a glimpse of him. Whether it be *American Idol* or *America's Got Talent*, or even Korean competitions like *K-Pop Star* and *Show Me the Money*, they always either skip or fast-forward the footage as the contestants walk backstage, and now I know why. The people who *aren't* obsessing over Henry Cho are all panicking, shouting in rapid Korean and firing directions at each other so quickly that my head spins. Bright lights flash overhead as the stagehands adjust the lighting onstage. Even from where I'm standing backstage, I can hear the loud chattering of the audience.

"Please wait here until the cameras start rolling again," the tablet lady says, sounding tired. She points at a blue taped-on X at my feet. "The judges are having a little break. I'll let you know when you can go onstage."

She taps at the earpiece in her ear.

I nod as my heart begins pounding in my chest. Other than the final episode, *You're My Shining Star* is prerecorded, but today, there is still a studio audience made up of various staff members and the hundreds of other people who showed up to audition. A handful of K-pop stars from PTS Entertainment—Park Tae-Suk's company—also sit in the audience, just so their fans will tune in to the show to see their reactions.

I've performed onstage countless times for my school events, but this is the first time I'll be performing in front of a camera that doesn't belong to my dad—who still insists that camcorders are better than phones—and the other parents who record our shows.

I wonder what my parents' reactions will be if they see me on Korean TV. Although we live in the US, our family subscribes to the special feature on our cable service that lets us watch Korean channels. I know Dad would be so stoked to see me on TV. But Mom? I'll be lucky if she doesn't ground me for a week. Knowing her, she'll probably squeeze her eyes shut and turn off the TV the moment she sees me, her biggest embarrassment—no pun intended—onstage.

"Okay, they're ready for you," the tablet lady says, interrupting my thoughts. She hands me a mic and waves me through. "Please walk over to the big X in the middle of the stage and wait for the judges to address you."

My heartbeat only grows louder with each step I take as I make my way out from backstage. The moment I'm within view, everyone stares. A few boys in the front row nudge their friends so that they, too, are gawking at me with their jaws dropped wide open. Some even laugh, like I'm the funniest thing they've ever seen.

Great. Okay. So they're going to be like this too.

For a split second, I'm afraid that this competition only let me advance through the preliminaries so people could laugh at me, like they did with the tone-deaf guy. It's disgusting how this is even a possibility, but on Korean TV, making fun of fat people isn't that uncommon.

One good thing about going to school in the States is that people don't subscribe to the same body standards as Asian media does. In performances at school, no one cares that I'm plus-size—or at least, they know better than to say anything or visibly react to it—because there are plenty of people who are from all sorts of backgrounds and have different body shapes. In Korean media, though, almost all the girls are super skinny. And if they are anything above a size 2—or, God forbid, a size 16 like I am—they're either comedians or supporting characters that are there to make the audience laugh and make the main character look pretty. Fat girls can only aspire to be the comic relief.

But I'm not here to make anyone laugh. I'm here to win.

I hold my head up high. So what if they're laughing at me now? They aren't going to be in a few minutes.

The judges, at least, are professional enough not to react like the audience does. But even though they're subtler about it, their reactions aren't exactly positive. Park Tae-Suk, the producer, raises an eyebrow at me. The other two, Jang Bora and Gary Kim, stare at me in stunned silence.

All three judges look surprisingly normal, and definitely not as larger-than-life as they seemed on TV or on promotional posters. I'm not sure I'd even recognize them if I passed them on the street. Sure, Park Tae-Suk, who's known for his eccentric outfits, is wearing a teal suit that clashes with his hot-pink tie. And Gary Kim and Jang Bora are dressed in cool, street-fashion-type clothes that make them look like they're about to drop the next hottest Korean hip-hop album. But aside from their designer clothes and professionally done hair and makeup, they actually look . . . human.

Which is a weird thing to say, I know. Of course they look human. They *are* human. But I always thought celebrities were on a whole other level from us mere mortals, who could only worship them like the ancient Greeks worshipped the gods. But now, I can see the tired black circles around Jang Bora's eyes, the wrinkles on Park Tae-Suk's face, and the sweat dripping down Gary's face, as if the room is a bit too warm for him.

Celebrities . . . They're Just Like Us! I always see tabloids with clichéd headlines like that, but I guess I never thought it was really true until now. In a way, it's oddly comforting. It makes me think that one day, I could be one of them.

I give them my best smile and bow deep and low, facing the judges and the audience.

"Hello," I say into the mic, properly introducing myself in

Korean. "My name is Skye Shin. I am sixteen years old and live in Orange County."

I may be my mom's greatest disappointment, but at least I'm not a heathen. Korean culture has its own standards of proper behavior about things American people don't even think about. Rules about bowing and properly introducing yourself would probably feel like trying to juggle while playing Twister if my parents hadn't drilled them into me since I was a little kid.

"Hello, Miss Shin," says Bora. Her voice is a bit higher—but not any less pretty—than it sounds on TV. "It says here that you're going to sing *and* dance for us today. Is that correct?"

As she says it, her lips twist into a slight smirk. It's barely noticeable, but it's enough to make me clench my fists. The audience's reaction as I walked onstage already shattered the ease I felt while I was talking to Lana. And Bora's smirk wipes away the remaining traces of it. It's clear from the way she's looking at me that she expects me to be a complete joke.

Fine, I think. *Just one more person to prove wrong. Added to the list.*

"Yup," I say in a cheery voice. If I have to pretend to be oblivious, at least for the time being, then so be it. "I'm dancing first, and then singing. Ready when you are."

A stagehand takes the mic from me and everyone waits in hushed anticipation, all eyes on me.

Park Tae-Suk nods and raises a hand.

The opening beats of my dance track boom out across the

auditorium, explosively loud and aggressive. They shake every nerve of my body and completely overwhelm me. I can't hear my own heartbeat, and it's probably for the best. I don't need anything to distract me from what I'm here to do today. Not even the frantic beats of my own heart.

Fat girls can't dance. I hear Mom's words in my head, over and over again like a broken record.

Well, Mom, I'm here to prove you wrong.

I jump forward and begin moving with the beat.

Chapter Three

DANCE ALWAYS HAS A FUNNY EFFECT ON ME. One moment, I'm all jittery and anxious about being onstage, and in the next moment, it's like someone has turned off all sections of my brain except the parts that control my muscles and ears. I'm the music and I'm the confident, bold movements of my arms and legs. Nothing else.

I've never rehearsed this choreography onstage before, but I adapt quickly, taking full advantage of the space by stomping and sashaying across the wooden surface. I pump my arms up and down to the beat of the girl-group power song I chose as my accompaniment. Instead of hearing my heartbeat, I *feel* it, like my chest is about to explode with energy that flares up inside of me from head to toe.

The crowd is completely silent at first. Shock and confusion flash across people's faces. But as I enter the chorus, a few and then a whole lot of people start cheering me on, until soon, the noise of the crowd is a deafening roar that only adds to the flames burning within me. I catch a glimpse of the guys who'd snickered at me just a few minutes ago. They aren't laughing now. They're still gawking, but they look more like they're about to have a heart attack.

I'm just about to wrap up my routine when Park Tae-Suk raises his hand.

The music cuts short. I recover quickly, sliding into a resting position so I'm standing on both feet. I'm panting and sweaty, but I directly meet the judges' gazes as I wait for them to speak.

I don't have to wait long. Park Tae-Suk sits back in his seat and picks up his mic.

"Miss Shin," he says in Korean. "When did you first begin dancing?"

His face is completely expressionless, so I don't have the slightest bit of idea about what he thought of my performance.

"I've been dancing since I was three," I say after a stagehand gives me back my mic.

Park Tae-Suk raises his eyebrows. "Impressive. And are you going to sing for us next?"

I nod.

I grip my mic tightly as I look out into the audience. I have everyone's attention now. Countless faces look back at me with varying expressions of mockery and awe.

The piercing opening notes of my accompaniment flood the auditorium. In contrast to my dance piece, which was fast and explosive, this music is a slower song that I specifically chose to show off my vocal range. Slow songs are always a gamble, but I made sure to pick an interesting song, a Korean rock anthem from the eighties that starts soft but gets loud and powerful in the chorus.

The moment they hear the opening notes, the older members of the audience sit up in their seats, their faces lighting up with recognition. Again, Park Tae-Suk raises his eyebrows. Bora doesn't react, but Gary gasps, leaning forward in his chair.

I first heard my audition piece when Dad was drunkenly singing karaoke at one of our many family parties. He couldn't reach any of the high notes but tried his best all the same, so he ended up sounding like a dying pterodactyl. It wasn't that Dad is a bad singer—he was actually the best among the people at the party—it was that this song is so freakin' hard, since it was originally sung by one of the greatest heavy metal legends in Korea.

Unlike Dad, I can reach all the notes. Or at least, I could when I rehearsed this song over the last few months. Although my heart starts to thump loudly in my chest again, I'm determined to sing this song just as well—if not better—as I did in the practice rooms at school.

As I sing, the expectant faces of the crowd fade away, replaced by all those years of going to choir events with Mom. Singing is the one thing Mom has supported me in throughout the years. She actually shows up to all of my choir concerts and even signed up to be the choir booster mom, which is a stark contrast to how, aside from the first few ballet recitals, she never went to a single one of my dance events in the last thirteen years.

I almost wish my mom *didn't* come to my choir events, though, because whenever she comes, she always makes these little remarks like, "You know, maybe it's a good thing that you're a bit on the large side. Like Adele! The additional girth must really help with the singing," and, "Honey, God gave you a big body for a reason. Maybe you should consider quitting dance and just stick with choir instead."

I never have the courage to actually speak up against Mom, because I know from experience that she'll come back with another hurtful comment. I've gotten in the habit of saying "mhm" over and over again until she stops talking, even though every word she says feels like a sharp needle piercing my skin.

Enough. I bring myself back to the present. I take a deep breath and let my voice take flight, so it soars above the thundering guitar and drums of my instrumental accompaniment. Fueled by the frustration and hurt I felt during all those conversations with Mom, I not only reach but blast through the high notes, like I was born to sing this song.

The crowd gasps. From where I'm standing onstage, I can see people staring back at me, transfixed. Some are even crying.

I'm about to close my eyes and fully immerse myself in the music when I catch sight of camera flashes coming from the crowd. But it isn't me that people are taking pictures of. Instead, they have their phones locked on Henry Cho, who's staring at me from where he sits in the audience.

They're taking pictures of him *with the flash on*. During *my* audition. Rude.

Despite the people around him, Henry's attention is 100 percent focused on me. His eyebrows are knit together in a slight frown, and his eyes look so sad, like he's fully immersed in the emotions of my song. When our gazes meet, I look away, my face flaring up in an undeniable blush.

Park Tae-Suk raises his hand. The music cuts short again, and I refocus my attention to the judges' faces.

Gary Kim is beaming. Park Tae-Suk and Bora, however, are still stone-faced.

I squeeze my hands into fists. It's the end of my audition. If they're not reacting positively now, it probably means that I didn't do well.

"Wow!" says Davey, popping onstage to stand in front of me. "That was an amazing performance. Everyone, please give another round of applause for Skye!"

People cheer, but the applause is scattered. Everyone knows that the lack of reaction from the judges is a bad sign.

Bora is the first to speak, daintily lifting the mic to her dark-red lips.

"Miss Shin?" she says. "You're talented, but would you ever consider losing weight? As someone who was a member of a girl group for five years, I can most definitely tell you the

25

camera adds ten pounds, and I'm afraid you're a bit too . . . rotund."

Gasps and whispers come from the audience, but no one outright boos or speaks out against her. I think about what'd happen if this were a Western talent show, try to think if there are any instances where Adele or Susan Boyle were outright fat-shamed on TV.

My blood boils. I'm embarrassed, yeah, but I'm also really, really mad.

I angle the mic right at my mouth so my words come out loud and clear.

"No," I reply. "I will definitely not. If I'm accepted into this competition under the condition that I lose weight, I'd rather not participate."

The whispers intensify. For a moment, I start to wonder why I'm here. I question why I worked so hard for this when people aren't even going to take me seriously.

The tension in the auditorium is palpable by the time Park Tae-Suk chimes in. "Although I respect your . . . confidence, I do have to agree with Ms. Jang, albeit for different reasons. As the head of PTS Entertainment, I've helped countless trainees become stars, but I have also been there to witness the ones who don't make it. Being a K-pop star requires a lot of discipline and hard work. And there just isn't anyone . . . your size in this industry. And if there was, they didn't last long. It's regrettable, but true. Is there any particular reason *why* you're so strongly against losing weight?"

The judges look expectantly at me, and suddenly, I'm back in our living room, watching a Korean talent show similar to *You're My Shining Star* with Mom. Because Mom is a sucker for anything related to fame and glory, it was a sort of mother-daughter tradition for us to watch talent shows together whenever they were in season. Since Mom was always busy working, I looked forward to this special bonding time with her, even though she sometimes pointed out contestants to provide me with "extra motivation" to lose weight.

"Look, Haneul! Look how pretty that girl is!" she'd say. "Everyone loves her! You can be like that too. We just have to figure out a way to get you to exercise more and eat less!"

And of course, every time she said that, she'd be talking about yet another skinny girl with perfect makeup and impeccable fashion taste. A girl who was a size 0 and looked nothing like me.

But when I was in seventh grade, everything changed.

I exhale slowly and start talking.

"A few years ago, when I was in seventh grade," I say, making direct eye contact with the judges, "a plus-size girl won a Korean talent competition similar to *You're My Shining Star*. I was so happy because it finally felt like fat girls like me could do anything they wanted to do. But during the first year of her debut, the same girl changed right before my eyes. In each Instagram post, news photo, and TV appearance, she was thinner and thinner, until one day, there was a breaking news story about how the girl was hospitalized for malnutrition and exhaustion. When they interviewed her, she said it was 'for her fans and her career,' and my own mom used her as an example of what I could be like if I 'tried a bit harder.'

"After that, I vowed to enter a K-pop competition and never change myself like that if I got in. That's why I'm here now. I want to show people that it's okay to not be model-thin and exhaust yourself to the point of hospitalization. That girl failed me, so I want to be my own hero."

By the time I finish, the entire audience is silent.

Bora opens her mouth, looking like she's about to protest, when Gary grabs his mic. He's been so completely silent this entire time that I almost forgot there was a third judge.

"Well," he says, giving me a huge smile, "you are clearly talented, so it's a yes from me. While it's true that the industry generally only has a . . . specific body type in mind, I think it's time to shake things up a bit!"

He slams his hand on the round button in front of him, and sparks fly above my head.

Only a few people cheer.

From beside him, Bora rolls her eyes and mutters, "You are *so* American."

She then turns to face me with a dead-set glare.

"Sorry, I'm going to have to say no," says Bora. "It's nothing personal, I'm just being realistic. Letting yourself gain weight like that signifies a lack of discipline. And being a K-pop star requires a lot of discipline and *not* that extra drumstick at the chicken place."

Did she not listen to a word I just said? I bite my lip to stop myself from snapping back at her, reminding myself that this is going to be on TV. Everyone from all over Korea and other parts of the world will see if I yell at Bora and give her a piece of my mind. So instead of replying to what she said, I nod at her curtly, which is about as polite as I can be right now.

Everyone turns to look at Park Tae-Suk. His eyebrows are raised again, but now, he's slightly grinning, like he heard a funny joke.

"Well, well," he says. "I guess it's down to me."

I swallow. My hands are shaking, but I try not to show any nervousness on my face. The last thing I want is for my mom to comment on how scared I look when this episode airs. If she even watches this episode.

"You're presenting me with an interesting conundrum, Miss Shin," continues Park Tae-Suk. "On one hand, I think you are brave and definitely very talented. I totally agree with Gary there. But on the other hand, I also agree with Miss Jang. I know firsthand what kind of rigorous discipline is required to make it in this industry. We push our artists, unapologetically, because we expect them to be superstars of not just Korea but the entire world. And like I said before, not everyone can handle that. In fact, most people can't. You're not the first plus-size girl to stand up on that stage and tell me that you can handle the pressure. Many have gone into training before you and ended up dropping out. How can I trust that you will be different?"

"I won't quit." I clutch the mic tightly between my hands, trying to think of what I could say that'll convince Park Tae-Suk to believe in me.

"If I quit," I continue at last, "I'll have to admit to my mom that she was right after all these years. And that'll never happen."

"Right about what?"

"That fat girls like me can't dance. That fat girls like me can't be up here onstage killing it like everyone else. You just saw me up here. You *know* I'm good. You said it yourself. So, please, just give me a chance. I can do way better than I did today. You haven't seen anything yet."

A quirk appears in the corner of Park Tae-Suk's lips. It's almost a grin. "Is that so?"

I nod, because I've already said everything I could think of saying. My brain and heart feel empty now, as if I've poured out my entire soul.

From beside him, Bora shakes her head. The two whisper to each other for what seems like an eternity. Park Tae-Suk frowns, and my heart sinks. I brace myself, expecting the worst as he finally turns to face me.

"You better prove your mother wrong, Miss Shin," says Park Tae-Suk. "Because you just made it into *You're My Shining Star.*"

He slams his hand down on the button in front of him, and for a moment, all I can see are bright lights.

Chapter Four

ON MY WAY OUT, I SPOT LANA, WHO'S STILL AT the front of the vocals line.

"You were *ah-mazing*," she says, drawing out the last word. "Everyone in line was cheering for you. No one could take their eyes off the TV screens! And that speech you gave at the end? A masterpiece. Did you rehearse that ahead of time? Because, man, if they don't use that as one of the highlight features for the audition episodes, they really don't know what they're doing."

"Nah," I say. "It all just came tumbling out. And honestly, that seems unlikely. Let's be real. There's probably going to be a fifteen-minute feature just on Henry Cho."

Lana snorts. "True. You should have seen what happened after you left. Everyone insisted that Henry cut to the front of the line. It was either that or they were acting like they were best friends with him and saying they 'saved a spot for him' or something. Thankfully, Henry just opted to go wait in the auditorium, but it was still one of the most pathetic things I've ever seen."

"Ugh. Meanwhile I stood in line at seven a.m. just to get my spot."

"Yeah, and thank God you got in! Tiffany and I had to wait in line outside for a long time too, but luckily we could switch off when one of us needed to go to the bathroom."

Just when I process that Tiffany must be the name of her blue-haired friend, my phone starts vibrating in my pocket. I check the caller ID. *Mom.*

"I have to go," I say. "Good luck with your audition and hopefully I'll see you at practice!"

"See you," she says with a smack of her gum. "And yeah, hopefully. Hey, want to exchange numbers? I'll text you if I make it in, I guess, since the show isn't airing until October."

"Sure."

I hand her my phone, feeling reassured that if Lana makes it in, I'll at the very least have one friend in this competition. Even though I know friendships are usually short-lived in cutthroat competitions like *You're My Shining Star*, it still makes me feel a bit better that I won't be going into all of this alone.

Plus, she's really pretty in a way that makes my bi heart squeeze a little. If I were allowed to date girls, and if my parents knew I wasn't straight, I'd totally date her.

A hand with black-painted nails reaches out and plucks my phone from Lana's grasp. I follow the hand up to see the girl with the blue bob—*Tiffany*, my brain reminds me.

"What's this?" she says. "Lana, you're not cheating on me, are you?"

Her voice sounds like she's joking, but her eyes are wary as they flicker toward me.

"Of course not, sweetie." Lana gives the girl a light peck on the cheek. "Tiffany, this is Skye. Skye, this is Tiffany, my girlfriend."

Tiffany gives me a self-satisfied smirk as she slings her arm around Lana's shoulders. I know it's meant to make me jealous, but all I can think right now is: *Oh my God, they're queer like me!*

I'm grinning really widely, and I can tell from Tiffany's confused face that this isn't the reaction she was expecting. But I can't help it. I'm just that happy. The LGBTQ Students Association at our school has plenty of queer girls, but none of them are Asian except me. Although I know queer Asian girls exist *somewhere*, I was beginning to lose hope of the possibility that I'd ever find them.

"It's so nice to meet you," I say, trying my best to not sound like a creep. I finally manage to control my face so I'm no longer giving them a weird grin, so there's that, at least.

Tiffany crosses her arms.

"Okay, what's up?" she says. "Why are you acting like this?"

Even Lana looks a bit concerned, although she doesn't say anything herself.

33

"We don't really have any other queer Asian girls at my school," I say. "At least, none that are out. Sorry, I know I probably look like a weirdo, but it's just so nice to see people like me. Like, freakin' *finally*."

Lana bites her lip, looking nervous for the first time since we met. "Oh," she says. "We're not exactly out. I mean, all of our friends know, and so do our families, but if we were *really* publicly out . . . I'm not sure if we'd even have a chance at this competition."

"Wait, but then why did you tell me?"

Lana shrugs. "Figured we could trust you. Besides, the way you were looking at me? It wasn't very hetero."

"Oops."

Both Lana and Tiffany burst out laughing. Despite my embarrassment, I join in, because there's no denying that I was totally checking Lana out.

At that moment, a staff member calls Lana's name.

She lets out a quick breath. Tiffany gives her a tight hug.

"Good luck, babe," she says. "Sing your heart out."

Lana smiles sweetly at her, then gives us both a little wave before heading to the stage.

I wave back. "Good luck!"

My phone vibrates again. Tiffany hands me back my phone.

Crap. I forgot about Mom.

I say goodbye to Tiffany and run out of the now-crowded building. The lines are now ten times longer than they were when I arrived.

"Haneul?" Mom's voice is frantic and sharp with worry when I call her back. She's the only person who still actively uses my Korean name, even though everyone else—including Dad—calls me Skye. "Your school called and said you didn't show up today. What's going on? Where are you?"

I sigh. Here we go.

"I just got out of an audition," I tell her, since she's bound to find out eventually.

A pause. "Did you try out for *You're My Shining Star*?"

"You know about it?"

"I heard a few of my customers talk about it. There was a spike in the number of appointments in the past few weeks since everyone wanted their skin to be in the best condition for the competition."

"Oh."

"Well? Did you get in?"

For a split second, I consider lying to Mom. I'm still kind of jittery from my audition, so I don't want to have this conversation with her at this very moment. But not telling her the truth now will probably only make things harder for me later on, especially since I'll have to attend the rehearsals every week. So, I slowly say, "Yeah."

"Oh, Haneul!" Mom says. The happiness in her voice is so genuine that it startles me. "I always said you have a good voice. You could be the Korean Adele!"

I wince.

"I didn't just audition for singing," I say. "I also auditioned for dance. I got in for both."

Silence. Any other parent would probably be even prouder of me, since it's twice as hard to get in for both than to get in for one category. But Mom doesn't say "I'm proud of you" or even "congrats." Instead, she says, "Oh, I see."

Her tone is completely different from just a few moments ago, when she'd been all bubbly and friendly. Instead, it's eerily flat, like her voice always gets when she's on the verge of yelling at me. But she doesn't yell. She just stays silent, and I wish we weren't talking on the phone so I could see the expression on her face.

"We can talk about it when I get to your studio," I say, when it's clear she isn't going to say anything else. "I'm about to hop on the metro right now."

"All right. See you soon."

She's going to try to talk me out of the competition. I can hear it in her voice. Before she can start, though, I hang up and run down the metro steps.

Mom's studio is only one metro stop away, but on this simmering-hot day, even that short trip is pretty soul crushing. The train is full of sweaty people who look just as miserable as I do. It smells like pee and the seats are sticky, so I stand and wait for the train to come to my stop.

My mom is one of the top aestheticians in LA, which means that she gives facials and does makeup for everyone, from all our family friends to major celebrities. It's how she single-handedly supported our family—working long, twelve-hour days six days a week—after Dad lost his job a few years back.

So, in a way, I get why she's so obsessed about my appearance. Her job is to literally make people more beautiful. But it still stings that she never thinks I'm beautiful the way I am now.

By the time I walk over from the metro stop to Mom's studio, it's five p.m., but it's still really hot and humid. I run inside, and I feel like I've died and gone to heaven when the cool AC air hits my face.

"Uhseo ohsaeyo!" Sally, Mom's secretary, greets me in cheery Korean. When she sees that it's me, her expression immediately changes to one of an older sister worrying about her baby sister. I'm an only child, but Sally, who's worked for Mom for five years and babysat me for the first two of those five, is the closest I have to an unni—an older sister. "Skye, are you okay? You weren't walking outside, were you? It hit one hundred degrees today!"

"I was," I groan.

"Were you really auditioning for *You're My Shining Star*? Your school called, and I had to transfer the phone to your mom!"

I nod, too tired to talk anymore. My head's starting to spin, so I plop myself down on one of the couches in the reception area. It's super nice, and the fabric is just as soft and smooth as it was when we first got it. I'm still dripping with sweat, and I belatedly realize I'm probably going to leave sweat stains on the fabric. But Sally doesn't say anything to stop me, and I'm too exhausted to get up.

"Did you get in?"

I nod again, vaguely surprised that Mom didn't tell her. It occurs to me that she might be so ashamed of me that she won't tell anyone. I feel sick, so I close my eyes.

"Here," says Sally. Something cool touches my hand. I open my eyes to see Sally holding out a glass of cold water for me. "Your mom is with her last customer, but in the meantime, have some water. You *really* don't look good."

A prickle of discomfort rises up inside of me as I think about the many times I've seen American movies and Korean variety shows make fun of the "fat, sweaty kid." In Korean shows especially, there are sometimes even laugh tracks and sweat droplets digitally drawn onto people's faces so viewers at home can laugh at how out of shape and breathless the fat people are. Even though I'm usually comfortable in my own skin, and even though a skinny person would be just as sweaty in the sweltering heat as I am, I can't help but wonder if that's what Sally's thinking when she says I *"really* don't look good."

I finish my water in just a few gulps, drinking so fast that I have to gasp for air when I'm done.

"Wow, that bad, huh?"

I nod, for what I hope is the last time. I love Sally, but sometimes she asks way too many questions. I rest my head back against the couch and close my eyes, pretending to fall asleep.

"Haneul-ah?"

I open my eyes at the sound of Mom's voice. I'd fallen asleep for real.

"She must have gotten heat exhaustion," says Sally. She hurriedly hands me more water.

I drink, slowly this time, wanting to make the glass of water last. As long as I'm drinking, I don't have to talk to Mom.

In some ways, Mom and I are exactly the same, and in others, we can't be more different. We have the same round, dark-brown eyes, the same button nose, and the same slightly wavy black hair. But she's petite, while I'm big-boned and sturdy like Dad, and she still wears soft kohl eyeliner and lush pink lipstick like an ABG—an Asian baby girl—while I usually only wear a pastel pink lip gloss and light mascara. The only reason I'm wearing red lipstick and heavier makeup today is because I knew I was going to be up onstage.

The thought of my makeup nearly makes me groan. I've sweat so much that I probably look like a sad half-melted clown right now.

Mom grabs the wooden office chair from Sally's desk and sets it down in front of me. When she's seated, she says, "So. You skipped school to go to a K-pop audition. Which . . . okay, I just wish you would have told me in advance. I could have at least called the school to get you excused."

"You wouldn't have let me audition," I say flatly. "Especially not for dance."

"Well." Mom huffs but doesn't correct me. "I just don't want you to make a fool out of yourself on TV, that's all. Heavens, Haneul. Imagine what Karen-imo would say if she saw you galivanting onstage in—in *that*." She pauses to wave her hand at my clothes for effect. "Or even all your imos and gomos in Korea!"

You mean, the same imos and gomos that you're too ashamed to let me visit in Korea? The response pops up in my head, although I don't say anything aloud.

Although here in the States I have lots of imos—maternal aunties—who are actually just Mom's friends and aren't really my blood relatives, I have tons of real imos and gomos— paternal aunties—that I haven't seen in person since I hit puberty. I asked countless times if we could visit Korea, but every year, Mom always made up some random excuse until it became clear what the real reason was. She's too embarrassed of me and, more specifically, my weight.

Usually, I just close my eyes and let her go on and on. But today, especially after what I endured from Bora earlier, I'm too fed up to stay quiet. I look Mom straight in the eyes and say, "My outfit is perfectly fine. I'm just wearing a sports bra and leggings."

Although I normally wear flashier things onstage, I wanted the audience to focus on me and my skills as a performer today. So I opted for a chic black sports-bra-and-leggings set from Torrid, one of my favorite plus-size-friendly brands. I look sleek and sexy in my outfit—or at least I did before sweat-pocalypse happened—and I know it. It's not my fault people like my mom think that fat people wearing tight or revealing clothing is "inappropriate."

"People watch that show all over the world, not just in the United States and Korea," Mom continues like I never said anything. "Does it really not bother you that everyone will see you dance with your arm flab shaking all over the place and your belly jiggling like Santa Claus? The least you could—"

Something clatters loudly onto the floor and Sally gasps, "Omo!"

When Mom and I turn to look at her, she sheepishly grins. "Sorry."

A glass lies shattered by her feet. Water's splashed all over the floor, and some of it seeps into Mom's plush rug.

"Sally, be more careful! Are you hurt at all?" Mom's attention immediately focuses on Sally, momentarily forgetting about me.

"I'm fine," Sally replies. "Sorry, Ms. Kang, I'll clean everything up right now."

When she walks past me to get paper towels from the bathroom, Sally gives me a wink. I shoot her a grateful look.

Mom, oblivious to our little exchange, bends down and says, "Here, let me help."

As they clean up the mess, I slowly exhale, feeling like I can finally breathe again for the first time since Mom started talking. I get up to help too but Mom shakes her head at me.

"We're done," she says. "It wasn't that big of a mess. I'd rather you worry about the things that actually matter, Haneul. Like that competition. Is it too late for you to call them and ask them to pull the footage?"

Sally freezes from where she'd just thrown the glass shards into the trash can. I pause too, wondering where this is coming from. Can't Mom just let this go? But of course, she can't. She's my mom. And I know exactly what kind of person she is.

"I don't want them to pull the footage," I say. "I think I did great. And I got in, for both singing *and* dance. If *some* people can't see past what I look like to see how good I am, it's on them."

"Well, honey, just because you got in, it doesn't mean they have to use your footage."

I abruptly turn to face her. "They do, Mom. They always use the footage for the people who get in. They're only accepting the top one percent of thousands of people auditioning this year. Can't you just be proud that I made it?"

I don't mention the fact that most of those thousands of people were weeded out during the preliminaries, which I couldn't have auditioned for without Dad. The last thing I need is for Mom to get mad at Dad because of me.

"I—" Mom starts, falters, and then tries again. "I *am* proud of you. I just think you should care more about how you look. Do you really not care that people might make a laughing-stock out of you?"

I think about the hours I spent in front of my bathroom mirror this morning. Today was a special occasion, but there was a time when I used to always spend several hours in front of the mirror, wishing I could "fix" myself. Every time I looked, something seemed off about me. But I could never tell what. It wasn't just that I wanted to be skinnier and prettier, like Mom wanted me to be. Everything seemed *wrong*. I cared so much about how I looked that nothing was okay.

When I steel myself to talk again, my voice is low. "Caring more about how I look is the last thing I need right now. And if people want to laugh at me, well, let them. I'm still going to win. I'm going home. You don't have to write me a note if you don't want to. We're allowed one unexcused absence."

I'm almost out the door when I hear a scribbling sound from behind me.

"Here," Mom says. "Use this as an excuse letter. And don't be ridiculous. I'm done for the day, so I'll drive us home in a bit. You can go wait by the car."

She holds out a piece of paper with her signature on it like it's a peace treaty.

I take it, unsure what to say except, "Thanks."

"Have you eaten yet?" Mom asks all of a sudden. It's such a complete one-eighty from the way she was fat-shaming me just moments before that I need a few seconds to recover. Asking if someone's eaten is a common way for Korean people to show we care for one another, but it feels so out of place in this current moment.

"No," I say. "I will when we get home."

"All right. You really shouldn't skip meals, Haneul. We're

not in North Korea. Think about how lucky you are compared to the poor, starving children."

"Okay," I say through gritted teeth. That's the frustrating thing about Korean moms. One moment, they're telling you that you need to lose weight, and the next, they're shaming you for not eating.

Mom gives me a small nod before closing the door.

Chapter Five

"SO, DID SHE TELL YOU TO DROP OUT OF THE competition?" Dad asks as I walk to school the following Monday.

I have my earphones plugged into my phone, and I'm Face-Timing Dad like I do every Monday morning before school. Luckily our neighborhood is pretty quiet, so I've never gotten hit by a car or come even close to it. Not yet, anyway.

Dad now works in the Bay Area, so he only visits us every other weekend at most, since he has to fly down from San Jose. I do miss him from time to time, but our weekly calls are usually enough.

"Yup," I say. "You should have heard her voice when I told her I auditioned for the dance portion, too. It was like I told her I murdered someone."

Dad chuckles. "That's just your mom being your mom, Skye. I, for one, am so proud that you got in. For both vocals and dance."

"Thanks, Dad."

His words make my heart hurt a bit less, even though it doesn't really help with the fact that he's almost never home while *Mom* is the one who I have to deal with every single day.

"Your mom grew up in a way different culture than you and me," Dad continues. "You've got to understand that, you know?"

"I know."

Dad always says stuff like this to me, like it's his second job to remind me that unlike the two of us, Mom was born and raised in Korea, where her parents brought her up with extremely high expectations during a huge recession. When he used to live with us, he was better at calling Mom out when she fat-shamed me. But since he moved away, he's been more about "keeping the peace." I think he just wants to enjoy what little time he has with us, minus the drama.

"I'm almost at school," I say. It's somewhat true. I'm still a few minutes away, but from where I'm standing, I can see the orange-red Spanish-style roofs of the high school. Besides, it's not like my dad can tell if I'm lying or not. From the way I'm holding my phone, he can only see my face.

"All right, well, I'll talk to you later," Dad says. "I have to go to work, anyway."

"See you."

When I walk into school, it's like nothing's changed. And I guess in a way, nothing has. Not yet anyway. Even though I got into *You're My Shining Star* this past weekend, no one else will know about it until the show premieres in two months. And even if it airs, it's not like the majority of the school will care. Although BTS is pretty popular now, most people in our school probably don't even know what K-pop *is*.

I go to the cafeteria, which is bustling with people.

It doesn't take long for me to spot my usual group of friends, since one of them—Clarissa Han—has bright auburn hair. Our school's dress code is strict about the colors we can dye our hair—natural colors only!—but it isn't really specific about the shade. And Clarissa took full advantage of that by dying her naturally black hair the brightest red she could manage.

Clarissa and my other best friend, Rebecca, are playing Rebecca's Nintendo Switch. Technically, game consoles aren't allowed in school, but we're usually allowed to play before classes start as long as we don't take them out in the classrooms. I've never really been into games, but I always like watching my friends play, since it gives me something to do before the school day starts. Today, they're playing Pokémon.

The three of us have been best friends ever since we were in the same homeroom class in fifth grade. All three of us haven't been in the same class since, but we've stuck together as much as we could, hanging out whenever we can. None of us really have any reason to get to school early, but since we all have different schedules, hanging out at the cafeteria before school is our daily tradition.

Rebecca pauses the game when I sit down next to her and says, "So. Did you really audition? How did it go?"

"Yeah," I say. "It went okay. I got in."

"You *what*?" Clarissa squeals, hitting me in the arm. "Oh my gosh, congratulations! You go, girl."

My friends' faces light up with surprise and pride. Mostly surprise. I realize that my own friends didn't think I could actually make it into the competition. It stings, just a bit.

"I heard *Henry Cho* showed up to the audition!" Clarissa continues. "How was he? Was he really good?"

"Yeah, I saw him."

"You *what*?" Rebecca exclaims.

"Did you get a picture of him?" Clarissa jumps in. "Or an autograph?"

I wave a hand at my friends. "Guys, guys, chill. No, I was too busy *auditioning* for my own place in the competition to do anything like that."

Rebecca and Clarissa exchange looks. Clarissa's eyes are still kind of wide, like an excited puppy's, but Rebecca calms down and clears her throat.

"Right," she says. "So, when are they airing the episode?"

"Mid-October," I say. "That's when the show premieres. Although honestly, I don't know how much of the footage they'll actually use from my audition. I guess I'll just have to see."

"Well, you made it in, didn't you? I'm sure we'll see at least one glimpse of you. They'd be complete fools to leave you out." Rebecca gives me a small, playful nudge, and I grin.

"Wait," says Clarissa. "They'll probably show Henry a lot,

right? Is he big in Korea like he is here? Do you—*ow!*" She winces as Rebecca elbows her in the ribs.

"Let's try to be a little more supportive, all right?" Rebecca says. "Skye might become famous one day. This is only just the beginning."

"Right," Clarissa says, rubbing the place where Rebecca elbowed her. "But can you get me Henry's autograph, on the off chance that you see him?"

I sigh, taking in the bright, hopeful look in her eyes.

"Fine," I reply. "No promises, though. I don't even know what he auditioned for."

I don't mention that it doesn't really matter, since I got in for both. I'm salty about the fact that Clarissa seems to care more about Henry than she does about me.

"Dance!" Clarissa chirps. "Official footage hasn't come out yet, of course, but I saw people's Instagram stories. He was *amazing.*"

She sighs dreamily, and I can tell from the definitely-more-restrained-but-still-admiring look on Rebecca's face that Clarissa isn't the only one who has a crush on Henry. She's just more transparent.

"Fine," I say again. "I'll get Henry's autograph. *If* I happen to bump into him or something. But I won't go out of my way to look for him. I have better things to do."

"Of course," Rebecca says with a sharp nod. "You prioritize you first, okay? This is just if you have time during your breaks or something."

Clarissa squeals. "You're the best! Thanks, Skye!"

At that moment, the bell rings. Everyone gets up from their seats. Both Rebecca and I have AP Psych for first period. The room is pretty close to the cafeteria, so we're in no rush to get to class. Instead, we just stay near our table and watch as Clarissa fights her way through the crowd leading out into the hall.

"I always tell her she should leave before the five-minute bell, since her first class is on the opposite side of school," says Rebecca. "But she always forgets."

"Yeah . . ."

"For the record, I don't care *that* much about Henry. He's . . . okay, fine, he's hot. But you're my number one, okay?"

"Thanks, Rebecca."

I give her arm a light squeeze.

But even after we're settled into our seats in psychology class, and even after Mr. Peterson starts his lecture on operant conditioning, I still can't forget how Clarissa cared a lot more about seeing Henry Cho than she cared about my audition.

I'll just have to show her I'm better, I think. I have no idea how good Henry is, but he probably only auditioned to gain more social media followers. No matter how good he really is, he's my competition, and I've worked way too hard and too long to lose to someone like him.

We might have both gotten in, but in the end, everyone will be talking about me.

~

About halfway into fifth period, I get an email containing detailed instructions on the next steps for *You're My Shining Star*, along with our rehearsal schedule and elimination-round dates. Since we're allowed to have our laptops out during history, I sneak a quick look at it while pretending to take notes.

It's a long email, but it's pretty straightforward and summarizes our schedule at the very end. There are "boot camp" rehearsals every Saturday, alternating between vocal and dance each week—which means rehearsals every weekend for me. Three Saturdays are devoted to elimination rounds, leading up to the live final elimination. The competition schedule itself looks like this:

8/29	First vocal boot camp session
9/5	First dance boot camp session
9/12	Round one eliminations (TBD: Top 20)
10/10	*You're My Shining Star* premiere (episodes air every Sat. at 6 p.m. PST)
10/17	Round two eliminations (TBD: Top 10)
11/7	Round three eliminations (TBD: Top 5)
11/28	No rehearsals or elimination rounds (US Thanksgiving holiday weekend)
12/5	Final round (live broadcast; TBD: #1 from each category)
6/6/2021	Winners start training at PTS Entertainment in Seoul

It's pretty daunting, but I'm glad they're only flying us out to Korea if we win. As long as we're in LA, I can still go to school. And I still haven't even worked out how I'm going to get to practice every weekend.

A text message pops up on my screen.

LANA MIN: Hey, did you get the schedule???

It's only then that I remember that I exchanged numbers with Lana back at the audition.

ME: Yeah!

LANA MIN: FORGOT TO TELL YOU EARLIER BUT TIFFANY AND I BOTH GOT IN TOO! ISN'T THIS SO EXCITING?

I grin at the all-caps message, and then immediately regret it when Ms. Blankenship says, "Miss Shin? Is there something funny you'd like to share with the rest of the class? I'm hoping it wasn't about colonial diseases. Because there's nothing funny about disease, and especially not smallpox, one of the deadliest diseases in human history."

There are a few snickers from the rest of the class, but they're cut off by a sharp glare from Ms. Blankenship.

"I think we're due for a pop quiz. Everyone, clear your desks. You have Miss Shin to thank for this."

Everyone shoots daggers at me. But instead of being mortified, I'm still a little giddy about the prospect of going to Korea. Even though LA Koreatown *is* like a mini Korea in and of itself, I still want to visit to see how everything's changed since I last went.

Ms. Blankenship passes out the pop quiz. It's printed on

bright blue paper that's still warm from the copy machine, so I know she's been planning to give us one all along. She only used me as a scapegoat.

It sucks, but I have bigger problems right now. The most pressing one being that I need to figure out how to get to LA every week when I don't even have a car. The truth is, I never expected this to be a problem, because I didn't think I'd get in for both vocals *and* dance. Dad promised to give me a ride, since he's home every other weekend, but now I have to figure out how to get to LA on the weekends Dad isn't here.

Even though I'm old enough to drive, I never learned because of Mom. Whenever I brought up the idea, she'd asked, "Why are you in a rush to learn how to drive? I learned to drive when I was thirty, after I got married and had you. School is close enough to walk from home!"

Dad and I tried to explain to Mom about how the culture is different here in America, where everything is so spread apart that you can't do everything by just walking around and taking public transportation like you can in Korea, but she never budged. Dad promised to teach me, but he never got around to it. I guess it's hard when he's almost never here.

Ms. Blankenship clears her throat as she walks by my desk, and I belatedly realize that she's already finished passing out the quiz. There's no way that Mom will let me stay in the competition if I do badly in school. Deciding to worry about everything later, I push all thoughts of *You're My Shining Star* out of my head and focus on the paper in front of me.

Chapter Six

THE FIRST DAY OF BOOT CAMP IS IN A WEST LA
recording studio, which is about an hour away from my house.
Dad's not coming down from San Jose until next weekend,
and Mom left early for work in the morning, so I end up asking Lana for a ride. Luckily, our house is on her way from
Irvine to the studio.

On the outside, Lana's car looks pretty normal. It's a Toyota
sedan, like the ones all my friends' moms drive. But when I
open the door to the passenger side, a pair of pink Converse
sneakers tumbles out, almost hitting my feet.

"Sorry!" says Lana. "Tiffany and I drove down from Nor-
Cal, so my car is still a mess."

I hand her the sneakers, and she chucks them into the back
seat, along with a few other things. She's moving too fast for
me to see everything clearly, but I could have sworn I saw
a rubber duck and at least five to-go boxes. I decide not to

comment on the mess and instead just say, "Hey, thanks for driving me," as I get in the car.

"No problem!" Lana gives me a bright smile before she pulls into the highway. She's as dazzling as she was in the auditions, with her reddish-blond hair done in long curls that elegantly spool out to her shoulders. This time, her lips are a magenta red and are incredibly shiny in a way that makes me wonder how she manages to get them to stay that way. At this point, I'm convinced that she's just magic. If little cherubs sing out in a heavenly choir every morning this girl gets up from bed, I wouldn't be surprised.

Traffic is pretty light, or as light as it gets in LA. Even though there are cars lined up in every lane of the highway, we're at least still moving. Typical LA traffic is bad enough to make every brave soul have a nervous breakdown while on the road.

"It's Saturday morning." Lana groans, resting her head on the steering wheel. "Where are all these people going?"

"Brunch?" I suggest, although I really have no idea.

We live less than thirty miles away from LA on the map, but I rarely go up north to the city because I can't drive.

"So . . . are you guys from NorCal?" I ask after a few minutes, breaking the awkward silence. "But you live in Irvine now, right?"

"Well, I'm originally from down here but went up north for college," Lana replies. "And my parents moved up with me because, well, they have no sense of boundaries. Right now, though, Tiffany and I are staying with one of my Irvine friends for the competition. It's honestly a relief. We live together up north, but our parents live there. They're always trying their best to separate us. It's really annoying."

I bite my lip, because I know this is probably what would happen if I ever dated a girl, too. I've thought about it plenty of times, and sometimes I'm attracted to girls more than I'm attracted to boys. But there's no way my parents would be okay with it. Korea didn't have a Pride festival until 2000, and even now, groups show up to Pride just to call people "sinners." Police have to be present to make sure no one gets hurt.

Things might be better with the younger generations, but my parents are still way too old-fashioned to be okay with me dating a girl. If anything, they'd probably think it was a phase until I "met the right guy."

My heart aches just thinking about what kind of hurt Tiffany and Lana must have suffered from their families. I can tell she's trying to be cool about it, but there's a slight quiver in Lana's lips as she stares resolutely at the road ahead.

"How long have you guys been dating?" I ask, trying to steer the conversation to something happy. "How did you two meet?"

It works. Lana beams. "We've been dating for two years. Met at an intro to music theory class in our freshman year. She asked if I could help her make a music video of her dancing for her friend . . . but it turned out that that 'friend' was *me*. Then she asked me out at the end of it! The video was the cutest thing I've ever seen in my life. I'll show you sometime!"

I can't help but laugh, because it's so clear by how fast and how excitedly Lana talks that she really, really loves Tiffany. I'm very happy for both of them, even though I do feel a slight twinge of jealousy that this is probably the kind of relationship I'll never be able to experience for myself.

"Hey, we're here!" Lana says, and I startle awake. I must have fallen asleep for the rest of the way.

The studio looks like a pretty normal brick building, with tall brown doors and long columns that make it seem more like a bank or museum. If it weren't for Lana's phone telling us we've reached our destination, I would think we got lost somewhere along the way.

"Apparently a *lot* of famous people worked here," Lana says, lifting up her Gucci sunglasses to get a better view. "Lady Gaga, Rihanna . . . and even people like Bob Dylan and Ringo Starr."

I already knew that from looking up the studio's website yesterday, but just hearing it out loud makes everything feel so much more real. My skin tingles with excitement as I think about working in the same space that all those famous artists did.

"A friend of mine works for the competition behind the scenes as a techie, and he told me that apparently the *You're My Shining Star* staff had to reserve the place nearly a year in advance for us," Lana continues as we walk toward the entrance. "I don't even want to think about how much money went into booking this place."

Inside, the studio is much nicer than it looks on the outside, with wood-paneled walls and gleaming rows of gold and platinum records commemorating best-selling albums and soundtracks that were made in this very building.

The studio staff ushers us back to a large conference room where the other vocalists who made it into the competition are sitting, along with Gary Kim and Park Tae-Suk. Since I didn't stay long enough to see who else got in, I don't recognize anyone except the Adele-singing SpongeBob-shirt girl, who's sitting at the middle of the table wearing yet another Sponge-Bob T-shirt—this one is pink and has the "F Is for Friends" song lyrics on it.

"Great," whispers Lana. "The child prodigy is here. Might as well give up now."

Everyone, including the judges, is dressed in normal street clothes, so the camerapeople standing with their backs against the wall are the only indicators that this isn't just a normal meeting. Although most of the people are Korean, or at least Asian, there's a handful of Black, Latinx, and white contestants. Since the competition is specifically a Korean music show, people who aren't fluent in Korean were required to audition with K-pop songs. From what I heard, a lot more non-Korean people got into the dance category since they didn't have to deal with the language barrier.

"Welcome, ladies," Park Tae-Suk greets us in Korean. "We're waiting on a few more people, and then we will begin."

He checks us off on his tablet and then hands each of us a sealed envelope. Both of our envelopes are personalized, with our names written in fancy cursive.

The conference room is about the size of one of my classrooms at school, barely big enough for the forty people who supposedly made it into this first round. Most of the seats are taken and it's pretty tight quarters, and I can't help but notice the way some people stare at me as I try to squeeze my way through to an empty seat.

I'm fat and I take up space, but that's okay, I tell myself, repeating one of the mantras I always say to myself in moments like this. *I'm allowed to take up space just as much as anyone else.*

"Move!" Lana yells to a guy who's manspread all over a row. "We're obviously coming through, and there's clearly two empty seats next to you, so it's not rocket science for you to get up and let us through."

The guy stumbles out of the way, a baffled look on his face. Lana rolls her eyes as we settle into our seats.

"Men," she hisses quietly so only I can hear her. "They always expect us to move for them, but they never think to move for *us*. This is why I only date girls. Like, I honestly don't get the appeal."

"Lana, I love you," I say. "In a friend way, of course."

She winks at me. "Girl, you know it."

Someone else comes in while we're getting settled, and I count the number of other vocalists in the room. Thirty-nine, including Lana and me. We're still missing one person.

I look down at my watch. It's twelve fifteen p.m., and we were supposed to have started at twelve. Park Tae-Suk must have thought the same thing, because he looks down at his smart watch and exchanges a look with Gary. Gary only shrugs at him, and Park Tae-Suk turns to face us.

"Well, hello, everyone," Park Tae-Suk says in English. "My name is Park Tae-Suk, but you can call me Mr. Park. If the last individual doesn't show up in the next five minutes, we have no choice but to disqualify her. Please note that we are being lax since this is the first day of practice. In future practices, you are expected to come exactly at noon."

Everyone says, "Yes, sir," and shifts uncomfortably in their seats. A few people look relieved, though, like they're glad that there's one less person in the competition.

Just then, there's a crash from outside the room. People shout, and rapid footsteps approach us from across the hall. Through the glass walls of the conference room, I see Henry Cho turn the corner, storming about like he owns the place.

What's he doing here? I could have sworn Clarissa said that Henry got in for the dance part of the competition, not vocals.

Everyone gapes as Henry opens the door and peers into our room, rapidly glancing this way and that like he's looking for someone. His hair is disheveled, and his face is full of panic and hurt—the complete opposite of the blasé coolness he gave off the last time I saw him. I'm struck by how different he looks now, and I realize this is my first time seeing him as an actual human being and not as a model in an Instagram post or a celebrity addressing his fans.

The camera crew in the back of the room immediately jumps into action, repositioning themselves so they're facing Henry. They're eating this up.

Shooting them a glare, Henry closes the door and ducks out.

More footsteps come from down the hall, and a blond white girl walks into view, yelling at Henry.

The sound is too muffled by the thick glass walls for me to make out exactly what she's saying, but I can tell she's talking really fast. Mascara runs down her face, and her eyes are all puffy, like she's been crying for the last several hours. Henry, on the other hand, stays silent, his jaw set in what looks like barely suppressed anger.

"Oh wow, that's Melinda Jones!" says one of the other girls in the room. "She was in last month's issue of *Teen Vogue*! What *happened* to her?"

It's only then that I recognize the girl outside as the sun-kissed blond-haired model I frequently saw on Henry's Instagram stories. I remember reading some rumors online about how she and Henry broke up a few months ago, and I guess those rumors were true. Henry and Melinda look like they can't stand each other.

The camera crew rushes out of the room to capture footage of the fight.

"Oh God," I hear Gary say from behind me. "What is up with all this drama? You'd think this was *Keeping Up with the Kardashians*."

Henry and Melinda freeze when they see the camera crew. And then, as if they weren't fighting just a few seconds before, Henry reaches over and wraps his arm protectively around Melinda. She curls into him, and I'm wondering how she forgave him so fast when Henry turns her around so she's facing away from the cameras. Melinda still looks pretty mad, but her anger is mixed with fear and unmistakable gratitude.

Henry makes conversation with the camera crew, casually running a hand through his hair while the other one still holds Melinda. I can't see his face from where I'm seated, but I can tell from the way the camera crew is laughing that he's working his charm again.

He's protecting her, I realize as I stare at the strange scene unfolding in front of us. Even though I barely know Henry, I can't help but feel a bit proud of him. A lesser guy would have just let Melinda be or even walked away from the whole thing.

Finally, Mr. Park walks out of the room and comes back with Melinda.

"This is Miss Melinda Jones. She's our final contestant for the singing competition this year."

Melinda quickly wipes the mascara from her face and greets us all in accented Korean. "Ahnyeonghaseyo. I'm Melinda. I taught myself Korean, so I'm not very good, but I can speak it well enough to sing it."

Switching back to English, she goes on to explain how she first got interested in Korean culture through BTS and other boy bands. While she's talking, I can't help but glance back to look at Henry, who's still in the hallway.

Henry's alone now, since the camera crew followed Melinda into the conference room. He looks so drained, and there's no trace of the smile he gave the camera as he stares down at his feet. Suddenly, he stiffens and looks up. It's only when our eyes meet that I realize I was watching what was supposed to be a private moment.

Like a startled deer, Henry stares wide-eyed at me before briskly walking away.

"So much *drama*," Lana whispers into my ear.

I nod in agreement, wondering what the heck just happened.

After Melinda finishes talking, we each go around and introduce ourselves. Everyone is mostly from LA and Orange County, although there are some people from other parts of the United States. Most of the Asian contestants are Korean American, like I guessed, although some are Chinese, Vietnamese, or Japanese. My brain admittedly tunes out after the fifteenth-or-so person, but I do catch some snippets. A girl with green hair sings trot, a more old-fashioned and rhythmic type of Korean music. One of the Latina girls lived in Korea for longer than I have and is really into Korean hip-hop bands like Epik High. And of course, there are a ton of people who are BTS Army and hope they can meet the members one day.

Once we're all done, Gary claps his hands.

"Welcome! Welcome," he says. "For this first round, all of you have been sorted into groups based on age and/or similarity in vocal style to even out the playing field for the members in each group. From there, we will pick the best of you, or, if none of the members are worthy of moving on, we will eliminate the entire group. There will be ten groups of four people. However, this isn't an exercise in group dynamics. That will be tested later. In this round, everyone in the group will be individually practicing and performing. They will just be onstage at the same time and be compared against each other. Before anyone says it, let me be up-front and say that yes, this *is* a ploy to eliminate people faster."

He laughs, and there's some nervous laughter around the room.

"We're not just being cruel, however," Mr. Park chimes in. "This method has been proven to be very effective and efficient in pinpointing the best and worst of you. The K-pop industry grows more saturated every day. If you don't stick out in a group within this setting, you will never stick out in the actual industry."

Gary then leads us in a brief session of vocal warm-ups, before telling us to open our envelopes.

From my envelope, I pull out a small slip of paper that says 3.

Lana leans over and whispers, "Hey, what did you get?"

"Three. How about you?"

"Same! I guess our styles *are* pretty similar."

I grin. This whole group-elimination round sounds scary, but I'm glad I at least know someone in my group.

"Please proceed to the practice room that corresponds with your number," instructs Mr. Park. "The rooms are large, so you are encouraged to spread out and use earphones to individually practice your songs. If you don't have your own earphones, please ask the front desk for a pair. You may choose any song from either the Korean or American pop genre for this first round."

This is it, I think. *Let the competition begin.*

My heart thumping loudly in my chest, I head to our practice room.

Chapter Seven

THE TWO OTHER GIRLS IN OUR GROUP TURN OUT
to be Isabel Martinez, the girl who said she had lived in Korea,
and Melinda, Henry's ex. Since we only have this one official practice to select and practice our song for the elimination
round, everyone starts working right away, each of us sitting
against one of the four walls of the practice room.

Like everyone else is doing, I pull up music on my phone. I
already know what song I'm going to do—it's a song I know
by heart and always wanted to perform if I got into a K-pop
competition. But I could still use a refresher and need to figure
out how to reinterpret it in my style.

I'm well into my fifth sing-along of Lee Hi's "1, 2, 3, 4" when
I notice Melinda hovering over me. This is the first time I've
seen her up close, so it takes me a second to recover from just
how flawless she is.

If Lana and Tiffany look like they could star in a K-pop
music video, Melinda looks like she could be in a music video

with Taylor Swift. I think she *was* in a music video with Taylor Swift, or was at least one of her backup singers. I still remember how her photos with Henry on Instagram looked like spreads from a fashion magazine.

"Um," I say. "Can I help you?"

"Oh my gosh, ahnyeong," Melinda says. "That is such a good song. And Lee Hi, what an inspiration, right?"

Trying really hard not to laugh at "oh my gosh, ahnyeong," I say, "Yeah. She's pretty amazing."

"You especially must find her so inspiring. She was fat-shamed so much, but now look at her! She's doing so well for herself! Pretty and thin, too!"

And just like that, Melinda's put herself on my list of enemies.

"She wasn't fat, but yeah, people did fat-shame her, which sucked," I say, trying to keep my tone civil. "Being fat and pretty aren't mutually exclusive traits, though. Fat people can be pretty, pretty people can be fat."

Melinda stares blankly at me, like I'm speaking a foreign language.

"Okay," she says slowly. "By the way, do you want to eat lunch together during our break? I brought some kimchi. It's *so* good for you."

I can't believe a white girl is telling me that kimchi is good for me. It's really weird, since she knows I'm Korean. Why would she think it's okay for her to explain to me about my own cultural food?

"Kimchi with what?" I ask, more out of morbid curiosity than anything.

"Pardon?" She blinks in confusion, and I don't know whether to groan or laugh.

"You're not supposed to eat kimchi by itself. If you do, it's the same thing as eating ketchup by itself. You're supposed to eat kimchi with rice."

Melinda scrunches up her nose. "I don't eat rice. I'm on a no-carb diet."

I don't know what to say after that, so I look around the room to find both Isabel and Lana staring at Melinda. Isabel has a look of horrified fascination on her face, while Lana has a hand over her mouth like she's suppressing a laugh. They both shoot me a sympathetic look before we all get back to work.

Melinda, thankfully, returns to her spot soon afterward.

Well, I think. *That's one person I won't feel bad about winning against.*

Lana has some errands to run with Tiffany after practice, so I ask her to drop me off at Mom's studio.

"See you in two weeks!" Lana says as I get out of her car.

"See you! Thanks for driving me!"

She blows me a kiss before speeding away, and I'm left alone to deal with Mom.

The logical part of me knows I really shouldn't expect Mom to mention the boot camp at all, but at the same time, some part of me hopes she'll give me a chance to talk about it, even if it's just with a simple "How was your day?"

But when I enter her studio, she only says, "Oh, you're back."

She doesn't ask how my day was, and she doesn't even ask where I've been. Without a second glance back at me, she rearranges some purple orchids in a vase on Sally's desk.

"Where's Sally?" I ask, since she's nowhere to be seen.

"She had to go run some errands. Today's a slow day, so I told her she could take care of them and come back later," Mom replies, still looking at the orchids like she's talking to them and not me.

"I see." It's the only thing I can think of to say.

Sally is usually the one who fills the gaps in conversation between Mom and me. She's the bridge between us that makes us seem like we're at least acquaintances and not just total strangers. But the truth is, we barely know each other.

I make myself comfortable at Sally's desk and pull up some homework from our school's Google Drive. This is what I usually do on Mom's slow days, and it's how I used to do most of my homework as a kid when Mom didn't want to leave me alone at home. Sally never minds; in fact, Mom and she always encourage it because they know all my schoolwork is online.

Despite how strained things are between Mom and me, this routine feels familiar. Comforting, even. Physics is as confusing as usual, and I'm so caught up in one of the questions that I don't notice that Mom is staring at me until she says, "Haneul, we have to talk."

Immediately, my hands clench into fists as I look up at her, all traces of whatever comfort I was feeling gone with just those five words. For some reason, she's unhappy with me again. I can see it written all over her frowning face.

"Do you really have to go to dance *and* voice practice?" Mom asks. "I read the email you forwarded me, and it sounds like you'll have to go to LA every weekend. I suppose, next week, your father can drive you, but what about after that? How on earth are you going to get there?"

I should have known this was coming. Luckily, I already worked out the kinks with Lana during our drive back.

"My friend Lana said she could drive me on the weekends Dad's not here," I say. "It works out, since she lives in Irvine. She can pick me up on the way."

"I see."

I don't tell her that our arrangement only works for as long as both of us remain in the competition. It *is* a pretty obvious predicament to have, but if Mom suspects anything, she doesn't show it. I expect her to say more, but she just goes back to rearranging the orchids. She's moved them back and forth in the same exact place multiple times already. I don't know which is worse, her explicit disapproval of me dancing in the competition or this passive-aggressive show she's putting on now.

I wonder if she'll even acknowledge the show when it airs.

After watching her rearrange the flowers for a bit more, I get out my earphones from my bag. If she doesn't want to talk to me, fine. I'm not wasting any more time waiting for her too.

Sally comes back later in the day, while Mom's with one of her afternoon clients. She only has to take one look at my face before she says, "What did Ms. Kang say this time?"

I groan, but not loud enough to be heard over the classical music blaring out from the facial room.

"She was giving me a hard time about the competition again."

Sally gives me a sympathetic look. "Sorry, Skye."

"It's fine," I say, even though it's not.

I go back to my homework—APUSH just might be the death of me this year—and I'm about to put on my earphones again when Sally says, "I can't understand why she can't be more supportive of you. I mean, she's shown me clips of you dancing and singing. You're so talented!"

"She's shown you clips of me dancing?" I ask, momentarily taken aback.

"Yeah, she has them on her phone."

I'm struck speechless. Before he moved to NorCal, Dad was the only one who ever showed up to my dance performances, so I always assumed Mom didn't care about that part of my life. It's not totally unbelievable for her to have seen the videos Dad recorded. After all, knowing him, Dad probably made her watch them. But for Mom to have the videos saved on *her* phone? It's enough for me to doubt whether Sally and I are talking about the same person.

"Oh," Sally says. "You didn't know she has them."

"I didn't know she even *saw* them."

Sally sighs. "She's watched all of your performances. And shown me a couple. I really do think she's proud of you, in her own weird little way. She's just too afraid of other people. And what they might think. I'm not saying that this makes the things she says to you okay. None of what she says is okay. I just . . . spend too much time with her, I guess. Since it's usually just her and me in this office all day."

"She's mean to me because she's afraid of . . . other people? How does that make sense?"

Sally comes over to where I'm sitting in front of her computer. "Scoot over for a second."

I immediately get up from the seat, because after all, it's her desk.

As I watch, Sally navigates through several nested folders until she finds one labeled "old family photos" in Korean.

I frown. I didn't know these even existed.

Sally nervously glances back at the closed door of the facial room before whispering, "Don't tell her I showed you these, okay? She usually only opens this folder after she's had some wine after a particularly exhausting day."

She clicks on the folder, and then on one of the first image files. It's simply labeled "03_15_1989."

72

I have to blink a couple of times to believe what I'm seeing.

"Is that . . ."

"Yup, your mom," Sally says. "She was fat, like you."

The girl in the photo looks like a miniature version of me. She's a bit younger, maybe twelve or thirteen, and she's shorter, too. But other than that, she's a dead ringer for me. Or, I guess, I'm a dead ringer for Mom. And she's beaming at the camera while happily lounging at the beach in her swimsuit.

Mom's rail thin now, so skinny that you can clearly see her collarbone and ribs. And I don't think I've ever seen her smile like that. Not in person.

"What *happened*?" I flip through more of the photos, just in case the first one was a fluke. But the girl is there again. And again. In one of them, she's playing with a cute white dog, while in another, she has her arms linked with her friends in front of what must be her old middle school in Korea.

Why has Mom never shown me these? I wonder as I keep flipping. But I know why. She wanted to hide this part of herself from me. From everyone.

As I flip, I get flashes of the things Mom has said to me throughout the years.

Haneul, don't eat so much! Think about what everyone will think of you when you're freely eating like this. Haneul, what will everyone think if you're wearing such tight clothing? Americans might think curves are sexy, but not Koreans. Everyone will think I'm a bad mom!

73

For Mom, what "everyone" thinks of me is always more important than what I want. "Everyone" could be our neighbors, our relatives, or even my friends. Regardless of who she's talking about, she's always scared about what other people might think of me, like everyone in our lives is scrutinizing my every move. *Our* every move.

And now, seeing Mom's pictures makes me sad. She looks so happy in them, and I wonder what happened to make her so afraid of what "everyone" thinks of us.

"I think she was bullied in high school. Like, a lot," Sally says, as if reading my mind. "The only time she's talked about it was when she had a bit too much to drink, but yeah. Things were—still are—really different in Korea. The antibullying rules are more lax there, or at least, they were back in the day. And in Korea, people think the ideal weight for a young woman is one hundred and ten pounds. If you're any heavier, people give you a hard time about it. Including family and friends."

The photos suddenly stop.

Wordlessly, Sally navigates out of that folder and into the next one. The photos in this folder are labeled with the year, 1998. Sally clicks on the first one.

The girl with the easy smile is gone. Instead, there's Mom in her twenties, and she's every bit the model-thin woman with steely eyes that I've always known. And she's not alone. Suddenly, Dad's there with her, ever his goofy, smiley self. I recognize UCLA in the background, although I know Dad went to USC.

"This must be during one of the times your dad visited your mom at her school," Sally softly says. "She told me she hated taking photos but started liking them again after she met your dad."

Before I can fully process everything I've just seen, Mom calls out, "Sally? Ms. Moon is ready to check out."

"Crap." Sally immediately exits out of all the folders. "Coming!"

I stare at the computer screen. In a way, I feel like how Harry Potter must have felt when he stared into the Mirror of Erised and saw his dead parents. Except, instead of my parents being alive again, my deepest desire was for Mom to understand what it's like to be me. And of course, instead of just being some illusion, the photos I saw are real. Unfortunately.

The fact that Mom was once fat herself makes the way she treats me even worse. If she understands what it's like, then why can't she just let me live and be happy the way I am? Is she really *that* afraid of other people?

My phone chirps. It's a text from Rebecca.

Is it just me or does the APUSH DBQ look IMPOSSIBLE? Hard to believe that these guys were responsible for creating our nation when their writing was so convoluted. Is this why America doesn't make any sense???

Pushing all thoughts of Mom out of my head, I go back to

work, all the more determined not to let other people treat me the way they treated her. I feel sorry for Mom, I really do. But I have my own problems and responsibilities to deal with right now. And what she went through in the past doesn't give her an excuse for how she treats me now.

Chapter Eight

DAD IS THE COMPLETE OPPOSITE OF MOM IN HOW he reacts to the show. On our way up to the dance studio in North Hollywood where rehearsal's being held, he asks me about every single little thing that has to do with *You're My Shining Star*. He asks about the audition, about the judges, and even about Lana and Tiffany.

With any other parent, it'd probably feel like an interrogation, but with Dad, it feels like catching up with an old friend at a party. I know I should probably tell him about what's been happening with Mom, but I don't bring it up. I don't want to ruin a good moment like this. We're both laughing and joking around so much that it's a wonder he doesn't crash the car.

There's an actual accident somewhere down the highway, so traffic is awful. I see so many people scowling behind their steering wheels, but I'm having so much fun catching up with Dad that I can't relate. By the time he drops me off at the dance studio, I'm actually wishing the car ride was just a bit longer, so I'd have more time to talk to him before he flies back to the Bay Area tomorrow morning.

Unlike the recording studio, the dance studio looks modern, even from the outside. It's shaped like a cube and painted bright orange. The parking lot is full, so I know I'm late even before I run into the building to find Mr. Park and Bora waiting for me with their tablets.

"I believe I mentioned punctuality last week, Miss Shin?" Mr. Park says with a raised eyebrow.

"I'm so sorry," I say. "I left my house at ten, but there was this huge accident on the 5."

Bora rolls her eyes. "Next time, leave at nine. Everyone had to drive here and yet only *you* were late."

Great, as if I weren't already on Bora's bad side.

Since Dad's never been a morning person, there was no way I could have left any earlier. And it's not like I could have driven myself, either. I don't say any of this out loud, though. If I told her about my car situation Bora would probably just tell me to drop out like Mom did.

"This is your first and last warning, Miss Shin," Mr. Park says. "Talent isn't an excuse for laziness. You're lucky this is the first dance practice, because otherwise, you would have been eliminated."

"Yes, sir," I say, bowing deeply in respect. "I won't be late again."

"Everyone else already went around and introduced themselves," Bora says curtly. "And unfortunately, we don't have time for you to do the same. Please go sit down and wait for further instructions."

I expect everyone else to be staring at our conversation, but when I look away from the judges, I see that only Tiffany is looking in my direction.

You okay? she mouths at me.

I nod, because I am. I'm surprised by the concern on her face—I thought Tiffany didn't like me after the awkward first encounter we had—but before I can dwell much on it, I spot Henry Cho, who's currently the center of attention.

Everyone—including the camera crew—is crowded around where he sits at the back of the studio. Henry is in the middle of some story, and he's all smiles and charm, making the people around him laugh. Some even slap their knees and look like they're about to cry because they're laughing too hard.

I find a spot to sit in the very back, since that's the only place with any space left. The dance studio is pretty fancy, with floor-to-ceiling mirrors and shiny wooden floors, but it's barely big enough to fit all forty of us.

After I'm settled down, I try to ignore Henry. But it's hard to do so when everyone around him is so loud. I don't turn around to face him, but I can't stop myself from staring at him and everyone else around him through the mirror.

There's a greater variety of people in the dance group, so less than half the people in the room are Asian. The rest are a good mix of black, brown, and white kids, and we're all dressed in hip-hop street clothes. Together, we look like one big, awesome dance crew.

"Henry, Henry. So, what happened after that?" It's a question, but the guy who says it practically yells his words, clearly a bit too excited.

"Oh, well, I was just standing there, wondering what the heck was going on . . ."

He's so different from the Henry Cho I saw last week that I start to doubt whether last week even happened. I tune him out, focusing instead on the people sitting next to him.

Henry's sitting with a petite Asian lady who's frowning down at a Surface Pro tablet, and a big professional-wrestler-type guy who reminds me of the Rock. From the looks of it, I'd guess that the woman is his manager and the guy is his bodyguard.

Henry's about to continue his story when Bora claps her hands.

"Okay," she says. "We're going to get started. When we call your names, please come down to the front of the room. You will be put into ten groups of four. Mr. Park and I have grouped you by age and/or similarity in style. Since each studio only has one sound system, each group has been preassigned choreography that you will learn together. During the elimination round next week, the other judges and I will either eliminate the entire group, choose to save a few from the group, or allow everyone from the group to advance to the next round. When we call your names, please proceed down the hall to find your assigned dance studio."

I let out a small sigh in relief. Somehow, it's less stressful knowing that they're doing the same thing for the dancers as they did with the singers last week.

Everyone waits in nervous anticipation as the groups are called.

"Studio one," Mr. Park says. "Elisabet Hernandez, Tiffany Lee, Prithi Reddy, and Katerina Kovacova."

Tiffany gives me a little wave before she gets up to join her group. I wave back before I refocus my attention on Mr. Park.

"Studio two: Henry Cho, Doug Barton, Skye Shin, and Imani Stevens."

I jump up from the floor, and so do the other members of my group. Everyone else in the room stares at us as we stand. Most of the attention is focused on Henry, but I also feel some eyes following me, as well as the others in our group. And of course, the cameras also watch our every move.

Since I'm sitting at the very back, I end up leaving way later than Imani and Doug, who both bolt out of the room. Henry, however, lingers behind. He has his full attention on me.

Well, that's awkward, I think.

I rush past him, since I really don't have time to socialize. I'm busy enough with school and prepping for the singing portion of the competition. I need all the practice time I can get out of today.

When we're more than halfway down the hallway, Henry says, "Hey, wait up."

I begrudgingly turn around to see that Henry's giving me his flawless Instagram grin. Both members of his team flank him, one on each side, and the petite lady looks like she's struggling to keep up, so I slow my pace. We're almost there, anyway.

"Thanks," Henry says when everyone's caught up.

Up close, he's a whole head taller than me, which is surprising since I'm five six. I wish I could say he isn't as hot in person as he is in pictures, but if anything, he's even more attractive up close. Henry looks like he could be the love interest in some old rom-com movie, like an Asian Hugh Grant or Ryan Gosling. Except younger, of course, and cuter, if that's even possible. He's probably the hottest person I've ever come face-to-face with.

Even though I live near LA, the closest thing I've had to a celebrity encounter was when I saw Halsey drinking a latte at Urth Caffé. Even then, she was sitting across the café from me, not inches away like Henry is. It still feels surreal that the same Henry Cho my friends obsess over is standing right next to me.

"Hi, I'm Henry. Nice to meet you."

He holds out his hand, and I shake it. "Hi, I'm Skye."

I must have shaken a bit too hard, because Henry slightly winces. He's nice enough to not say anything, though. Instead, he gives me the same calm and collected smile I've seen countless times in his Instagram photos. Only, now that I'm seeing it up close, I can see that the smile is definitely fake. His mouth is undoubtedly smiling, but his eyes are distant and guarded, like he has a huge secret. I resist the urge to flip out my phone and check his Instagram to see if his eyes look like this in all his pics.

What does his real *smile look like?* I find myself wondering, long after Henry's let go of my hand.

I expect him to say something else—he *did* tell me to wait, after all—but he doesn't. He seems content just to walk with me. I guess he only wanted the company.

Henry seems so at ease that I wonder if he knows that a cameraman from the main room has broken off from the rest of the crew to silently trail behind him. But then, I notice how set back his broad shoulders are, like he's going down a runway. He definitely knows.

Somehow, I'm not surprised that the show has one camera exclusively following Henry around.

"Doesn't that bother you?" I ask, gesturing behind us. "Always being followed around by a camera?"

Henry shrugs. "Kind of. But I'm also used to it. My family is always in the spotlight back at home, and my job is literally to be in front of cameras."

I'm taken aback by Henry's frankness, so much that I almost don't notice the mason jar in Henry's hand. It's full of a mysterious yellow liquid that I really hope isn't what I think it is.

"Ew!" I say. "What is that?"

Henry's face instantly melts into a lopsided grin. It's not a full smile, and it's definitely not as polished or friendly as the smile he saves for the cameras, but it looks a lot more natural. Combined with the way his eyes crinkle up in the corners, for a split second, he looks so adorable that I almost trip and fall on my face.

Luckily, Henry's too amused by my reaction to his drink to notice the blush on my face. Or if he does, he's nice enough to not mention it.

Stop it! I tell myself. *You're not allowed to get charmed by Henry freakin' Cho. He's your rival, for Pete's sake!*

"It's kombucha," he says. "Brewed it myself. Do you want to try some?"

"No thanks. I don't know which tastes worse, kombucha or . . . another yellow liquid," I say, because the last thing I want to do is mention *pee* on television. "And I don't intend to find out."

From behind us, I hear a muffled giggle, but whether it's from the bodyguard, the manager, or the cameraman, I can't tell.

"Harsh," Henry laughs as we reach the studio door. He opens it for me and says, "After you."

The doorway is pretty narrow, so I brush past him on my way through. As I pass, I get a whiff of his sea-breeze-scented cologne.

Ugh, I think. *He even* smells *nice.*

"Kinda sucks how we only have a week to prep while the singers get two weeks, huh?" Doug is saying as we walk into the room. He's stretching with Imani, who looks so done that I can only assume Doug's been talking her ears off. "I mean, I guess it's still fair because both groups have only one official practice. But I wish Mr. Park could clone himself so both the voice prectices and the dance practices could be on the same days."

Imani immediately gets up when she sees me, a look of immense relief on her face.

"Oh, thank God," she says as she holds out a hand in my direction. "Hi, I'm Imani. You must be Skye. So glad there's another girl in our group."

My eyes are immediately drawn to Imani's pink dreadlocks, which look really cool. They fashionably stand out against her black tank top and leggings.

"Hey, nice to meet you too."

"Isn't it so awesome that we're here?" Imani asks. "I've been dancing since I was a little kid and I love K-pop, so this is like a dream come true."

"Same here!" I smile. "What's your favorite K-pop choreography?"

We gush over our favorite dances as we stretch together, and I feel myself relaxing more with each passing second. Melinda may have been a total bust, but I'm so glad I'm bonding with Imani.

A tall, muscular Asian guy in his late twenties walks into the room. He's dressed in a blue muscle tank and sweatpants, so I can only assume he's our instructor. And sure enough, he goes to stand in front of the room after giving the cameraman a slight nod.

"Hey, guys," he says in a really low voice. "My name is Chad. Your group has been assigned 'Idol,' by BTS."

Doug lets out a piercing shriek that earns raised eyebrows from all of us. It's hard to tell if it's a shriek of joy or panic. Maybe it's a mix of both.

"I love BTS," he says. "But oh my God, that dance is so hard."

We all mumble our agreement. It's one of my favorite choreographies, but it's a dance that the BTS members themselves have acknowledged is one of their hardest, since it mixes in elements of traditional Korean dance with lots of high jumps and intense footwork.

"It *is* pretty challenging," admits Chad. "But I can assure you, the other groups have been assigned equally hard choreos. Let's try not to be the group that gets eliminated, eh?"

"Easier said than done," says Imani.

I have to agree with her. This is *not* going to be easy in the slightest.

Well, worst-case scenario, at least I still have a chance at vocals.

Since the choreography requires a lot of space, Chad has us stand in two neat rows behind him. Doug and Imani end up standing next to each other—I shoot Imani a sympathetic look—while I end up next to Henry.

After everything is set up, Chad starts us off right away,

guiding us through all the moves for the first stanza at half the original speed and then repeating himself a couple of times until we get the hang of it. I breathe deeply, slow and even, as I follow along. At this pace, the dance isn't that bad, and soon I feel confident enough to let my eyes wander away from Chad to check on everyone else.

Doug is a stumbling mess, nearly face-planting multiple times. In contrast, Imani makes everything look really easy. Her execution of the choreo isn't perfect, but I can tell just by the fluid way she moves that she's probably the most experienced dancer out of all of us. Henry's somewhere in between, moving in a graceful way as he follows all the steps. Watching him dance makes me wonder why he's never danced in one of his videos before. Then again, it's probably for the best that he never has. I can only imagine what kind of chaos would happen if he uploaded a video of himself dancing. He'd probably break Instagram.

Just then, I trip on my own feet, falling flat onto the ground.

"Careful!" Chad says. There's a hint of a laugh in his voice. "We haven't even done anything at the actual speed yet."

My cheeks burning, I quickly get up and rejoin the others like nothing happened.

Focus! I tell myself. Too embarrassed to look anywhere else, I keep my eyes locked on Chad's reflection.

By the time Chad goes over the choreography in real time, we're all struggling. It takes all my effort not to make a complete fool of myself in front of the camera. Doug's face is filled with unbridled terror, Imani is stone-faced with concentration, and even Henry's highly controlled expression falls into a grimace every so often.

The more I practice the dance, the more I'm determined not to get eliminated in this first round. Despite how hard it is, I really am having lots of fun, and it'd suck to be eliminated while dancing a choreo I love. I also don't want to give Bora the satisfaction of seeing me eliminated from the dance part of the competition right away.

I can do this, I think, gritting my teeth as I try to keep up. *I am* not *going to get eliminated in the first round.*

Chapter Nine

I END UP SPENDING MOST OF THE FOLLOWING week at school, either doing homework in the library or practicing for the elimination round on Saturday. Because of *You're My Shining Star*, I had to drop out of the dance team and choir for this semester, but my teachers were nice enough to let me use the dance studio and practice rooms when no one else is using them.

"Just don't forget us when you're famous!" my dance teacher said after I told her what was going on. "And say hi to BTS for me!"

I was too amused to tell her I'm probably not going to see BTS anytime soon.

The first elimination round for singing goes even better than I thought it would. Lana, Isabel, Melinda, and I totally kill it, so much that the judges only listen to a minute or two of each of our songs before evaluating us.

"This is a group of angelic voices," says Mr. Park. "You all have so much potential that I wish I could make a girl group out of you four right here and now."

"The world needs to watch out for you ladies," says Gary. "Wow, just wow."

"Congratulations, ladies," Bora finally says. She makes eye contact with and smiles at everyone in the group . . . except me. "You are all advancing to the next round."

Despite the fact that Bora totally pretended I didn't exist, I'm still glowing from the other judges' comments when I rush backstage to change for the dance portion of the competition. My singing group was one of the last ones to perform, leaving me with less than thirty minutes to get ready. I'm rushing around like a headless chicken when I run smack-dab into Henry Cho.

Henry grunts. We both stumble back. I barely suppress a groan of frustration.

Why is my life literally *a K-drama right now?*

"Hey," I say. "Sorry, are you okay?"

For a second, I'm worried Henry might say something about how I should watch where I'm going since I take up so much space. It's something a few of the meaner guys said back in middle school, and I've always been careful not to run into anyone in the hallway ever since.

Really wishing I weren't blushing, I reluctantly look up at Henry.

Instead of being mad, Henry's expression is a mix of

amusement and concern. When I meet his gaze, his eyes crinkle a bit at the corners.

"I'm perfectly fine," he says. "You're in a hurry to get ready, right? Go ahead. I think everyone else is done prepping."

He steps out of the way with a grand flourish, his lopsided grin telling me that he's just fooling around.

Ugh, I think. *How does he manage to be* both *gentlemanly and goofy at the same time?*

I'm still reminding myself that Henry is *competition* and not potential boyfriend material as I run into the nearest bathroom to change. Since we're only performing for the judges today for both vocals and dance, I just brought a really cute pink tank top and black workout leggings as my dance outfit.

I feel energized the moment I put them on my nervousness transforming into raw determination. My mom always says that I shouldn't wear bright colors. Every time we go shopping together, she always tells me to go for "slimming" colors like black and navy. I got the pink tank top from Torrid while shopping with Rebecca and Clarissa over the summer, and it's one of my favorite things. It has a split in the back, and the color complements my skin tone perfectly. I look dang cute in it and I know it.

After retouching my makeup and making sure my hair's not a wild bird's nest, I run over to where my group is waiting backstage. Doug and Imani say hi, but Henry doesn't say anything. All the mischief from earlier is gone from his slightly widened eyes as he slowly gives me a once-over from head to toe.

"Wow, Skye," he says. "You look really nice."

Henry opens his mouth like he wants to say more, but Doug cuts in with, "I am so nervous. Are any of you nervous or is it just me?"

"We're all nervous," Henry says flatly. "Who wouldn't be? We're—"

"Oh my God, Henry, you're nervous too? Oh wow, we're all doomed. I heard that *everyone* in the group before us got eliminated. Jesus, take the wheel!"

Henry closes his eyes for a split second before focusing his attention on me. The expression on his face clearly says: *Help.*

"Well, I think it's okay to be nervous," I try. "We're about to perform a choreography we only started learning last week, and the judges might eliminate us at any moment."

"Yikes," says Imani. "When you put it that way . . ."

"We'll just have to try our best," I continue with a shrug. I'm not usually optimistic, but I feel the need to say something to reassure everyone. We can't *all* be freaking out like Doug. "There's nothing else we can do at this point anyway."

"True," Imani replies. "Hopefully at least some of us will make it to the next round."

"I bet you'll make it. Sorry if this sounds creepy, but I watched you in the mirror while we were practicing in the studio. You're definitely the best dancer out of all of us."

"Aw, thanks, girl! You aren't so bad yourself."

I'm about to respond when I hear a low keening sound, like a dying animal would make. Startled, Imani and I look up to see that Doug is *crying* like he's been given a death sentence.

"I don't think I'm cut out for this," Doug says. "I barely managed to audition. What was I thinking?"

"Doug, calm down," says Henry through gritted teeth. His jaw is set in a firm line, and his shoulders are visibly rigid. And that's when I realize: Henry has *stage fright*. Maybe just as much as Doug. I wonder if that's why Doug's meltdown is bothering him so much.

I've been through enough choir recitals and dance performances that I'm perfectly fine with being onstage. Sure, I'm still nervous, but that has more to do with what'll come afterward, with the judge's evaluations, than performing onstage itself.

Imani, too, seems okay. Tense from anticipation, but still pretty calm. Henry, though . . . he's better at hiding it than Doug, but I don't miss the way his eyes are slightly widened, or how his breaths come out in shallow gasps.

"Are you okay?" I ask Henry out of genuine concern. *How did he even audition for this competition when he's this afraid of being onstage?* I wonder. Why *did he audition?*

He glances down at me again, his cheeks turning beet red. And I have to admit it. It feels nice to not be the only one blushing, for once.

"I'm fine," Henry says. "Don't worry about it."

At that moment, the stage manager ushers us onto the stage. We're barely situated when the opening notes of "Idol" start blaring from the speakers.

I immediately fall into a half crouch, sliding my feet back and forth across the floor in time to the music. Even after hours of practice, "Idol" still remains my favorite BTS song, if only because of how loud and bombastically Korean it is. The unapologetic confidence and swag in the dance moves electrifies me, so much that by the time we reach the chorus, I feel like I'm flying.

I'm in the middle of a spinning jump when I hear Henry yell, "Ow! Watch it."

There's a loud crash, and I manage to follow through with my momentum enough to land safely back on the ground.

The music stops. I glance back to see both Doug and Henry sprawled on the stage. From the looks of it—and from where we were in the choreo—my guess is that Doug must have accidentally spun into Henry during the jump, causing both of them to come crashing down.

"Oh my God, are you guys okay?" I say. I'm all out of breath—something I didn't even realize when I was dancing but is so apparent now as I gasp for air.

Imani's also panting as she stares wide-eyed at the two boys, and the confusion on her face tells me she has no idea what just happened either.

"Doug Barton, you are officially eliminated from the competition," Bora says. "Please go pack your things."

Doug, looking dazed, slowly gets up and leaves without another word.

During all this, Henry remains still, and I find myself caring a bit more than I should about his well-being. *Get up*, I can't help but plead in my thoughts. *Please be okay.*

"Hey, Henry," says Gary, sounding concerned. "Are you all right, man?"

At the sound of his name, Henry slowly sits up, his arms wrapped around his abdomen.

"Yeah," he says. "He missed my ribs, thankfully, but he knocked the breath out of me."

At that moment, the backstage door bursts open, and Henry's team comes rushing onstage.

"Stop the cameras," the bodyguard says. "Stop them right now or there will be consequences."

The manager kneels beside Henry, who looks just as embarrassed as he did before the performance.

"I'm fine," he quietly says to her. "It'll probably bruise, that's all. I'm not doing any shirtless shoots anytime soon, so we should be okay."

I suppress an urge to snort. *Of course* his ability to be shirtless in front of a camera would be a major concern to Henry right now.

"If Mr. Cho is okay," says Mr. Park in a loud, authoritative voice, "I would like to recommence shooting. We still have to give evaluations to the group and can't afford a delay in an already tight schedule."

Henry's manager whispers something, and Henry says again, "I'm okay. Really. I'll let you know if it still hurts later. Thanks, though."

His team leaves the stage, and Mr. Park has the remaining three of us line up onstage.

"Aside from Mr. Barton, this group has proven to be exceptional," Mr. Park says once the cameras are rolling. "It was not revealed to you until now, but this group was put together because the members demonstrated the most energetic dance performances out of all the auditions. You could say Mr. Barton, too, had lots of energy, even though he unfortunately didn't know how to harness it. The other three of you showed not only a tremendous amount of energy, but also a great ability to perfectly control it. Well done. All of you have my vote."

"Imani Stevens and Henry Cho," says Bora, "congratulations, the judges have unanimously voted to advance you to the next round. You may leave the stage."

Both Imani and Henry shoot me concerned looks as they leave.

Oh great, I think as the cameras focus on me. *It's just me now.*

As I wait for the judges to continue, I try to wrap my head around what might have happened. I'm pretty sure I had the chorcography down to a tee. What went wrong?

"Skye," Gary starts. He shoots Bora a wary glance that I don't miss. "You're fantastic. You took that BTS choreography and made it your own. I admit, I'm more of a rapper than I am a dancer, but I do know talent when I see it. And I love, love, *love* your style."

"Thank you," I say.

I turn to Bora, and really, I should have seen it coming. Instead of looking me in the eyes like the other judges, Bora stares down at her mic as she says, "Miss Shin, you already know my opinions about your dancing. You *are* talented, yes. But I frankly think you ruined this choreography."

I wait for her to explain herself, but she doesn't. And honestly, I'm relieved. Her reasons are probably the same crap she said after my audition.

"Miss Shin," says Mr. Park. "Well done. I look forward to seeing you in the next round."

I'm still thinking about Bora's words when I'm dismissed from the stage, but instantly forget about them when I see Henry Cho standing *shirtless* backstage.

Henry's bodyguard is standing in a way that blocks the view of all the cameras as his manager sprays something over his bruising skin. From where I'm standing, I catch a glimpse of Henry's broad chest and chiseled abs.

Holy crap. How is that even real?

At that moment, I fully understand why Henry's inability to go on shirtless shoots would be a major concern. Heck, a part of my brain is even convinced that it'd be an international crisis.

"Like what you see?" Henry says with a little quirk on his lips.

"Yeah—I mean, no," I stammer as I avert my eyes. "Okay, yes, but sorry! I was totally invading your privacy."

Henry laughs, his face completely lighting up for a split

second before he winces in pain. "Ow, guess I should avoid laughing for the time being. But yeah, it's fine. I don't mind."

"Of course you don't," I grumble. "Freakin' models."

Henry's manager finishes spraying him, and he grins as he puts his shirt back on.

"So," he starts. "I—"

But before he can finish, Tiffany rushes over with her group in tow. Since I was busy getting ready, I missed Tiffany's group performing. But I heard whispers in the hallway about how amazing they were. Apparently, they were total goddesses in their rendition of GFRIEND's "Love Whisper."

"Skye!" Tiffany exclaims. "Thank God you made it. I was worried for a second."

"Yeah," I say. "I don't think I was ever in any real danger of getting eliminated, though, since I had Gary's and Mr. Park's votes. Bora just wanted to give me a hard time. Either that or she just wanted to make things extra dramatic for the show."

Tiffany rolls her eyes. "Probably both."

"Yup. Everything turned out okay, though. I mean, Henry got hurt, but I think he's okay . . ."

I trail off when I realize that Henry's no longer behind me. He and his team must have left while I was talking to Tiffany.

That's it, then? I think. *I'll just see him next week?*

I know it's silly, but I can't help but feel a little hurt that he left without saying bye. Even though we didn't interact that much, we still practiced together for several hours last week. He could have at least waved before he left.

It's for the best, I tell myself. *At the end of the day, he's just another person you have to beat.*

Tiffany raises an eyebrow at me but thankfully changes the subject. "So, the girls and I are going to grab some cupcakes at Sprinkles. Wanna come? Lana's getting the car right now."

Cupcakes sound absolutely perfect after the day I've had.

"Sure," I say. "I'll go see if Imani's still around and ask if she wants to come."

"Perfect, meet you at the front!"

Shaking away all thoughts of Bora and Henry, I head farther backstage.

Chapter Ten

GRABBING CUPCAKES WITH THE OTHER GIRLS turns out to be so much fun that I almost forget that we're supposed to be competing against each other. We all exchange numbers, follow each other on Instagram, and promise to boost each other on social media once the show premieres next month.

In a way, it's nice. I didn't go into this competition looking for new friends, but I'm really enjoying the fun little moments I share with Lana, Tiffany, and Imani. Throughout the week, Lana sends me links to #positivity posts on Instagram and gorgeous shots of the beaches she and Tiffany are frequenting, while Tiffany sends out hilariously relatable memes in our group chat. Imani and I bond over our favorite choreos and music videos, as well as the new restaurants popping up in LA.

After the utter chaos that was last week, this week is eerily chill. Besides a few assignments and projects for school, I don't really have anything to do, and I even have time to hang out with my school friends. Clarissa and Rebecca ask me all about the competition, but I'm careful not to tell them any details. Telling Dad about everything is one thing, but I still want my friends to be able to enjoy the show without any spoilers when it airs.

On Saturday, I carpool up to the recording studio with Lana again. Her car is just as messy as it was last time, and today, the rubber duck flies into my face when Lana makes a particularly sharp turn. I'm more amused than anything, though. I have a feeling that this is something I'm just going to have to get used to when I ride in Lana's car.

There must have been a major accident on the road again, because even though it's a Saturday, the cars are moving at a slow crawl. Luckily, unlike Dad, Lana's a morning person, so we left really early.

Lana sits back in defeat after it becomes clear that traffic isn't going to get better anytime soon.

"So," she says. "Any guesses on what the next challenge will be? Apparently, they carved out two weeks of official practice for both vocals and dance before the second elimination round, so it must be pretty big deal."

"Not sure," I say. "But hopefully it won't be that bad. Maybe it'll be a group thing? Didn't they mention something about testing us on group dynamics or whatever in another round?"

Lana gasps. "That'd definitely make sense. That would explain the extra practice time, too. Wow, an intensive group challenge right after the last round. They *really* want to get rid of us ASAP!"

A few days ago, the competition committee sent out a text telling us the number of people still left in the competition. Like they warned us they would, the committee had eliminated half of the people in both vocals and dance, leaving a total of twenty for each group.

For better or worse, I turn out to be right, and as soon as we arrive, Mr. Park tells us to choose our groups.

"Many of our past winners have gone on to join K-pop *groups*, rather than break out as individual artists," he explains. "In my company, at least, there is a greater chance of debuting as a group member than as a solo artist. And even solo artists frequently collaborate with other people. Knowing how to sing or dance as part of a team is an essential skill to have in this industry."

"Even though most K-pop groups have more than two or three people in them, we're limiting the number of people you guys can have in a group to give you more flexibility," Gary chimes in. "We care just as much about your interpretation of the song as we do about your performance, so be creative! Rappers, feel free to improvise! Singers, try out new keys! As artists, the ability to make songs *yours* is super important, so consider this a golden opportunity."

I, of course, pair up with Lana. She was amazing during the last round, and I want to be with someone I know I'll get along with.

Each group gets their own practice room, and one of the cameras follows Lana and me into ours. Although I didn't mind the cameras while I was up onstage, or even in the bigger rooms, its constant presence in such close quarters is unnerving. I have to try really hard not to squirm. Lana, though, is a complete natural, like she grew up being chased around by cameras. She even gives the one in our practice room a friendly wave.

I don't even dare look at the camera. Knowing me, I'd probably stare at it like a raccoon about to become roadkill. Instead, I focus my attention on a piece of paper taped to the music stand in our practice room.

It reads, first in Korean and then English:

For your second challenge, please pick either an American or a Korean pop song. Make sure that everyone in your group approves of the choice, as you will not be able to make changes. Once you've made your selection, please text your song choice and your names to 54311. No two groups will be allowed to sing the same song, so first group to text their choice gets the song.

Here are some suggested song choices, although you are welcome to choose one that is not listed below.

Lana and I both look at the suggested songs below the instructions. In a short while, it becomes clear that Lana and I have way different tastes in music. She likes more indie stuff, like Guckkasten and Humming Urban Stereo, while I like more mainstream artists.

"Okay," Lana finally says. "We're short on time, so let's try picking a song we both know." She puts a perfectly manicured finger on one of the suggested songs. "How about 'Crazy in Love'? I don't listen to many Top Forty artists, but Beyoncé is a queen."

I look back down at the list. Although doing a Beyoncé song seems daunting, it really does seem like the best choice for us out of the suggested songs on the list.

"Okay, sure. Let me text them."

I get out my phone and start composing the text.

"I really hope we get that song," Lana says as I send the message. "I guess we *could* do another Beyoncé song if that one's taken, but that'd just be plain repetitive."

A few agonizing seconds later, I get a text saying: You have been assigned: Crazy in Love. Best of luck in the competition!

Lana and I high-five each other and get to work.

I was afraid that singing with someone else would be awkward and restrictive, like stepping on their toes. But Lana is so chill and playful that singing with her feels like we're just messing around in the best sort of way, experimenting with different harmonies and playing off each other until we're both smiling and laughing.

After a while, the cameraman leaves to go record another group, but I hardly notice. I'm having *that* much fun.

We're still belting along to "Crazy in Love" when my phone vibrates against my leg. I fish it out of my pocket to see that I have a new message from Mom, which strikes me as odd because she's been pretty much ignoring me for the past few weeks.

Maybe it's because Dad's home, I think. Mom tends to be a lot less obvious about her disapproval of my life choices whenever Dad is around.

I read the text.

MOM: When are you going to come home today? It's late.

I only then realize that it's already around seven p.m. Mom must have just gotten home from work.

ME: I'm probably going to leave within the hour. I have a ride back so it's okay.

MOM: OK.

And that's it. I half expect Mom to say something else, to acknowledge the fact that the last time we had a real conversation was when I got back from my first competition rehearsal. But of course, she doesn't. I guess it's more wishful thinking on my part than an expectation.

Well, at least she still cares about me? I think. But even I know that doesn't even remotely make up for how long she's been giving me the cold shoulder. Dad probably asked her to check in on me.

"Hey, what's up?" Lana asks, looking concerned. "You okay?"

"Yeah. I just need to head back soon. That was my mom." I gesture at my phone, and Lana nods.

"Okay, yeah, let's wrap things up for tonight."

We drive back down to Orange County in silence. Lana stopped trying to talk to me after her last few attempts at conversation ended with me giving monosyllabic answers like "yeah" and "nah." I feel really bad about not being better company, but I also can't bring myself to pretend that everything is all right. Mom has that effect on me.

Lana pulls up to the curb in front of my house.

"Hey," she says. "I know you probably don't want to talk about it, but whenever you do, I'm here for you, okay? I know things aren't great between you and your mom, and even though my reasons are different, I know what it's like to have a strained relationship with a parent."

"Thanks," I reply. "I really appreciate it."

"Don't sweat it," Lana says. "Well, actually, yes, sweat it. Let's totally kill it with this performance. Show the haters what we've got."

Lana makes a big heart with her arms above her head. The gesture is so cute that, despite my panic, I can't help but smile and say, "Okay."

"See you in two weeks!

"See you."

By the time I reach my doorstep, I feel a bit better. So what if my mom isn't supportive of me? At least I have friends like Lana who are. And I have Dad, who's probably waiting on the other side of the door, eager to hear how my day was.

I put a smile on my face and enter the house.

Chapter Eleven

AFTER THE COMPLETE SILENCE THAT WAS OUR house before Dad came home, his presence is a breath of fresh air. We talk almost nonstop during what we have left of the weekend, and Mom even smiles and nods along to our conversations. She's always on her best behavior whenever Dad's in town, so much that I doubt Dad even knows what's been going on between Mom and me.

Too soon, we have to drop Dad off at LAX and I'm again alone with Mom. And then we're right back to how things were before. Pretending the other doesn't exist, for the most part, anyway.

When I have to go up to LA for the next dance practice, I don't even bother asking Mom for a ride. Instead, I take an Uber to the train station and then the metro once I'm in the city. It takes me about twice as long to get to the studio, but LA public transportation is so bad that I consider myself lucky that I even make it to my destination at all.

"Okay," Bora says as I walk in. "We're going to get started. When we call your names, please come down to the front of the room. You have been paired off for the second round of eliminations."

Everyone tenses up. Some people grumble under their breath about how it's not fair that people in the vocals category got to choose their groups. I stay perfectly still. Since I'm in the vocals category, too, I don't think I have a right to say what's fair or not.

"You will thank us later," Mr. Park declares loudly, like he's some gracious king. "Freedom of choice is not the blessing you all think it is. By dancing with the person we assigned you, you won't have to blame yourselves if you end up getting eliminated."

No one really complains after that, not because they agree with him, but because there's no use in protesting. I stretch a bit, reaching to touch my toes and then bending my torso from side to side, as I wait for the judges to call my name.

"Skye Shin and Bobby Lim."

I get up as a guy walks up to the front of the room. From his loose pants and snapback, I can already tell that he's a break-dancer. I can't break-dance to save my life, so I'm trying to figure out how we're going to dance together when I realize he's full-on *glaring* at me. You'd think I ran over his dog or something.

"I have to dance with *her*?" he practically yells. "Are you trying to get me kicked out? Of course I'll lose if I dance with the fat girl."

Mr. Park freezes. Even Bora has the decency to look scandalized. The entire room goes silent, and I look around to see that everyone is staring at me now. No one speaks up to defend me or to tell Bobby off for being such a jerk. Not even the girls I hung out with after the first elimination round.

I guess I can see why they don't. We're on camera, after all, so they probably don't want to stir up additional drama. But still, it stings. Why can't they be friends with me on *and* off camera?

Instead of letting it get to me, I take a deep breath. I'll just have to speak up for myself.

"Hey," I say. "I'm not a bad dancer. I wouldn't have made it into this competition if I were. You think the judges went easy on a fat girl?"

He scoffs. From behind him, Bora rolls her eyes. I'm always fed up with Bora, but today, I'm even more done with her. It sucks that a fellow woman is hating on me so much like this. As if the industry weren't already sexist enough.

Mr. Park fixes a cool gaze at Bobby. "Partners were chosen randomly. If you have a problem with your match, you're going to have to see if anyone else wants to swap with you."

Bobby groans, glancing back at me again like I have some contagious disease. "That's practically a death sentence. *Of course* no one is going to want to trade partners with me. I mean, look at her!"

He motions at me, and my lip quivers, just a bit. I can't help it. I feel like a little kid again, standing in the middle of the room as my ballet teacher singles me out to the class as an example of how a kid like me could never look graceful in a tutu. I feel the same way I felt all the times Mom made a comment about my body. And I know this is how she must have felt during all the times she was bullied as a kid.

But as much as it hurts, I am *not* giving Bobby the satisfaction of seeing tears fall down my face. I squeeze my hands into fists, putting all my willpower into the effort not to cry.

"How in the world did someone like her get in, anyway?" Bobby continues, still raging on like he's reciting a monologue from a play. "It's obvious she won't get that far."

Someone like her.

"Hey," I say again. "Stop talking like I'm not here. And, come on, double standards much? You're not skinny either. Shouldn't fat guys like you support fat girls like me?"

I didn't want to go there, but it's true. Bobby is a pretty big guy, which makes the fact that he's hating on me, a fat girl, even more yucky.

"Did you really just call me fat?" Bobby crosses his arms against his chest.

I sigh and try my best to keep my voice level as I say, "Fat isn't a bad word, Bobby. It's just an adjective to describe our bodies, which, by the way, are beautiful just the way they are."

"Now you're calling me beautiful?" Bobby's face is all scrunched up in confusion, like I'm blowing this guy's mind.

Body Positivity 101! I want to yell at him. *Look it up and educate yourself!*

The entire room's still quiet around us, and I don't have to look to know that the cameras are all focused on Bobby and me. It'd be nice to have some backup instead of just a bunch of spectators, but I guess life can't always be good.

"Enough," Mr. Park says, stepping in between us. He doesn't even look at me as he tells Bobby, "Mr. Lim, please remember that we have a schedule to follow. If you really do wish to switch partners, I advise that you get it sorted it out on your own time so you don't keep the rest of the contestants waiting."

It bothers me that Mr. Park only seems to care about his freakin' TV show, but it's not surprising. He's a producer, after all. He probably only cares about the money.

I catch a glimpse of Bora and almost groan out loud. She looks so amused, like she's the embodiment of that guy-eating-popcorn meme. For the first time since the audition, I wonder if all of this is even worth it.

If I make it into the industry, I'm going to have to deal with people like this all the time. Even though I really do want to prove Mom, Bobby, and Bora wrong, I don't know if this is the life I want for myself. I'm tired. Why should I have to stand up for myself all the time? Just because I'm fat doesn't mean I have to let myself get hurt by these people over and over again. I'm not some spokesperson for all fat people, nor am I some martyr. I'm just one girl trying to achieve her dreams and live her own life.

I'm about to turn on my heel and walk out of the studio when a voice comes from the back of the room, "Don't know about you, Bobby, but I'd kill to be her partner. Skye's an amazing dancer. And if you're really that insecure about your ability to stay in this competition, I suggest you walk out right now."

Everyone turns around and gasps when they see that *Henry Cho* was the person who just spoke. His voice is colder than I've ever heard it before, so much that I didn't recognize it.

"But," Bora says, "Henry—"

Henry doesn't even acknowledge Bora as he turns to look straight at me.

"Skye, I'd love to be your partner," he says. "If you'd like to be mine, of course."

Chapter Twelve

IN AN INSTANT, MOST OF THE PEOPLE IN THE ROOM turn around to *glower* at me, like I got the last piece of food on a deserted island. I balk. This is so not fair. It's not like I *asked* Henry to be my partner.

For a moment, I consider saying no. I don't need any more drama in my life, and I definitely don't need the help of some celebrity to win this competition. I think back to how my friends were obsessing over him back at school. If he's my partner, they probably won't even pay attention to me when we perform.

But then I take one more look at Bobby, who's gone back to glaring at me like I'm the worst thing that happened to him. I may not need Henry's help, but I can already tell that staying Bobby's partner would be shooting myself in the foot.

As I'm mulling things over, the cameras have somehow gotten even closer, so they're practically in my face when I say to Henry, "Okay, sure. Let's be partners."

Henry beams, and it's freakin' annoying how dashing he is, even when he's just wearing a simple gray shirt and sweatpants. He joins us at the front of the room.

As he walks by, people casually take out their phones and snap pictures of him like he's walking down a red carpet. One girl doesn't even bother putting her phone on silent first, so I can hear the loud, rapid CLICK-CLICK-CLICK-CLICK! of her camera app. I can't help but think how rude it is to just casually snap pictures of someone like that. Even though Henry told me he's used to it, I can't imagine how scary and annoying it must be to not be able to do anything without someone recording it.

When Henry reaches me, Bobby blurts out, "Wait, what about me?"

Henry and I break eye contact, and it's only then that I realize we've been staring into each other's eyes *this whole time*. In the split second it takes for Henry to glance at Bobby, the smile drops from Henry's face and he takes on a cool, blasé look.

Jeez, I think. *This guy should be an actor. Not a model.*

"Well, you can be with Henry's originally assigned partner, Cassie Chang," says Mr. Park.

"What?" A girl who I assume is Cassie jumps to her feet and furiously marches up to us. "You mean Henry was supposed to be *my* partner?"

She shoots Bobby a death glare, and Bobby actually shrinks back.

"Well, yes," Mr. Park continues. Even he seems taken aback

by Cassie's rage. "Unless Bobby still wants to partner up with Skye?"

Bobby takes one good look at me and laughs. He actually *laughs*. "Hell nah."

"Well then," says Mr. Park, "there you go."

Henry starts walking away, and just when I'm wondering if he's forgotten about me, he looks over his shoulder at me and says, "Come on, let's get started."

Cassie gives me the stink eye as I walk away.

I join Henry at the back of the room, where he'd been sitting with his team. Henry introduces me to Portia, his manager, and Steve, his bodyguard and driver. Since I've seen them around for a while now, it's nice to finally know their names. I give them both my friendliest smile.

Portia glances at me nervously, as if she's not sure if my being Henry's partner is a good idea.

"Portia, relax," Henry says, giving her a reassuring grin. "She's probably the best dancer in this competition. And she's pretty awesome in general. You saw her last week."

Portia still looks pretty dubious, but she nods before she turns away.

"Don't take it personally," Henry whispers to me. "She's just annoyed that there was a last-minute change. Portia got the *You're My Shining Star* team to tell her beforehand who I was assigned to and already ran a background check on Cassie. She's nervous because we don't know anything about you aside from the fact that you were in my group in the previous round."

A *background check?* It seems a bit extreme, but I guess this is what happens when you're from a jaebol family.

"Well," I say, "I don't know much about you either, so I guess the mystery is mutual."

Henry grins, throwing me off guard. "I know, right? How exciting. Just don't try to sell my underwear on eBay, okay?"

My mouth drops open, and I'm about to ask Henry if this is a problem he's actually had when Mr. Park raises his hands to get everyone's attention.

"All right, now that that's settled," he continues, "I will run through the rules for this second round. In K-pop, dance is rarely a partner act, but mastering not only your own body but also how it works with other people is the greatest testament to the skill of a dancer. While the previous round was about seeing how well you stuck out in a crowd, this one is about teamwork. Dancing as a couple requires the same amount of training and synchronization—if not more—than dancing in a group. Many of our past winners were scouted for groups, so it's important for you to show your mastery of working with another person. Although there will be a few exceptions, we will generally eliminate by pair rather than by individual. To even out the playing field, the basic choreography will be the same for everyone. *You* are responsible for changing it in a way that best fits your own style. Anything is permissible as long as you stay on the beat and keep things appropriate for children. Only ten of you will make it past this round."

"What's the music?" Tiffany asks.

"I was just going to get to that. Or rather, Miss Jang was. Take it away, Miss Jang."

From where she's standing by the mirrors, Bora flashes everyone a confident smile. The dance studio door opens, and Chad comes in wearing sweats and a black snapback. He joins Bora at the front of the room and they get into position, tangling their limbs together in dramatic positions like a pair of figure skaters about to execute a passionate routine.

Then, music starts blaring from the overhead speakers. It's a really fast song, with a pounding bass line and dubstep interludes. Bora and Chad begin dancing with each other tango-style, then burst into an energetic pop-and-lock routine. The choreography is complex, mixing a whole bunch of different styles in a way that somehow comes together to form a really awesome whole.

Almost instinctively, I track Bora's movements, taking note of every flick of her wrist and which foot she uses to pivot during a turn. I even visualize myself moving along with her, syncing my breaths with hers so I get a sense of her flow. As I watch her, my entire body feels all tingly with excitement. Even though I don't like Bora (and I know she *really* doesn't like me), I can't deny that she's an amazing dancer. She's flawlessly executing what looks like an impossible routine.

I'm so lost in her dancing that I only barely process when the music stops. Everyone cheers for Bora and Chad. Despite the enthusiasm, though, everyone looks terrified.

"That . . . was interesting," says Henry.

"Tell me about it," I groan. "They really *are* weeding us out as much as possible."

"Yup."

I look around, and see variations of panic and despair in Tiffany's, Imani's, and Henry's faces. This choreography is basically a death sentence.

"Don't panic yet," Mr. Park says with a chuckle, addressing the entire room. "The first few hours of today's practice will be learning the dance. Then, after everyone learns the basic moves, we will branch out into the individual pairs. After that, you will have an entire extra session of practice in two weeks. Please stand up and join Bora in front of the mirrors."

It's only when I'm standing next to Henry that it occurs to me that dancing with him means that Henry will touch me and I'll touch him. I know it's a pretty duh thing to realize just now, but I guess I'm still processing the fact that all this is even happening.

Even though I already danced in the same space as Henry, what we're about to do now seems *a lot* different. I'm not sure how I feel about the fact that I'm about to dance quite intimately with him for the entire world to see.

Heat rises up in my cheeks. In my reflection in the mirror, I'm blushing bright red like a tomato. Something else in the mirror catches my attention. I look away from my own face to see that Cassie is glaring daggers at me. And she's not the only one.

I sigh. *Better get used to it now*, I think. After all, this is just the beginning. Soon, I'll have to dance with Henry in front of thousands—maybe even millions—of viewers watching *You're My Shining Star* in the audience and on TV. My own friends are going to see me dance with Henry. Mom, Dad, everyone. If I can't dance with him now, in the relatively private confines of a studio, I won't be able to do it in front of all those people.

In the end, I just try to forget he's famous. It's the only way I can get myself to relax and focus on learning the choreography.

Bora and Chad slowly lead us through all the steps, going at half the tempo so everyone can follow along. Slowed down, the dance is a lot less intimidating, but even then, people are stumbling here and there. It's a really hard routine.

"You're a pretty good dancer," I say as I sync my movements to Henry's. "I have to admit, I had my doubts when you showed up to the audition."

"So did a lot of people." He shrugs, and before I can fully process what's going on, Henry spins me around, gently raising my hand and guiding it so my body turns 360 degrees. Thankfully, my instincts take over, so even though my head is spinning, my body gracefully executes the turn without awkwardly twisting my legs.

"And you're a *really* awesome dancer," he says with a grin. "Although I never doubted that."

"Well done!" exclaims Mr. Park from the front of the studio. "Looks like Mr. Cho and Miss Shin are off to a good start!"

I glance up to see that the entire room is staring at us again.

Even Bora and Chad stopped dancing to watch. Bora full-on glowers at me like she wishes I'd messed up.

Her annoyance only makes me want to do better. I hold my head up high and give her a look that says, *Yeah, I can dance. What are you going to do about it?*

She glances away first, scoffing like she can't believe my nerve. I know it's probably not a good idea to make an enemy of one of the judges, but I just can't keep being intimidated by someone who's so clearly a bully. Enough is enough.

We're running through the choreography again and again when something happens. At first, I think I imagined it, but then it happens again. Henry's stomach *growls*. It's quiet and barely audible over the music, but I'm positive it's not my stomach, and everyone else is too far away.

Henry notices my stunned expression and gives me a sheepish look. "Had to skip breakfast to beat traffic."

I frown at him. It's past two now. He must be starving.

"Don't you have . . . people responsible for feeding you or something?" I ask, gesturing to his team at the back of the room.

Henry gives me a startled look. "Oh, they're just my PR team. Portia posts my pictures and takes care of logistics for me, while Steve makes sure I get where I need to go safely. I can't ask them to fetch me food . . . that's below their pay grade."

I shrug. "Some people do. I've heard stories about how celebrities order their staff to do chores and stuff like that."

He shakes his head. "I'm not that type of person. That'd be so insulting. I didn't even ask Portia to spray me when I got injured during the first elimination round. She insisted on doing that herself."

I can't help but respect him a little bit for saying that.

Then, I get a pretty wild idea. I have no idea if he'd be down for it, but I figure it's worth asking.

"Hey, do you . . . wanna grab tacos after this?"

Chapter Thirteen

AS SOON AS THE WORDS LEAVE MY MOUTH, I realize it sounds like I'm asking him out.

"Not as a date or anything," I quickly add. "It's just that if you're hungry, I know this really good taco truck in Koreatown. And I've been craving tacos for *weeks*."

I think about asking Tiffany and everyone else if they want to tag along, too, but then I remember how Henry's manager was nervous about me not being vetted, so I can't imagine how she'd react to more strangers. As awkward as it'll probably be, maybe Henry and I are better off going by ourselves.

Henry cocks his head in a contemplative gesture and runs his hand through his hair as he glances behind us at Portia and Steve. "I'll have to ask Portia about my schedule, but if she says I'm free, I'm down. Come to think of it, I don't think I even ate dinner last night."

"You don't think?" I practically yell. A few people turn around to see what's going on. I'm glad the camera crew is on break, because this is *not* something I want on camera. "What were you even doing yesterday?"

Even as I'm saying all of this, I inwardly cringe. Everyone's stares make me self-conscious, and for a half second, I'm afraid Henry will crack a "joke" about why I'm so "obsessed with food," like a lot of people think fat people are. But he doesn't. In fact, he actually looks kind of touched that I'm bringing this up.

"I honestly don't remember," he says. "My schedule's so busy these days that I just . . . forget to eat or sleep sometimes. It's really bad, I know. But yeah, let's definitely go get tacos afterward if I'm free. Thanks for the suggestion."

Henry's team doesn't seem happy about the idea, but they still meet us in front of the studio after practice. Henry himself, however, has a really bright smile on his face, like a little kid about to go to the candy store.

"How did you convince them to let you go?" I whisper to Henry as we walk across the parking lot.

"Oh, I just told them it'd be a great partner-bonding activity. Which is true. We're going to have to become *very* comfortable with each other for the next few weeks."

He raises his eyebrows, and I look away before our eyes can meet. I'm still reeling from today's turn of events, but that doesn't mean I want to let my guard down around him. We might have to get through this round together, but at the end of the day, he's still competition. With only ten people left after this round, I definitely can't afford to get distracted by him.

I only asked him out for tacos because I was genuinely concerned for him as a fellow human being. Or at least, that's what I tell myself as we pile into the car.

Henry's car is a black Suburban SUV like the ones I've seen celebrities riding around in LA. Henry gets in the back with me, while Portia rides shotgun.

"Okay," I say when I'm settled in my seat. "So, what's the real reason *you* agreed to come with me for tacos?"

"Oh, you know. You're probably my biggest threat in this show, so I need some time to get to know you and figure out your weaknesses."

He says it in such a deadpan voice that it's hard to tell if he's kidding or not.

"Seriously?"

Henry shakes his head with a laugh, his face instantly melting into his dorky grin. "Nah, I'm kidding. I'm a total Hufflepuff. No backstabbing here. Just a lot of emotional crying."

I snort. "Can't relate. I'm Slytherin."

I don't mention that I was *just* thinking about us being competition and how I need to beat him—in true Slytherin fashion.

Henry gasps, looking scandalized. "Oh no, should I fear for my well-being? Check for poison in my kombucha?"

"Kombucha *is* poison," I reply in the same deadpan tone Henry used before.

Henry guffaws, and I can't help but smile.

"Just kidding," I continue. "You're safe. For now. I still need you for this round!"

"Oh, of course." Henry's smiling too. "Well, that's a relief. Okay then, let me ask you the same question. What's the *real* reason you asked to get tacos?"

I hesitate and then say, "Well, first of all, I love tacos, so I'm always down to get some. And then . . . well, you just seemed really hungry. And exhausted."

As I say those words, I realize how right I am. I was too preoccupied with practice to notice before, but now I see the slight dark circles around his eyes.

"You noticed?" Henry asks, his voice growing soft. But I pretend not to hear him. Instead, I give Steve the directions to the taco truck and stare out the window as we drive through LA.

The sky is light blue and cloudless as always, and tall palm trees line both sides of the street. The trees and sun are the only consistent things about LA, since the buildings change depending on which neighborhood we're driving through. As we approach downtown, the hipster cafes and Spanish-style houses give way to concrete office buildings and glass skyscrapers.

"So," Henry says after a while. "Would you believe me if I said that I've never had tacos before?"

I give him a skeptical look. "No, I'd say you're lying."

"What can I say, I only eat kale. And kombucha. Or I guess I eat kale and drink kombucha. You know what I mean."

"*What?* Really?"

He smiles, and I realize he's joking again.

"Nah. But that's a decent part of my diet. I mostly eat vegetables and, like, lean protein. Not really allowed to have much else, except in special circumstances. Not allowed to have soda, either, so I get all the fizz I want from kombucha."

"Not allowed?"

"Yeah, I have a personal nutritionist who determines my diet for me. Minimizes breakouts and any other disasters that can ruin shoots."

I remember then that Henry literally makes a living off his looks. And not just his looks, but how good he appears on camera. *The camera adds ten pounds,* Bora said at my audition. It sounded so ridiculous when she said it, but I can't imagine how stressful it must be to have your entire life depend on how you look in pictures or how your skin decides to behave that week.

"Still," I say. "There *are* vegetarian options for tacos. You never thought to try one?"

"Well, I guess it's also largely because of how I was brought up. I moved to the States when I was in seventh grade, for school. And my parents were pretty strict about not eating food that required me to use my hands or food that comes from food trucks, because they think it's dirty."

"Ugh, they sound like my mom," I groan.

Henry shrugs. "It's a very old-fashioned Korean mind-set. I think people *just* started finding out about food trucks in Korea, and only because they've seen the ones in LA. But yeah, I guess I was so used to that attitude that I never thought to try tacos myself."

After a few minutes, we arrive at the parking lot where the El Flamin' taco truck is. El Flamin' is like any other taco truck except for two distinguishing features: 1) it's painted with orange-red flames like a Hot Wheels car, and 2) its tacos are *amazing*, with freshly cooked and sliced al pastor meat that they grill on a giant stick right in front of the truck. I've only been to El Flamin' one other time, but it was so good that every other taco place has paled in comparison ever since.

Steve pulls up to the curb. As I reach for my bag under my seat, I see Henry pulling a sleeveless white hoodie, a white baseball cap, and a pair of blue aviators from the back of the car.

"So no one will recognize me," he explains as he puts everything on.

"Does that really work?" I ask, amazed. He still so clearly looks like Henry Cho to me. His height and cheekbones aren't exactly average, especially not for an Asian guy.

He shrugs. "Usually, yeah. Honestly, most people are really bad at spotting celebrities when they're not expecting it. You've probably passed by at least a dozen celebrities without noticing."

"Probably," I grumble, knowing he's probably right. That would explain why even after sixteen years of living around LA, I've only seen *one* celebrity in the flesh.

"Have fun, guys," Portia says with a strained smile as we get out of the car. She's all tensed up, like Henry and me going out for tacos is a PR nightmare waiting to happen.

For a moment, I wonder why she doesn't stop us if she feels

so nervous about the whole thing. But after one look at Henry, I kind of understand why. Even though I can't see much of his face anymore, I can still see how he's practically bouncing up and down in his seat like a little kid. It makes me wonder how often—if at all—Henry gets to hang out with people. From the way he's acting now, I doubt it's a lot.

I can't help but think about the Henry Cho I saw last month, so confident and grown-up as he responded to Davey's questions that first day at auditions. And then there's the other Henry Cho I saw a few weeks ago, when he was barely suppressing his anger because of whatever had happened with Melinda. It's hard to believe that those two Henrys and this really happy, almost puppylike dork are the same person.

"Thanks, Portia. Thanks, Steve. See you guys later," he says, cheerfully waving at his team before closing the door behind him.

The SUV drives away, leaving us in the parking lot.

Chapter Fourteen

HENRY TURNS AROUND AND TAKES ONE STEP back when he catches sight of the taco truck.

"Wow . . ." he says. "It's . . . really red."

I beam. "Yup. It's called El Flamin' taco truck for a reason."

Even though it's midafternoon, there's a long line snaking around the parking lot in front of the bright red truck. It's a hot day and some people are sweating so much that they're soaking through their shirts. The heat and smoke from the al pastor spit next to the truck don't help either. But the food smells so amazing that no one seems to care.

We get in line. As we slowly approach the truck, Henry takes out his phone and starts snapping pictures.

"I like it," he says. "Has a quirky charm to it."

"Is this going on your Instagram?"

"Yup."

I can't say that I'm surprised.

When we finally get close enough to see the menu next to the service window, Henry's mouth drops open. He looks completely overwhelmed, like he has no idea where to even begin.

"Honestly, you can't go wrong with any of the choices," I tell him. "Although if you want the complete experience, you should get the carne asada fries with whatever tacos you end up picking."

"All right. I'm trusting your judgment."

When it's our turn to order, Henry gets the al pastor pork tacos and carne asada fries while I get chicken tacos. Before I can pay for my own food, Henry holds up his card to the taco truck vendor.

"My treat," he says. "A thank-you for showing me this place."

Although I normally don't like owing anyone, I let Henry pay this time. The entry fee for *You're My Shining Star* took out a good chunk of my Lunar New Year money, so I'm pretty broke right now. And it's no secret how rich Henry is, even without his modeling career.

We manage to find seats at one of the plastic picnic tables set up nearby. While we're waiting for our food to come out, Henry takes pictures of everything from the rack of al pastor meat skewered on the vertical spit to the line behind us. I guess some people would find it annoying, but I don't mind. All of my friends pretty much live on Instagram, and, like Henry, they also take pictures of everything whenever we go somewhere new.

The way Henry takes pictures, though, is different from how

my friends take them. Every shot he takes is really methodical, like he's photographing a crime scene. He even snaps a few shots of me, but I don't say anything since I doubt Henry will post them on his Instagram. Aside from Melinda (back when they were dating) and a few of his celebrity acquaintances, I've never seen Henry post pictures of anyone but himself or his dog.

"Sorry," he says when he notices I'm staring at him. "I don't know which pictures will be worth posting later on."

"It's fine. I don't mind. There's a reason why you have so many followers on Instagram, right?"

I mean it in a good way, but Henry only gives me a tight grin that's almost a grimace. "Right."

I debate with myself whether I should ask him my next question. It's something I've always wondered about celebrities.

"Um," I say.

Henry cocks his head to the side, reminding me a bit of his dog. "Hm?"

"Do you ever get tired of . . . you know, all this?" I gesture first at his "disguise" and then at his phone.

He deflates, and I suddenly feel really bad, even though I'm not sure why.

"Yeah, honestly, I do," Henry says after a while. "I mean, a lot of the time, it's fun. But on some days, it feels like work. It *is* work for me, even though I'm sure some people don't see it that way. Even though I primarily do modeling in the traditional sense, I do get a lot of informal requests from brands to do sponsored posts for their products. It's an extra source of income."

"Sorry," I quickly say. "I didn't mean it like that. I guess I'm just always curious about what it's like to, you know, be a 'celebrity.' It must be hard, always having to hide from paparazzi and stuff."

Henry nods. "Occasionally, yeah. But getting into modeling was actually a relief for me because people finally cared about me because of what I did, and not because of whose kid I was."

"Are your parents supportive of your modeling career?"

"They are now. But they weren't always. Most of the time, they asked me why I felt the need to do what I want to do."

"Ugh, I can definitely relate with that," I say.

At that moment, the vendor calls out, "Harry? Your tacos and fries are ready."

Henry gets up from his seat.

"Harry?" I ask.

"I gave them a fake name in case someone recognizes me. Don't blame me, blame Harry Potter."

I barely suppress a smile. *Who would have thought Henry Cho would be such a big Potterhead?*

As Henry comes back with our food, all smiles and happy excitement, I can't help but think that if people had Patronuses, Henry's would be a dog. A big, fluffy one.

"Holy crap," he says. "You were totally right. Everything looks so good. It *smells* amazing, too."

Henry sets down a tray with all four of our tacos and a plastic to-go container with his fries. Our tacos look just as good as I remember them being, brimming with juicy, still-smoking meat, onions, pineapple chunks, and chilies.

When he's settled back in his seat, Henry opens the container of fries and gapes at it. I don't blame him. The carne asada fries take up the entire to-go container and are topped with avocado and generous layers of cheese and sour cream.

He takes pictures of our food, but after that, he just sits there, like he isn't sure what to do next. Trying my best not to laugh, I give him a small nudge. "Go ahead. Try the food!"

"How am I supposed to grab the tacos off the plate without everything spilling out?" Henry asks, looking overwhelmed.

"Tacos get messy no matter how hard you try to be neat. It's fine. It's not like we're at a fancy restaurant. We're literally in the middle of a parking lot!"

"Fair."

Before he picks up his first taco, Henry sheepishly hands me his phone. "Do you mind?"

"Not at all."

I don't even have to ask to know what he means. I focus the camera on him and it's like he's a totally different person, suddenly every bit the model I know him to be. Even with the hoodie and glasses, his easy, sexy smile shines through, making him look ridiculously attractive. He looks like he belongs in an actual advertisement for tacos. If I sent El Flamin' taco truck his picture, they'd probably gladly post it on their Instagram.

"God," I say as I take the photo.

He frowns slightly. "What's wrong?"

"How are you so photogenic?"

A startled laugh escapes from Henry's lips, but he doesn't say anything as he puts his phone away. He looks pretty embarrassed by how I've been scrutinizing him this whole time, so I take out my phone and snap a picture of our food.

"You know what? I rarely post on Instagram, but I'll post a pic of our tacos, just for you. Consider it a little memento of our meal together."

A little smile plays on Henry's lips as he watches me post the picture on Instagram.

"Thanks," he says, laughing. "I feel honored."

In the end, Henry chickens out from eating first, so I grab one of my tacos, being careful to keep all of its contents within the tortilla as I take a bite. Henry watches me for a moment and then follows my lead, gingerly lifting one of his tacos to his mouth. At first, I'm worried that he'll be too preoccupied with not making a mess to enjoy what he's eating, but fortunately, he loosens up. By the time he's done with his first taco, he's reaching for the fries without a second thought, a bright, satisfied smile on his face.

"Feel free to have some of my fries, by the way," he tells me as he happily digs in.

"Thanks!"

The food is so good that I actually forget how to talk until my plate is empty. Henry is equally preoccupied, so neither of us say anything until we're both finished with our tacos.

Henry leans back in his seat. "That was so good. Thanks for suggesting wc go here, Skye."

"Sure, no problem," I reply. "I'm glad you got to eat something."

We're finishing off his fries, taking turns grabbing one long, cheesy stick after another from the container, when Henry asks, "Where are you off to after this?"

"Well," I say, "normally, I'd go to my mom's studio, since she works near here. But things haven't been so great between us since she found out about the competition, so I might just take the metro to Union Station and ride the train home from there."

"Let me give you a ride home. I'll ask Steve and Portia. Where do you live?"

"Orange County. But really, you don't have to. Traffic is probably bad right now."

"Traffic's always bad in LA."

"True."

Henry texts Portia, and we sit on the parking lot curb to wait. We end up talking about pretty much everything, and by the time the Suburban pulls up, Henry and I are deep into a discussion about our favorite Korean rappers.

"I really love RM," Henry says. "He's the backbone of BTS. It's really impressive how he can speak English, too, even though he's never lived in the US."

"Right?" I agree. "I really like Dean and Zico, too."

"Did you have a good time?" Portia asks when we get in the car. The almost mom-like way that she asks the question makes me realize that Portia is probably a lot older than I thought she was. People always joke about Asian people looking younger than they are, but even I have trouble figuring it out sometimes.

"Yup," Henry replies. "You should try the tacos here sometime. They're amazing."

"Oh, El Flamin' tacos? I've already been. Who *hasn't*?"

Portia and I share a laugh. Henry rolls his eyes in a good-natured way.

As we exit out of LA to turn onto the highway, I can't help but think that Henry is not at all like I thought he would be. I expected him to be stuck-up and obnoxious, but he's actually sweet and considerate, to the point that now I'm even more curious about what made him so angry during his fight with Melinda.

The highway headed away from LA isn't as clogged up as the one heading toward it, so we get to my house sooner than I thought.

"See you at the next practice," Henry says as I get out of the SUV.

"See you."

I get a glimpse of his smile—the real one, not the one tailored for the cameras—before he closes the door behind me.

Chapter Fifteen

ON MONDAY MORNING, I WAKE UP TO THE RATTLE of my dresser. At first, in one confused, half-asleep moment, I think there's an earthquake. Even though severe earthquakes are pretty rare where I live, they happen frequently enough that the rattling makes me bolt up from my bed. But it's just my phone. And it's buzzing with so many notifications that it freezes up when I try to swipe it open.

Make it stop! Panic flashes around in my head like emergency lights, and even more so when I see that I only have fifteen minutes to get to school. Yesterday, I worked my butt off late into the night, scrambling to finish my homework. I must have been so tired that I forgot to set my alarm before I went to sleep.

The time flies by way too quickly, and my hair is still dripping wet when I run out the door. Normally, I'd do my makeup and pick out a nice outfit, but not today. I consider myself lucky that I even remember to wear pants.

I only have time to actually look at my phone when I step through the school doors. The notifications are still popping up, with no signs of stopping. This time, though, I'm ready for them. I read what each bubble says.

Most of the notifications are from Instagram, but there are also a lot of texts. I don't recognize most of the people who requested to follow or message me on Instagram, so I go to my texts first, glancing up occasionally to make sure I don't run into people in the hallway. Since it's way too late for me to meet up with my friends in the cafeteria, I head straight to my locker to get my books.

Most of the texts are from Clarissa, and most of her messages are just full of emojis and long strings of "OMG."

CLARISSA HAN: OMG. OMG OMG OMG OMG. 😱 🫣 😳 DID YOU AND HENRY CHO GO ON A DATE? OMG SKYE, WHAT'S GOING ON???

Henry. I finally have an idea about what must have happened. I flash back to him taking photos of me. I didn't say anything when he took a picture of me, but only because I didn't think he would post any of them. But apparently, I was *really* wrong.

I tap away from the long string of "OMGs", exiting out of the conversation with Clarissa to read a text from Rebecca. Rebecca rarely texts, so it's a big deal that she did.

REBECCA NGUYEN: Um, Skye . . . You might want to check Instagram . . .

After taking a deep breath, I finally open Instagram to see

a post on Henry's account that went up just a few hours ago. It's a collection of four photos: the picture I took of Henry, the blazing glory that is the El Flamin' taco truck, our tacos and fries, and . . . me. Fortunately, it's a pretty good picture. I don't look weird and there isn't any food stuck in my teeth. I'm even smiling the perfect amount, so I'm not grinning too wide in a way that—according to Clarissa—makes me look like a serial killer. The caption simply reads **Had fun grabbing tacos with @newskye16**.

He tagged me on Instagram. This must be where all the requests are from.

I didn't tell Henry my username, but he must have seen it when I posted the picture of our food on Saturday.

I'm relieved that, all things considered, the post is relatively harmless. Sure, a few people stared at me when I walked past them in the hallway, but it's not like Henry is as famous as Taylor Swift or any other mainstream American celebrity. Even still, I'm overwhelmed by how many people thought it was okay to randomly request to follow my private Instagram account just because I was hanging out with Henry. I have two hundred new requests and counting. A lot of them are from complete strangers and bot accounts, but some are from people I know at school.

I feel utterly grossed out and don't add any of them. These people never bothered to give me the time of the day before I appeared on Henry's feed. Why would I become friends with them now?

Before I can stop myself, I read through the comments on Henry's post. And I instantly regret it.

Most of them are pretty harmless, with messages like, "Wow, those tacos look really good!" or "😍 So handsome!" But there are also endless strings of pig emojis and lots of "oink oink" responses and even some comments that say extreme things like "Go die! Henry is mine."

My face heats up as I scroll through the comments. I always hear about celebrities getting bullied off social media, but I never really understood what that was like until now. I know I'm going to have to get used to this if I want to be a K-pop star. And if I were more established, or if I even had a heads-up before this happened, I'd have been more okay with it. But now, I just feel like the wind's been knocked out of my lungs. And I hate how weak and crappy everything makes me feel.

I'm thinking about deleting my Instagram when the one-minute-warning bell rings. I grab my books and run to my psychology class, where Rebecca's waiting in her seat.

Worry flashes across her face when she catches sight of me.

"Hey," she whispers as I sit down in front of her. "Are you okay?"

Only then do I realize that I'm shaking from head to toe. Aside from the brief, stabbing feelings of hurt and panic, I've felt mostly numb this entire morning. But suddenly, under Rebecca's concerned gaze, I have to fight really hard to not burst into tears. Since I can't trust myself to say anything without dissolving into a human puddle, I just shake my head.

"Oh, Skye . . ."

The tardy bell rings.

"All right, class," says Mr. Peterson. "Clear your desks except for a pencil. I hope everyone's ready for a pop quiz."

As if this morning could get any worse . . .

The quiz is so big a disaster that it makes the *Titanic* look good. At least some people survived *that* sinking ship. I'll be surprised if I don't get a big, fat zero.

Rebecca tries to talk to me both during and after class, but I just shake my head. I've never been good at talking about bad things when they happen, and today's no exception. I don't want to think about the quiz. And I don't want to think about what happened on Instagram. The only reason I haven't already run out of the school doors screaming is because I have a precalculus exam during my last period.

I already failed in one class today. I can't afford to do the same in another. Mom made it clear multiple times this weekend that she won't let me go to rehearsals if my grades drop.

I'm not in the mood to talk to anyone right now—least of all my Henry Cho–worshipping friends—so I go to the library during lunch. My precalc grade is already hanging by a thread. And no way am I retaking the class.

My phone's still going off relentlessly, so I slide it to Do Not Disturb mode. I listen to music as I study, going through my usual playlist of K-pop girl-group power anthems. The songs are usually upbeat and loud enough to clear my head even on my worst days, and thankfully, today is no exception. I power through my entire lunch period without even a single thought about Henry or his Instagram post.

Even with all my studying, the exam is still pretty horrible. But I expected as much, since precalc is my worst subject. I'm glad that I at least finished all the questions this time. And I feel way better about it than I did about the psychology quiz.

With everything going on today, I've been in such a state of anxiety that I didn't even go to the bathroom. So as soon as the last bell rings, I run to the nearest restroom. Only when I'm sitting on the toilet do I open up my phone again.

The number of notifications has greatly increased since I last checked them. More follower and message requests on Instagram. More texts. Thankfully, my phone is freezing up a lot less now with Do Not Disturb on. But I still can't look at the screen for more than a minute before feeling like I can't breathe.

And this is all from *one* single post. *How does Henry handle this?*

Before I turn off my phone, I look at my text messages again. My friends kept texting me throughout the school day, and I can tell they're really worried about me. Even Clarissa stopped her stream of OMGs to ask if I'm okay. I feel bad about leaving them hanging, but I'm too drained to answer everyone individually. So I go to my group chat with Clarissa and Rebecca and say: **Hey, I'm okay. Sorry, busy day. I'll explain everything tomorrow.**

I'm washing my hands in the sink when I realize that I haven't heard from Henry during the entire day. None of my hundreds of Instagram notifications were from him. He either doesn't care about what happened to me today or has no idea that anything even happened. I really hope it's the latter, but heat still rises up inside me as I wonder if this was his plan all along. Was I part of some gimmick so he could get more attention on social media?

I dry my hands, and I'm about to shoot him a DM on Instagram when two girls I vaguely recognize enter the bathroom. They freeze when they see me.

"Is that . . ." whispers one of them. I think she's a freshman, and her name is either Brenda or Brenna Kim. We went to the same Korean school, but I haven't seen her much since then.

"It *is*," says the other girl.

In almost perfect unison, they take out their phones and send pictures of me to all their friends on Snapchat.

Chapter Sixteen

"HEY!" I YELL. "CAN YOU GUYS STOP? YOU'RE BEING incredibly rude."

The two girls gape at me before scurrying out the door. I try to run after them, but by the time I'm out of the bathroom, they're nowhere in sight.

"That's it," I say. "I've had enough."

I pull up Instagram and slide into Henry's DMs. I don't know Henry's number, and I don't know if celebrities like him even check their direct messages, but this is the only thing I can think of doing right now.

Hey, can you please untag me from the taco truck pictures? Your fans are targeting me on Instagram. And people in school are being ridiculous.

Almost immediately, the word "Seen" appears below my message. Henry types a response. Or at least, I think it's Henry until I see the reply.

Skye, this is Henry's manager, Portia, the message reads.

Henry's at a photo shoot right now. We're so sorry for the major inconvenience we've caused you. Henry actually doesn't manage his Instagram anymore. I do. We always have notifications off, so I didn't realize what happened until now. I'll take the post down immediately.

Hi, Portia, no problem, I reply. Thanks so much for the fast response.

I breathe a sigh of relief. Well, at least Henry and his team are nice people.

Suddenly, my phone starts vibrating. It's Clarissa.

I let the call go to voice mail, but Clarissa just calls again.

"Skye!" she screams in my ear when I finally pick up. "WHERE ARE YOU? Did you go home already?"

"No, but I'm gonna head back soon."

"Meet us at the front of school!"

I cringe, wondering if I should have lied and told her I already went home. Even though I do feel bad about isolating myself all day, I really just want to be alone. But I know my friends won't stop bothering me until I meet up with them.

Clarissa and Rebecca are waiting for me when I reach the front of the school. Rebecca looks just as worried as she did in first period, while Clarissa looks concerned but also kind of jealous.

"YOU WENT ON A DATE WITH HENRY CHO?" Clarissa screams at me. She rushes closer, like she's about to give me a hard shake, but Rebecca holds her back.

I shoot her a thankful look.

146

"Why have you been so unresponsive all day?" Rebecca asks. "We've been worried. *Right, Clarissa?*" She gives Clarissa a pointed look.

Clarissa frowns. "Well, yeah. Of course I was worried. But honestly, I've been so confused because I had no idea what was going on! I saw your picture on Henry's Instagram. Everyone's talking about you. Are you, like, famous now?"

"I . . . don't think so?" I say. "And sorry for being nonresponsive. I panicked when everything happened, and then I had to study for my precalc exam in seventh period."

"Man, brutal day," says Rebecca.

"Yeah," Clarissa says, looking a bit guilty. "Hey, want to go get some ice cream? Or shaved ice? You can rant about everything while we eat."

That's when I realize that's exactly what I need right now. My friends aren't perfect, but they know me. And sometimes, that's more than enough.

We end up going to a Korean shaved ice place, and I tell my friends about everything over bowls of matcha, red bean, and taro shaved ice. We split the cost of all three flavors and get three spoons, like we always do. Rebecca and I wait until Clarissa finishes taking pictures of our shaved ice before we dig in. We're pretty much used to it by now. She's not as obsessive about photos as Henry is, but she's close.

When I'm done telling them all about my last two weekends and about what happened today, Rebecca asks, "Did he at least ask for your permission before he posted that picture of you?"

I think back to what Henry said as he took the pictures. I'd said I didn't mind, without fully realizing what that meant. I tell Rebecca this, and she groans. Clarissa laughs, but then covers her mouth.

"Skye . . . you really just . . ." Rebecca trails off. "Wow."

"For the record," I say. "I didn't think he would bother to tag me! Or even post my photo."

Rebecca sighs. "What am I going to do with you?"

"Wait," Clarissa says. "Sorry for playing devil's advocate here, but I still don't get why all this is a bad thing. Aren't you in that K-pop competition? Shouldn't all this publicity be a *good* thing? I heard the show factors in popularity votes in the last round. You should be congratulating yourself on what happened! Not beating yourself up. All that exposure!"

In a way, she's right. And part of me knows I should just grow thicker skin and be thankful for the free publicity. But I also can't help but feel like there's no way my friends could ever understand what it was like to see those pig emojis flooding the comments of Henry's post. Neither of them wears anything larger than a size 4.

Instead of saying anything else, I look down at the sad puddles of melted shaved ice left in our bowls.

"Still," Rebecca says. "It's not like Skye was ready for something like this to happen so quickly. The audition hasn't even aired yet! No one knows who she is."

"True," concedes Clarissa. "I guess I didn't think about that."

I give Rebecca's arm a grateful squeeze. She always knows the right thing to say.

We're about to leave the ice cream shop when my phone starts ringing. I do a double take when I see the screen. It says, "No Caller ID."

Clarissa grabs my arm so abruptly that my phone almost goes flying out of my hand.

"Oh my gosh! I bet it's Henry Cho! He's calling you. He's *actually* calling you!"

"Shhh!" I say. "Everyone be quiet so I can talk to him. Clarissa, calm down. I don't want to scare him."

Clarissa rolls her eyes at me, but silently nods.

I accept the call.

Put him on speaker! Rebecca mouths at me.

I nod and tap the speaker button. "Hello?"

"Skye?" Henry's voice is so sharp that it catches me off guard. I've only heard him sound like this when he was telling off Bobby. "Are you okay? Sorry I was MIA all day. I just got out of a photo shoot. Portia got your number from the competition committee. Hope it's okay that I'm calling you right now. I just wanted to make sure you're all right."

"Yeah," I say. "I am now. Thanks. And I appreciate you getting in touch with me."

Even his voice is hot! mouths Clarissa.

Rebecca face-palms.

"Sorry," Henry says again. "I didn't realize that something like this could happen. That people would react this way."

"It's fine. You didn't know."

Rebecca elbows me in the gut, knocking the air out of my lungs.

"Ow!" I hiss.

"It was *not* fine," Rebecca blurts out. "He's a celebrity. He should have been more responsible!"

Oh. My. God.

We all freeze. Clarissa looks like she's about to scream again, this time in pure horror. I want to scream too. My face heats up, even though Henry is nowhere nearby. Even Rebecca seems shocked at her own outburst.

There's nothing but silence on the other end of the line. At first, I think Henry hung up on me. But then he slowly says, "Oh, am I on speaker?"

"Um . . . yeah, sorry. I was hanging out with my friends and—"

"We wanted to make sure you're not a creep!" Rebecca cuts in.

I love Rebecca, I really do. But right now, she's giving me serious Asian-mom vibes. Then again, I guess it's mainly my fault. I really shouldn't have put my phone on speaker.

I walk a few steps away from my friends and take my phone off speaker. "Sorry about that. You're not on speaker anymore."

"It's fine," Henry says. "I get it. It's great that your friends

are looking out for you like that. And the one that spoke up—
she's right. I *should* have been more careful. Sorry, I won't
bother you anymore. Hope you have a good rest of the day."

The call ends before I can say anything. Baffled, I stare at
my phone for a good long moment.

"Did he *hang up* on you?" Rebecca gasps. "After everything
that happened today? Wow, he's trash."

I expect Clarissa to defend Henry, but even she's pursing her
lips.

"I mean, he apologized," I say. "I don't know. He sounded
really weird. He wasn't like this before."

Except he was, once. I wonder what my friends would say if I
told them about what happened between Henry and Melinda.
I skipped over that part, since it didn't seem like my business
to tell, but now I wonder if I should have.

What if this cold and mean Henry was the real Henry all
along?

Chapter Seventeen

IT TAKES A FEW DAYS FOR THE EXCITEMENT ABOUT Henry and me to die down. Even though Portia deleted the original post, a lot of Henry's fans and even some online journalists had already taken screenshots of it and shared it elsewhere. Gossip articles popped up about how Henry and I are "dating," with a lot of them discussing how "interesting" of a rebound I am after Henry's relationship with Melinda.

I lose count of the number of times I've rolled my eyes. I hang out with Henry *one* time and people are already calling me a "rebound." And it's really disgusting how people think it's "interesting" for Henry to date "a girl like me." People are so transparent with their fatphobia sometimes.

My first instinct is to uninstall all my social media apps, so I don't see what the thousands of strangers who shared the gossip articles online are saying about me. But since we only have one other official dance practice before the second elimination round, I keep Instagram. I need it to contact Henry.

But when I message Henry's account to ask if he wants to meet up sometime to practice, neither he nor Portia responds. They just leave me on "Seen." After obsessively checking my phone for an hour, I make myself stop. Even though my chances at the dance part of this competition are crumbling into little pieces, I still have the voice portion. And at least *that* part I can do something about.

Since "Crazy in Love" is such a dance-dependent song, at rehearsal on Saturday I teach Lana a few moves that we can both dance during the instrumental breaks. Despite what Lana says about being "just okay" at dancing, she manages to follow along to the choreography with only a few mistakes. Practicing with Lana is going so well that I almost forget how horribly things are going with Henry. Almost.

During our lunch break, Lana catches me sulking behind the studio. Thankfully, everyone—including the camera crew—is on break now, so I'm taking full advantage of the fact that I don't have to smile and pretend everything is okay.

"What's up?" she asks, her eyebrows knitting together with concern.

"Ugh, it's Henry," I say. "I wish things were going well with him like they are with us, but he's avoiding me for some reason. Won't even answer my DMs."

She frowns, leaning against the wall beside me. "Why? I thought he was cool with dancing with you. Didn't he volunteer to be your partner? That's what Tiffany told me."

"He did. And he was fine with it for the first practice. But ever since we went out for tacos and the whole Instagram thing happened . . . well, I haven't heard from him since."

"Guys are so strange. I'm so glad I don't have to deal with them."

"I mean, it's not like I'm dating Henry."

Lana does a double take. "Wait, you two aren't dating?"

"Nope, those are all just rumors. I literally only invited him out for tacos because he said he hadn't eaten anything for the day."

"Skye . . ." Lana groans. "Henry's a celebrity. You can't just go out with him like that without expecting some scandal to break out."

When she puts it that way, what we did does sound pretty reckless. Still, I can't bring myself to really regret that day. What happened afterward sucked, but we had a good time.

"Honestly," Lana continues. "I've heard some really strange things about him. To be fair, I don't know him personally, so I don't know if any of it is true. But I have a few friends who went to Harvard-Westlake with him, back before his parents pulled him out of school. Apparently, he doesn't have any friends. Like, at all. He used to, a long time ago, but then something happened."

"Something? Like, what?"

"I don't know. My friends got really uncomfortable when I asked, so I didn't push. Seems like it was a big deal, though."

I think back to how excited Henry was to just be grabbing tacos with me. He definitely acted like he didn't get out much, so I can see how the rumors Lana heard could be true. A sinking feeling grows in my stomach. I don't know whether to be wary of him or feel bad for him.

After a while, Lana says, "Have you tried talking to him about everything? I'll never date a guy again, ever, but from what I know about my little brother, guys are awfully bad at talking about things. You can't just expect them to tell you what's wrong. You have to ask them first."

Just flat-out asking Henry about everything did occur to me before, but I couldn't bring myself to do it. Maybe it's because he's a celebrity, or because of what happened after we hung out, but I feel a bit intimidated by him. I know Lana is right, though. I can't just let this go on forever. And I don't want this to hurt my chances in the competition.

I make a mental note to *definitely* ask Henry what's up at our dance practice next week. If I message him, he'll probably only ghost me again.

I'm about to thank Lana for the tip when Barack Obama's voice suddenly booms out: "KAKAOTALK!"

I give Lana a look, and she grins like a five-year-old.

"I didn't know anyone actually used that ringtone," I say as I watch her open up her phone.

Everyone and their mom—maybe even their grandparents—uses KakaoTalk to message each other in Korea, and so do a lot of Korean people who live in the States. Since the only Korean friend I have from school is Clarissa, and she doesn't really use KakaoTalk, I only message my parents on it. The app has pretty hilarious ringtones and stickers that you can't get anywhere else, so I'm sad I don't have more opportunities to use it.

"They got rid of it in the app, but Tiffany and I changed our text notification sounds to it. It's an inside joke between us," Lana explains. "He was the most pro-gay president in US history, it was great."

I watch Lana excitedly text Tiffany back. Then, before I can stop myself, I blurt out, "What's it like?"

Lana startles, like she already forgot I was there. She looks confused for a moment, before realization slowly dawns on her face.

"It's amazing," she says. "When I was in high school, I was still dating guys and was always miserable. I couldn't understand why I didn't care about any of them or why I wasn't attracted to anyone. But then . . . when I started going out with Tiffany, well, this sounds cheesy, but it just felt *right*. I finally understood what all those love songs were talking about. You're not straight, right?"

"I'm bi," I say. "Or at least, I think I am. I'm still not sure about the whole pan-versus-bi thing . . . and I'm not sure if I'll ever be able to date a girl because, well . . ."

I sigh. Lana waits patiently for me to continue.

"Asian parents," I finish. "But no, I'm definitely not straight."

She nods sympathetically. "Yeah, I feel you. Both Lana and I got kicked out of our houses when our parents found out. We live together now, but . . . getting there was definitely not easy. And our families still give us a hard time about it. I mean, I wish they could just get over it and freakin' accept us already. But . . . it's been years and I think my parents are still waiting for me to get over my 'girl-dating phase' and find myself a guy."

Something in my heart cracks. It's one thing to see posts on Twitter and Tumblr about homophobic parents kicking out their kids, but it's a whole different level of pain to be friends with someone who's actually experienced it themselves. And as much as I hate feeling this way, I can't help but be relieved that I'm still safe. That my parents still don't know. That my parents might never even have to know.

"I'm so sorry," is all I can say.

Lana shrugs. "It is what it is. I can't change my parents any more than they can change me." She clears her throat and says, "Okay, enough sad talk. Let's get back to work. We're going to for sure make it to the next round, yeah? You better not fail me!"

"Okay," I laugh.

We bump our fists together, smiling.

After rehearsal, Lana and I are on our way out to the parking lot when Melinda steps right in front of me.

"So, you're Henry's partner."

Melinda's gray eyes give me a disapproving once-over, like she doesn't think I'm worthy. It's a stark contrast to how she looked at me the last time we interacted, when she was so desperate to be my friend.

And you're Henry's ex, I almost say back. But since I don't want to get slapped, I just say, "Yup. That's how things turned out."

A hand reaches out in front of me and gently pushes me back. It's Lana, and I shoot her a grateful look for coming in between Melinda and me.

"Excuse you," Lana says. "What do you think you're doing? Skye and I are tired after a long day of rehearsal, so you better not be stirring up some jealous-ex drama."

Lana is talking so loudly that the camerapeople—who were on their way home just seconds before—turn back around to circle us, switching their cameras back on so they can eagerly record our every move.

Melinda glances at the cameras and shoots us an annoyed look.

"Look," she hisses at me, completely ignoring Lana. "Henry and I are just taking a break. He's only dancing with you for this competition, that's it. So don't you dare try anything when you're clearly nothing but a charity case."

I was going to let everything Melinda said go, but that last bit makes me really mad. I never *asked* Henry to be my partner, and I never asked to be "rescued." And yet everyone's treating me like I just got lucky. I step away from Lana's protective arm so Melinda and I are face-to-face. I'm sick and tired of people believing that I don't have a rightful place in this competition.

"Listen," I say. "Henry and I aren't like that. The rumors

that I'm his 'rebound' are just that. Rumors. But don't go around calling me a charity case just because I'm dancing with your ex. If you wanted to dance with him, you should have tried out for the dance portion of the competition, too."

"I did," Melinda says through gritted teeth. "I didn't get in."

"Well then, I guess I'm not that much of a charity case."

By then, a crowd's gathered around us. I catch the Sponge-Bob T-shirt girl—honestly, at this point I'm wondering if she just has a closet full of SpongeBob shirts—and a few other people cheering for me. The cameras zoom in so they have a closer view of our faces.

Melinda narrows her eyes, but then she turns around and leaves without another word.

Chapter Eighteen

THE NEXT SATURDAY IS OUR LAST DANCE PRAC-
tice before the second elimination round. Things are bad. *Really* bad. Nothing is going right. Henry and I keep stepping on each other's feet. Our limbs get tangled up together, like we're playing Twister. I almost trip and fall flat on my face.

I can't stop myself from looking around at the other couples, and instantly regret it. Imani and her partner, Caleb Kim, are methodically going through each step of the dance, making sure they are perfectly in sync. Tiffany and Paul Johnston aren't doing as well, but they seem to at least be on the same page.

Envy creeps up in my head before I can stop it. The way Henry and I easily danced together just two weeks ago seems like a wild dream.

I'm on the verge of panicking. Not only is today's practice going horribly, but tonight is also the premiere of the first episode of *You're My Shining Star*. Clarissa and Rebecca have been texting me about it the entire week, but I've been mostly keeping my distance, only replying with one-word answers to their questions about the show. I don't mean to be a jerk, but it's hard to be excited about the show's premiere when things between Henry and me are so bad right now. My stomach twists into knots just thinking about it.

I'm still worrying about the premiere when Henry and I butt heads. Hard.

"Ow!" I yell.

Everyone—including, of course, the cameras—turns around to look at me. I'm in too much pain to care. My eyes water as I glare at Henry. He didn't cry out like I did, but his face is tensed up in a pained wince.

"Sorry," he mutters. It's the first thing I've heard him say since our phone conversation.

I think back to what Lana said and decide to follow her advice.

"That's it," I say. "Come with me. We need to talk."

I grab Henry's hand and pull him toward the studio doors. As we pass, people stop dancing to stare at us with their mouths open. Whispers fill the room.

"Where do you think you're going?" Bora says, stepping in my way.

The cameras are circled around us now, and I have to take a deep breath before I can say in a calm, matter-of-fact voice, "I need to go talk with my partner. We'll be right outside, but I'd like some privacy, please."

Bora shakes her head. "Absolutely not. Whatever private conversation you need to have with your partner can wait until lunch."

Lunch is in the middle of our day. We'll have wasted an entire half of the day by then.

"Just five minutes," I say. "Please."

"No," Bora snaps. She switches to Korean, speaking so quickly that I almost can't understand her. "You must think you deserve some kind of special treatment since Mr. Park saved you from getting eliminated, but I'm afraid that's not the case. Even now, you are causing such a disruption, wasting everyone else's valuable rehearsal time. I don't know how things work on American TV shows, but that's not how we do things on this show."

From behind her, I spot Imani, who mouths, *You need backup?* Even though Bora's talking in Korean, I guess it's pretty clear that I'm in trouble.

I shake my head. As much as I hate Bora, I have to admit she's right this time around. I never intended to cause such a big commotion, but it's clear from how everyone's stopped dancing that that's *exactly* what I did. I internally groan. This will look *great* on TV.

"Okay," I say. "Sorry."

I look back at Henry, surprised that he's been quiet this whole time. Unlike the charismatic celebrity he was on the first day, now he's barely responsive, just staring silently at the floor.

We go back to our places, and the rest of the morning is predictably horrible. By the time we break for lunch, I want to scream. Before I can say anything, though, Henry gently grabs my hand and pulls me out to the hallway while everyone gets in line for food.

"Okay," he says. "Let's talk."

"Ugh!" I say loudly, finally letting all my frustration out. "You *really* don't care about the competition, do you? We're definitely going to be eliminated in the next round if you keep dancing like a zombie."

Henry runs his hand through his perfectly swept-back hair. "I do care. I just . . . I don't know."

"Are you mad at me or something?" I try again. "Did I do something wrong?"

He blinks, as if he's having trouble processing what I said. For a moment, I think that's all I'm going to get out of him, but then he says, "You? No, how could I be mad at you? You didn't do anything."

I breathe a sigh of relief. It's the most he's said to me in the last two weeks.

"Okay then, what is it?"

He takes a deep breath and looks away, running his hand through his hair again. "It's me. I messed up."

"How so?"

"I shouldn't have let Portia tag you on the post, or at least I should've okayed it with you before she put it up. I'm so used to posting stuff with other celebrities, people who don't manage their own accounts and are used to that kind of exposure, that I didn't even think about how that might affect you."

I narrow my eyes at him. "Wait, so are you telling me that you were giving me the cold shoulder this entire time because you felt *bad*? You left me on 'Seen' because of *that*?"

Lana was right. Guys *are* stupid.

"I didn't let Portia respond because I thought you were forcing yourself to be nice to me. I don't know. Sorry, it's complicated."

"How so?"

"I realized I probably couldn't be friends with you after all. *Shouldn't* be friends with you. Honestly, hanging out with you after practice that day was great. I had so much fun, and it felt like a breath of fresh air, especially after the last couple of hellish weeks I've had. But what happened on Instagram was a wake-up call. I realized I couldn't just freely hang out with you. It was irresponsible of me, like your friend said."

"Or, you could just . . . not post pictures on Instagram."

It only occurs to me after I say it that I've been anticipating us hanging out again. Like it's something I can take for granted. If Henry thinks that's weird, he doesn't mention it. And even though I told Melinda that there was nothing between Henry and me, I can't deny that I liked spending time with him.

"But that goes against everything I am as a person," Henry says. His tone is completely serious, but his lopsided grin tells me he's kidding. His expression, as annoying as it is, is a welcome sight. He's finally loosening up.

When I don't say anything, he continues. The words flow out of him, like water rushing out from a faucet. "But yeah, I wasn't sure if I should have even volunteered to be your partner in the first place—not because of anything you did, but because of all the attention and drama that resulted from it. I also . . . well, I thought you were mad at me. Or you wouldn't want to deal with me again after what happened. And you'd have every right to not want to spend time with me. Not after what I did."

Henry's voice is now barely louder than a whisper. His vulnerability surprises me, and so does the pained expression on his face.

"I've had people stop being friends with me after similar things happened in the past," he continues. "Granted, the circumstances were really different. And I wasn't blameless then, either. But I was scared it was happening again. I'm sorry."

I wait for Henry to elaborate on what exactly happened between him and his friends, but he doesn't. So I say, "Well, what happened on Instagram definitely wasn't the happiest experience of my life. And I made the mistake of reading some of the comments. I've never seen so many pig emojis in my life."

Henry winces. "I'm so sorry."

I hold my head high, thinking back to what Melinda said about me being a "charity case." "Make it up to me by putting your all into this competition so we can move on to the next round. I won't accept any other apology."

"Okay, sure. I can definitely do that."

By the time we return to the main studio, everyone's already well into practice. I forgot how short our lunch break is.

Bora smirks at me from where she's observing everyone from the front of the studio, like she's pleased that Henry and I are missing out.

"Crap," I say. "We'll never catch up now."

Henry nervously drums his fingers on the door. "I know a place we can practice some more after this rehearsal is over. If you'd be comfortable with going there, that is."

"Where?"

"I . . ."

Henry sheepishly looks away and mumbles something. It's so uncharacteristic of him that I laugh before I reply, "What?"

"I have a private studio that I use whenever I want to dance by myself for a bit. It won't just be the two of us. Portia and Steve will be there with us, but I totally understand if you don't feel comfortable practicing there."

I'm desperate not to let this day go to waste. Besides, other than the whole Instagram incident, Henry, Portia, and Steve seem like good people. It's not like I haven't already hung out with the three of them before.

So instead of saying no, I ask, "Does it have AC?"

"Yup."

"Does it have a good sound system?"

"Yup."

"Then I'm good. Let's head there after practice."

∼

We drive down to Studio City, thankfully avoiding the busier areas with lots of tourists. Growing up near Hollywood is weird because countless people from all over the world visit here to take pictures of the Hollywood sign and go on the double-decker-bus tours. Meanwhile, to me, Hollywood is just another metro stop, and a huge inconvenience because of the exponentially bad amount of traffic it causes.

Steve parks the Suburban on the side of the street, and we go inside what looks like a run-down office building. But the inside is really nice, like the recording studio we practice in for *You're My Shining Star*. Aside from the dance practice rooms, there's a lounge area and a fully stocked bar, like we're in some exclusive club. Signed and framed photos of celebrities like Britney Spears and Demi Lovato hang on the walls.

"You rent out a studio *here*?" My voice comes out in a hushed, reverent whisper as I stare at the photos of famous artists who've practiced here.

Henry gives me a bemused look.

"Yeah. This room specifically." He taps a framed photo of Vanessa Hudgens and her backup dancers. "I don't think she still uses this room, though. That picture is pretty old."

Mouth wide open, I follow him up the stairs.

Thanks to Mom's small business and Dad's tech job, my parents make a decent amount of money, but I can't imagine being as rich as Henry's family. And even if we were, knowing my parents, they'd probably put a good chunk of that money into my college savings account and use the rest to visit family in Korea. Not rent an exclusive A-list studio.

I'm still thinking about Korea, and how badly I want to win this competition so I can finally go there again, when Henry stops to open a door.

"Well, this is it. Feel free to stretch and warm up. I'll go cue up the song."

Heart pounding in my chest, I walk into the studio. It's smaller than the one that we usually practice in for the competition, but it's twice as beautiful. The one they rent out for *You're My Shining Star* is more modern, with bright red walls and industrial ceilings, while this studio has strategically placed floor-to-ceiling mirrors and lighting that gives everything a soft, comforting glow. It's the kind of space I've always dreamed of practicing in.

Portia and Steve enter carrying a small plastic table and chairs and set them in the back of the room, next to the mini fridge and water dispenser. I ask them if they need help, but Portia just shakes her head and smiles.

"Okay, the song is ready," Henry says. He must have noticed me eyeing his team, because he adds, "Oh, they don't usually do that when it's just me. But we figured you'd feel safer if you and I weren't alone in the room."

Portia gives a friendly wave from the back of the room, like she's a soccer mom about to watch her kid play. Steve, as usual, doesn't say anything, but his gaze does look a bit less menacing than usual. The level of everyone's thoughtfulness is so extreme that it's simultaneously really awkward and really endearing.

Henry and I get into position in the middle of the room. Although we're doing the same thing we did countless times with everyone else, with just the two of us on the dance floor, it feels ten times more intimate. The studio we use for the competition is usually pretty noisy because everyone's always talking before the music comes on, but here, it's completely quiet. Even though Henry is standing just as close as he normally is when we practice, he seems even closer now, and I can hear the quiet, barely perceptible sound of his breathing. He always smells nice, but today, I can't help but notice how his ocean-breeze-scented cologne has undercurrents of wildflowers.

"God," I say. "You take the flower-boy thing a bit too far."

"Hm?"

"You know how in Korean, there's this phrase 'kkot minam'? Like, boys that are as pretty as flowers?"

Henry nods. An amused smile plays on his lips, and he looks down at me through eyelashes that are unfairly darker and longer than mine.

"Well, you're one of them," I continue. "But you also *smell* like flowers."

He bursts out laughing, and I nervously giggle with him. Being so intimate with a hot boy I barely know is pretty awkward, but at least we can both laugh about it.

As soon as the music starts, though, I forget about all the awkwardness. Like I always do, I throw myself into the elaborate choreography, spinning and twisting along with the beat.

Henry dances with me, and we move in sync, our bodies perfectly matched in our reflection in the mirror.

It's been so long since we've danced like this that I almost cry in relief. After hours of things being so mechanical and awkward between the two of us, it's ridiculous how everything comes so easily now. We're even *breathing* in sync.

I'm so glad I took Lana's advice.

As we're dancing, Henry smiles. And I smile back as he spins me into his arms.

Chapter Nineteen

HENRY IS QUIET FOR NEARLY THE ENTIRE DRIVE TO my house. He's tense, like he's nervous about something. Whenever we make eye contact, he smiles, but it's his fake, professional smile, not his real one.

Since Henry's clearly not in a talking mood, I plug my earbuds into my ears and listen to "Crazy in Love" on loop as I study some Quizlet flash cards I made for my psychology test on Monday. I have so much going on between school and the competition, I have to be as efficient with my time as I possibly can.

We're about to get off the 5 when I feel a gentle tap on my shoulder. I startle and look up from my notes to see Henry gesturing at his ear, like he wants me to take out my earbuds. I take one out and say, "Yeah?"

With uncharacteristic shyness, Henry holds out his phone. "Can I, um, have your number?"

"Huh?"

He glances away and runs his hand through his hair. "It'll make coordinating practices a lot easier this week. You said you wanted to practice during the week as well, right? Since we're so short on time."

I'd totally forgotten I said that during practice. Was that what Henry had been nervous about this entire time? "Oh, sure!"

I type in my number, and he texts me a quick message. My phone buzzes.

Henry's mouth slides into a lopsided grin. "Okay, good," he says. "So you didn't give me the number for the Rejection Hotline."

I snort. "I don't hate you, you know. At least not yet. Talk to me a week from now and that might change."

Henry raises his eyebrows at me in mock surprise. "Guess you're not one for 'friendly competition.'"

"We can be friendly," I amend. "But I'm still going to win."

He laughs, and his smile is so genuine that it makes me grin, too.

Wow, I think before I can stop myself. *I wish he smiled like that more often.*

I look away to add his number to my contacts. Or at least, that's what I tell myself I'm doing.

"Is this your personal number?" I ask.

"Yeah," Henry replies, sounding puzzled. "Why wouldn't it be?"

"Well, I don't know. Aren't celebrities supposed to be really secretive of their personal information or something? The last time you called me, it was from a 'No Caller ID' number."

"Oh, I was actually using Portia's phone because I didn't have mine with me. And she likes to keep things private since she has kids. As for me, well . . ." He grins. "I *am* secretive. You're the only person I've shared my number with in a long time. The only person besides Portia and Steve that I've genuinely interacted with for a long time, really."

He winces, as if he's mentally kicking himself for admitting the last part to me.

"Wait," I say. "What do you mean? Do you . . . not have any friends?"

"Not anymore. The last real ones I had were from school. Before my parents decided to homeschool me."

"Oh . . . did something happen?" I'm trying so hard to be sensitive that my voice goes way higher than usual. Hearing rumors that someone is friendless is one thing, but hearing them say it directly with their own mouth is a totally different, way sadder experience.

Just then, the car rolls to a stop.

"We're here," says Portia.

Unmistakable relief crosses Henry's face.

"See you later, Skye," he says.

Another day, another mystery, I think as I slide out of the SUV.

"Skye!"

I startle, because I wasn't expecting anyone to be home. But then I remember. Dad's back this weekend. It's not his regular week to be home, but he promised he'd be home to watch the premiere with me.

Sure enough, when I turn around, I see that Dad's out in the garden, pruning some of the bushes. Or at least, he was. Now he's just staring slack-jawed at the SUV as it drives off, his shears frozen in midsnip.

"*Ya*," he whispers, as though Henry and his staff could hear us from miles away. "Whose car was that? Is it some celebrity's?"

I give Dad a wary look, since I don't know how much he knows about pop culture.

"It's Henry Cho," I say. "He's a model—"

Dad gasps. "Henry Cho? I follow him on Instagram!"

"Y-you have Instagram?"

"Of course! Isn't Facebook on the decline right now? That's what I read in *Forbes*, anyway. All my college friends use Instagram now."

I groan. "Time to delete my Instagram."

I roll my eyes, but secretly, I'm more amused than horrified. Since he's an engineer, Dad tries his best to keep up with the latest technology, but he's also always saying things like, "Wow, this used to all be analog when I was your age!" or some equally embarrassing statement. I didn't know his hobby extended to social media, but I guess I shouldn't be surprised. Dad lives alone in NorCal, so he must have a lot of time outside of work.

"How on earth do you know Henry Cho?" Dad asks. "Is he in the competition too?"

"Yup, he's my partner."

"What? But why didn't you tell me that before?"

"It's still a secret! The first episode premieres tonight, remember?"

Dad's enthusiasm for Henry is so eerily similar to my friends' reactions that I almost walk away from my house right then and there. But it's Dad. Unlike Mom or my friends, I know he'll be my number one fan, no matter what. Or at least, I hope he will.

Dad excitedly throws his hands up in the air when I nod in reply. "Finally, our Skye will grace people's TVs with her talent! I can't wait. Watch party!"

I giggle. Only Dad can say silly things like that without making me automatically roll my eyes.

It's only then that I realize I've never really had the chance to update Dad about the competition. So I tell him about everything that's been going on in the last week or two, minus the Instagram debacle. Luckily, it doesn't seem like he saw Henry's post in the brief time it was up. And he doesn't read any gossip sites, either. Thank God.

When I'm done, Dad makes a really impressed sound. "Wow, look at you. You always work so hard. You're amazing, Skye. I hope you know that."

"Thanks, Dad."

He goes back to pruning the bushes, and I'm about to head

inside the house when he says, "Oh, so, Henry Cho. Is he nice? He better be treating you well."

I cringe. "You make it sound like we're dating."

Dad raises his eyebrows, and his expression becomes really stern. I almost laugh. It's been a while since I've seen him look so dad-like. "Are you?"

"No! Of course not. We're just dance partners. There are a bunch of rumors that we're together, but really, we just got tacos together. That's it."

Dad coughs and turns a little green. "Your mom had The Talk with you, right?"

"Dad! I told you, we're not dating!"

His coloring becomes slightly more normal, but his face is still unnaturally stiff in a way that makes him look constipated. "Okay. Good. If you two do end up dating . . . well . . ." He sighs, and his face finally relaxes like a deflating balloon. "I give up. It's probably better for you to go to your mom for that sort of thing."

"I know!" By then, I'm losing it, laughing really loudly despite my embarrassment. After a few milliseconds of looking absolutely mortified, Dad joins in. We laugh until we're both gasping for air.

"I know," I say again. "Don't worry, Dad. I know how to be safe."

Dad awkwardly scratches his head. "All right, well. Go wash up. I'll prep dinner in a few minutes."

"Nah, I got it. You probably need to finish up around the

yard, right? I can reheat some of the stuff in the fridge."

It's pretty amazing that Dad does the yard work for a house he barely lives in every time he visits from the Bay Area. But that's my dad. Prepping dinner is a small thing, but it's something I can do for him.

"You sure?"

"Yup. I always cook and prep food when Mom's working anyway. How about I make some jjajangmyun? I think we have some instant noodle packets left."

"Ooh, my favorite! Thank you, Skye. I really appreciate it."

He grins, and it's the sort of grin that makes my heart ache with how familiar it is. We have the same dimple on our right cheeks, which makes our smiles nearly identical. I wish I could see his more often. For probably the millionth time, I wish Dad lived with us again.

"Hey, Dad?" I begin.

"Hm?"

I open my mouth to reply when the garage opens, rumbling like thunder as the gate climbs slowly up. I look back to see that Mom's BMW has pulled into our driveway. Even through her tinted windows, I can tell that she's scowling. Probably at me.

"Never mind," I say. "See you at dinner."

Before Mom can get out of the car, I walk the other way to the front door.

Chapter Twenty

AFTER DINNER, DAD AND I SIT DOWN IN THE LIVING room to watch the first episode of *You're My Shining Star* on SBC, one of our main Korean channels. My skin feels all tingly with excitement, since I know the show is being broadcast simultaneously here, at six p.m. on Saturday night, and at ten a.m. on Sunday in Korea. I wonder if my family back in Korea will see the show, and what they'll think of my audition.

Dad and I cuddle up together on the sofa, and he clutches me tightly like *he's* the one about to make his TV debut.

"Oh my gosh, this is really happening," he says as he turns on the TV. "My daughter, woori Haneul-i . . ."

He trails off, and I crack up. Unlike Mom, Dad pretty much grew up in the States, so he rarely speaks Korean to me. He must be way more nervous than I thought if he's calling me "our Haneul" in Korean.

"Ya," Dad says, looking embarrassed. "Why aren't you

more nervous? You're the one who's going to be on TV in two different countries!"

I shrug. "I am, but at this point I've pretty much accepted that it's going to happen. And seeing myself on TV can't *possibly* be worse than auditioning in the first place, right?"

"I guess so."

At that moment, the TV screen momentarily goes black, before fading back in to a shot of Mr. Park sitting at a large mahogany table. It must have been prerecorded a while ago, because he's sitting in his office back in Seoul. The walls of the room are covered with framed posters of the countless K-pop groups he's nurtured from all the way back in the nineties.

"Welcome," Mr. Park says, "to *You're My Shining Star.* Over the last few years, K-pop has become an international phenomenon, with groups like BTS and Blackpink performing sold-out concerts all over the world."

As he talks, the show plays clips from various K-pop concerts in cities like London, Mexico City, Tokyo, and, of course, LA.

"After watching the rise and fall of countless K-pop competition survival shows in Korea, my colleagues and I decided it was time for a new type of competition to reflect the widening scope of the Korean music industry. Why should competitions be held in only Korea, when our audiences become more international every day? Thus *You're My Shining Star* was born, the first major K-pop competition set exclusively outside of Korea. We've had an exciting few weeks in sunny Los Angeles, as you will soon see today. Come witness the astounding talent and heart-stopping drama our participants have in store for us. We welcome you to *You're My Shining Star*."

The screen fades to black again, with loud trumpets blending into an obnoxiously happy K-pop song by Pixel, PTS Entertainment's lead girl group. Bright pink bubbles and sky-blue clouds display the credits, interspersed with footage of our auditions and practices. Every time my face pops up, Dad yells, "THERE SHE IS! MY DAUGHTER!"

His reaction is so cute that I almost forget the fact that Mom isn't here to watch the show with us. Ads for the premiere were plastered all over K-town, so Mom must know it's airing tonight.

By the time the opening credits end, Dad must have noticed Mom's absence too, because he says, "Hm, I wonder where your mom is."

"I'm honestly not surprised she isn't here," I say, trying to keep the disappointment out of my voice. "She's been pretty much ignoring me ever since I got into the competition."

"Is that so?" Dad says, looking worried. He glances upstairs, where my parents' room is. "I'll be right back."

Before I can dwell much on Dad's absence, my phone starts vibrating in my pocket. I look at the screen. It's a group Face-Time request from Clarissa and Rebecca. I accept the call.

"OH MY GOD, SKYE, IT'S REAL. YOU'RE ACTUALLY ON TV!" Clarissa squeals as soon as I pick up. "And they have clips of you dancing with Henry! I can't wait for that episode!"

I wince at the loudness of her voice, but I can't help but laugh at her enthusiasm.

"Do you know when they're going to show your audition?" Rebecca asks.

"No idea," I say. "Since so many people auditioned, they're dedicating the first two episodes to auditions. I might not even be in this one."

My friends and I watch the show together, and I laugh at the dramatic zooms and instant replays they've added into the footage. These effects are pretty standard for Korean TV shows, but it's so hilarious in a bizarre way to see the final footage after having personally experienced everything myself.

All the drama and exaggerated humor gets old pretty quickly, though, and I find myself laughing less and less, especially when the show starts making fun of people who I saw while I was standing in line. Sure, there are a lot of auditions where people absolutely kill it and are amazing, but there are just as many—if not more—auditions of people embarrassing themselves onstage.

I guess that's the entertainment value of the show, though, because my friends never stop laughing. After a while, I find myself tuning out and wondering why Dad isn't back yet.

"OH MY GOD," Clarissa shrieks. "IT'S HENRY!"

I turn my attention back to the screen, where, just like Lana and I predicted, there's an entire feature on Henry, starting from him entering the audition building to him performing onstage. I've never seen him dance solo before, and okay, my friends aren't wrong about how hot he is. With the same confidence and agility I recognize from dancing with him these last couple weeks, Henry perfectly executes the dance for NCT 127's "Cherry Bomb," popping and locking to the beat. NCT 127 is a pretty big group, and Henry somehow channels the energy of all ten members into his performance. Every time he jumps really high or drops down to break-dance, the audience screams.

I try really hard not to, but I smile. I can't help but be proud of my partner.

Then, finally, I hear someone coming down the stairs.

I hang up on my friends. **Sorry, guys,** I text in our group chat. **My parents are coming. I'll call you later.**

The show finally moves on from Henry, and at that moment, my phone buzzes. It's a text from Henry Cho himself.

Oh God, it says. **I thought they'd never stop talking about me.**

I laugh so loudly that Dad asks, "What's so funny?" when he comes back to the living room. He's alone, and although he's trying to smile, I can tell something's bothering him. I guess talking to Mom didn't go well.

"Nothing," I say, trying to keep my voice casual. "What's Mom up to?"

"She's actually watching the show on our bedroom TV," Dad says. "I tried getting her to come down here and watch with us. but . . ." He gives me a frustrated shrug. "No such luck. Sorry, Skye, I tried. At least she's watching, right?"

"Yeah, it's okay," I say. No matter the result, I can see from the tired look on Dad's face that he really did try. And I don't want Mom's negativity to ruin our watch party anyway.

Trying to ignore the uneasy feeling in my stomach, I refocus my attention to the TV screen, where Imani is dancing onstage. She does such an amazing job with her dance cover of one of Exo's songs that by the time she's done, Dad and I are cheering her on with the audience.

"Wow, she was fantastic!" says Dad.

"Yup!" I reply. "She was in my group for one of the rounds. Imani's probably one of the best dancers in this competition."

I send Imani a quick text.

You were so good!!! My dad and I were losing it while watching you on TV.

A reply comes almost instantly.

IMANI STEVENS: HAHA, thanks <3 Can't wait to see your audition.

Next up is Lana, who is unsurprisingly good, and then the SpongeBob T-shirt girl, whose name, I learn, is Mindy.

"Wait, did they show you yet?" Dad asks during a commercial break.

"No," I say. "I think they're showing people out of order. Henry auditioned sometime after me, but they showed him already. We might not even see me today, since they split the auditions into two episodes."

A few more people perform, and then I see myself walking across the stage.

My phone starts blowing up again, but before I can check

it, Dad squeezes me tightly into a bear hug. "THERE YOU ARE!" he exclaims.

"Dad, I can't breathe!" I yell, laughing as I pull away. We both watch as TV Me introduces myself.

"*Hello*," she says. "*My name is Skye Shin. I am sixteen years old and live in Orange County.*"

I cringe, not because I'm embarrassed of myself but because it just feels *weird* to see myself on TV. I'm not sure I like it. Suddenly, I understand why so many actors say that they can't watch their own movies.

"Wow, this is weird," I say. "It's like having an out-of-body experience."

"My daughter is so cool!" says Dad. "This is the best day of my life!"

"Dad, I haven't even performed yet!"

I spoke too soon, because at that moment, TV Me starts dancing. Dad is yelling, "Go, Skye!" and various other things so loudly that I can barely hear the TV. I have to admit, even though watching myself on TV isn't an experience I want to repeat anytime soon, I'm really proud of myself. I absolutely kill it, in both my dance piece and my vocal audition. And I hold my ground, my head high and voice mostly calm, even when the judges ask their fatphobic questions.

Dad starts cursing in Korean. "How dare they talk like that to my daughter?"

Seeing him get so mad at the judges makes me happy and sad at the same time. I'm glad that Dad has my back when it comes to strangers, but I wish he was the same way when it comes to Mom. Something clearly happened between him and Mom tonight, but what about the other times? I wonder if it's selfish for me to wish that he'd get more involved with stuff happening between Mom and me, when he spends so little time at home in the first place.

Dad suddenly wraps his arms around me in another bear hug, and I realize my audition is done. TV Me is walking off-stage.

"I'm so proud of you," he says. "Your audition, what you said, everything was amazing. I'm sure your mom is proud of you too. Even though she can't bring herself to admit that yet."

"Is she really?" I ask. "Have you seen the way she looks at me? It's like she desperately wants to switch me out for another, thinner daughter."

Dad winces. "Yes, she is proud. Take now for instance. If she really wasn't proud of you, would she be watching this premiere in her room right now? Her unwillingness to accept what you look like is . . . how do you kids say it . . . 'nothing personal.' I am not saying that her behavior is okay. I'll try to talk some more with her about that."

"Thanks, Appa," I say, calling him the Korean word for Dad.

My phone starts vibrating from an incoming call.

I check my phone again and nearly drop it. Not only do I have another incoming FaceTime call from Rebecca and Clarissa, but I have a hundred notifications and counting on Twitter alone.

By the time I recover, the call drops, but my friends make up for it by texting me in our group chat.

SKYE. SKYE. OMG!

CALL US BACK!!!! AND CHECK TWITTER!

SKYE, YOU'RE GOING VIRAL AHHHH!

Chapter Twenty-One

MOM DOESN'T COME OUT OF MY PARENTS' ROOM until almost midnight, long after Dad went to sleep. I almost wish she'd stayed in the room for the entire night, because she does not look happy. Or proud. Not in the slightest. Either Dad didn't get the chance to talk to her, or it didn't work.

"Haneul," she says flatly as she approaches my bed. I'd just finished getting ready to go to sleep, but now I'm wide awake, my heart pounding in my ears.

"I saw you on TV," Mom continues. "I really think you should drop out of the competition."

Heat rises up inside of me, and I clench my fists. "Why, did you think I was really that bad?"

She takes a deep breath and holds the bridge of her nose with her fingers.

"Not exactly, no. You were good . . . unfortunately."

She sits on the edge of my bed and taps her phone to show me a list of Google search results. Some of the results are in

Korean but a good amount are from English K-pop fan sites. It takes me a moment to realize that they're all about *me*. Right after my friends told me I was "going viral," I turned off my phone, because tonight felt too much like a repeat of what happened when Henry posted my picture on Instagram. I brace myself now before reading the headlines.

Is She the Korean Adele?

LA Teen Shocks Many with Stellar Performance

Skye Shin: New Teen Sensation and Henry Cho's Girlfriend?

The results go on and on. Most of them are positive, but I don't miss the ones that aren't. It's only been a few hours since the episode aired, but there are already tons of people posting about me on social media and message board websites. And a lot of them are saying stuff about my weight, pig emojis included.

It's the same hurtful things I saw on Henry's Instagram comments, but worse, since some people are even saying that the judges only accepted me as some sort of sideshow entertainment, so the audience can get a laugh out of seeing me dance.

She's just comedic relief, one comment says. **To relieve the tension, you know?**

It all hurts. So much.

Past feelings of shame burn bright again as I remember the

boys and skinny girls who teased me in middle school. One day after eighth grade PE, I returned to my locker to find a folded note with a piggy drawn on it. The drawing itself was actually pretty cute. The pig had anime-style chibi eyes and was drawn in a pink gel pen. But the meaning behind it, and the fact that someone had stuck this drawing into my locker, made me sick.

I never found out who drew it, but I didn't have to. I'd already seen the stares from the other girls as I changed out of my clothes.

"Clips of your audition are on YouTube already," Mom says. "And people are commenting nonstop."

My heart beats even faster than it was before. Of course, I *knew* people would watch my audition, and yeah, I *was* hoping I would make enough of an impression that people would know who I was, but I never thought everything would be this big of a deal. At least, not this early. I always thought that if I did "make it," I would become famous at the end of the competition, not at the very beginning. And I never imagined that everything would be this . . . stressful.

Honestly, I think I'd be okay with everything if Mom weren't right in front of me looking like she just found out I'm going to jail. I'm half expecting her to ground me when she asks, "Is there no way for you to drop out of this competition now?"

"Of course not," I say. "We're already almost two months in, and the second elimination round is next Saturday."

In reality, I'm sure I *could* drop out if I said there's an emergency, but there's no way I'm telling Mom that. I worked way too hard to even get into this competition in the first place. And the fact that Mom is even suggesting that I quit only makes me want to stick with the competition even more.

"And an episode of this show is going to come out every week?"

"Yup."

She cringes. She actually cringes. "How am I going to show my face to everyone after this? What am I going to tell my customers? Your relatives in Korea are already messaging me about the audition."

I can hardly believe my ears. She's thinking about how my going viral will affect *her*.

"Why can't you ever be proud of me?" I blurt out before I can stop myself. Some part of me, though, is glad I said it. I needed to get it off my chest. "You know I'm good. You even admitted it. *Why* is that not enough?"

"I just wish you were more self-conscious! People all over the world are commenting on how fat you are. And they're probably thinking I'm a bad mom for letting you become like that. I have to hide my face whenever I go to the Korean supermarket and pray I don't run into someone we know. I couldn't even open any of my KakaoTalk messages past the notifications because I'm afraid of what our relatives are saying."

Her face is full of real terror, like her worst nightmare has come true. I think about the photos Sally showed me on her computer. About how Sally said that Mom's this way because she's afraid of other people, not because she hates me. I also think back to what Dad said about how Mom's lack of support is nothing personal on my part. Now, I almost wish it *was*, because then I could figure out what to do about it. How am I supposed to fight this when it has nothing to do with me, and everything to do with Mom herself?

"Well, maybe they're just messaging you to say how proud they are of me," I say. "How do you know what they're saying without reading the full messages?"

"I just know," Mom says. Her eyes are steely, and I can't tell if she's mad at me or at what our relatives might have said.

I wish I could shake Mom and get her to see that none of that really matters. That all of her fears are more of a testament to how low her own self-esteem is than anything else. That no one cares about us and our image as much as she does. These are all things that Dr. Franklin, the school counselor, told me whenever I went to see him last year, and that's probably one of the few reasons why I'm so okay with who I am now.

Mom, though . . . I'm not sure if even Dr. Franklin would have any luck with her. She's so set in her ways.

But there is one thing that I know *will* change her mind. Or at the very least will get her to really see me and respect me more than any words will.

"What if I win the competition?" I say. "Will you still be unable to show your face around then?"

Mom looks like she's not sure whether to gasp or laugh.

"Haneul," she says softly. "Do you *really* think you have a chance?"

I ignore her patronizing tone and shrug. "I can try my best. I'll prove to you and all the haters out there that size doesn't matter. I'm a good dancer and singer, period. Me being fat doesn't mean I can't do things. And I'm going to show everyone that I didn't let anyone—not even you—stop me."

At that moment, her phone rings. She pauses for a moment, staring blankly at it without answering.

I get out of bed, in no mood to sleep anytime soon.

"I'm gonna go walk around the block," I say. "I need some fresh air before I go to bed."

Mom doesn't even look up at me as I leave.

Luckily, our neighborhood is really safe, even late at night, so I walk around while scrolling through my phone. Without Mom looking over my shoulder, I can actually process everything in peace.

Despite the pig emojis, most of the tweets I got tonight are pretty nice, with people saying how much I inspired them. I reply to texts from Lana and Tiffany, who missed the show when it was airing but are catching up now after coming back home from a night out. Finally, I FaceTime Rebecca and Clarissa again, and they go on and on about how proud they are of me.

"I, like, cried," Clarissa says, dabbing her eyes. "Look, I love Henry, and I'm still *so jealous* that you're his partner. But, wow, that speech you gave in front of the judges. And your performance! Consider me your number one fan."

"Ahem," Rebecca says. "I'm number one. You're number two."

"You can *both* be my number ones. Duh."

We all laugh. Talking to my friends is such a relief after what happened with Mom.

I'm about to head home when my phone buzzes with another incoming FaceTime call. This time, it's Henry.

It's silly, but I suddenly feel shy, so I let my phone ring a couple of times before I pick up. Even though we've interacted with each other plenty in person, I've never FaceTimed with Henry before. And somehow, accepting his call feels really intimate, like a step forward into uncharted territory.

"Hey," Henry says when I pick up. His surroundings are dark, and there's just enough light for me to make out his face. "Wait, are you outside?"

"Yeah," I reply. "I had a fight with my mom after the premiere, so I wanted to clear my head before I went to bed."

"Ah. Want to talk about it?"

"Not really. It's the same crap I've been hearing for all my life, just amplified a lot more."

"Got it. Well, here's a pic of my dog, Snowball, to cheer you up."

My phone dings, and I switch back to our texts so I can see the picture. It's of Henry's gorgeous white husky, dressed in what looks like a sky-blue onesie with cloud-shaped white buttons.

"OMG," I say. "Why haven't you posted this one on Instagram yet?"

I switch back to our conversation so I can see his face.

"Portia actually gave me a limit on how many pictures of Snowball I can post per week." He makes his voice higher, in a hilarious imitation of Portia. "'This is your professional Instagram! Not Snowball's dog-stagram!'"

I laugh. "Honestly, Snowball deserves her own Instagram. She's the reason I started following you in the first place!"

For a millisecond, I'm afraid Henry might be offended, but he just exclaims, "Aha! So maybe dog-stagrams are my true calling after all. Maybe I should talk to Portia about reevaluating our social media strategy."

I snort. "You're so silly. But also, please send me *all* the cute dog pics. I can't get enough. I've always wanted a dog but can't have one because my mom is allergic."

"All right, I will. My phone is mostly pictures of Snowball, anyway." He smiles shyly, before clearing his throat. "Anyway, I just wanted to tell you that I watched your audition and you were absolutely amazing. I mean, I knew that from the moment I saw you perform live, but I wanted to tell you that again. You deserve all the hype you're getting online."

"Aw, thanks. You were pretty great yourself. Your audition was really cool!"

"Between you and me, I almost broke my back on that stage. Like, literally," he admits with a wince. "But I'm glad it doesn't look like it. Really wish I'd started dancing as a kid."

"Well, you *were* going at it pretty HAM."

"I know," he groans. "Let's stop talking about it."

His pained expression makes me laugh.

By then, I'm back at my house, standing on our front porch.

"Well, thanks for the call," I say. "I have to go back inside and sleep, though. Talk to you later this week to coordinate extra practices?"

"Yup, I'll be in touch."

"You better be. You already ghosted me once."

"How about I message you so much that you get sick of me?"

"Forget messages," I say. "Just spam me with dog pics. That, and plans for practice. Nothing else."

Henry draws back in mock hurt. "Wow, I see how it is."

"I'm kidding," I laugh.

"I know. Good night, Skye."

"Night."

We hang up, and I'm left with this warm, fuzzy sensation inside my chest.

Oh no. Now it's my turn to groan. But there's no denying it. Even though I've been trying hard to avoid it, I guess it was inevitable.

I'm starting to have feelings for Henry Cho.

Chapter Twenty-Two

THE NEXT WEEK FLIES BY IN A FLURRY OF TESTS and extra practices with Henry and Lana. They're both nice enough to give me rides from school to LA, and I make it up to them by paying for gas. Or at least, I try to pay. When I offer to pay for Henry's gas, though, he just shakes his head.

"It's fine," he says. "Besides, I owe you for ghosting last week."

Henry and I text throughout the week to coordinate things, although admittedly, we text a lot more than necessary. I mostly talk about school and how I'm drowning in homework, while Henry tells me about the various fashion shoots he's in and, as promised, sends me pictures of Snowball to cheer me up.

On Friday night, the day before the second elimination round, I get a text from Henry. I open it expecting another dog pic. Instead, it's a selfie of Henry making a heart with his thumb and pointer finger, the way I've seen K-pop stars do.

He's got his face snuggled up against Snowball, and the white husky's looking directly at the camera with her mouth slightly open, so she looks like she's smiling.

Snowball and I are wishing you good luck tomorrow morning, says the accompanying text. You'll do amazing, I know it. And I'll see you in the afternoon.

Probably the worst thing about qualifying for both vocals and dance is the fact that I had to prep for both elimination rounds tomorrow—vocals in the morning and dance in the afternoon. I was feeling pretty anxious today, but Henry's picture is so cute that it makes me feel a bit better.

Thanks, I reply. Let's kick butt tomorrow.

I don't get much sleep, and way too soon, it's go time.

Bright and early in the morning, Lana, Tiffany, and I head to the performance venue. Per Lana's suggestion, the three of us are already all dressed up and in full makeup. Lana's driving, while Tiffany rides shotgun and I sit alone in the back with the bag of stuff I'm bringing so I can change in between my two performances.

"Ah, I'm so nervous," Lana says, anxiously drumming her fingers on the steering wheel. "What if I trip and die?"

"You won't *die*," Tiffany replies. "You'll just probably fall offstage in front of hundreds of people. Not to mention the thousands and maybe millions watching back home."

Lana playfully nudges Tiffany's side. "That's not very reassuring."

"I'm kidding. Of *course* you'll do fine. You and Skye have been working really hard. You two are totally going to rock it. Right, Skye?"

I've been silently wrestling with my own nerves in the back of the car, but I manage to cheerfully say, "Yup! We'll be okay."

"You do your best." Tiffany plants a kiss on Lana's forehead. "Regardless of whether or not you make it past this round, I'm so freakin' proud of you."

"Aw, come here, you."

At that moment, we reach a red light, and Lana kisses Tiffany full on the lips. Tiffany practically melts in her seat, her usually confrontational posture relaxing as the scowl disappears from her face. It's so cute that I don't even mind that I'm totally third-wheeling.

Just then, my phone buzzes in my pocket. I quickly put it on silent, because it'd be so bad if it went off during the competition.

I open up my phone to see a picture of Snowball with a pink-and-yellow flower crown. It's so adorable that I squeal out loud.

Lana startles in her seat. "What? What is it?"

I show Lana and Tiffany the picture of Snowball, and they both instantly "aww." The white husky is just that cute.

Coachella Snowball wishes you good luck and sends you good vibes, Henry texts as a caption to the picture.

ME: You can take pets to Coachella???

Knowing people in SoCal, I wouldn't be surprised if that

was a thing, but I've never heard of anyone mentioning bringing their pets.

HENRY CHO: Nah. 😊 But I still like to dress her up for that time of year. Have you been?

ME: No. You need to be 18 or older to go alone and there's no way my parents would go with me. Can you even imagine? Uptight Korean parents at Coachella?

HENRY CHO: 😂 😂 😂 😂 We should go sometime. Either Steve or Portia goes with me every year, depending on who's free. It's chill.

I try to imagine the life he lives on a day-to-day basis. How could someone be only one year older than me but have a life that's so different?

ME: Sure.

I don't ask him the question floating around in my thoughts. *Does this count as you asking me out on a date?*

I shake my head, as if that'll knock the thought out of my mind. This is going too far. Regardless of how I feel about him, I don't even know if Henry and Melinda are really broken up yet. Sure, the press and everyone else says they are, but if Melinda herself says they're not . . . I just don't know. Melinda may be a jerk, but I'm not one to steal other people's boyfriends.

I have to admit, though, texting Henry is a nice distraction. Almost all the tension I was feeling before fades away, and I feel a lot more relaxed than I was only a few moments ago.

When we get to the venue, Tiffany switches seats with Lana

so she can park the car while Lana and I head backstage. As soon as the stage manager sees us, she gives us instructions.

"You're team number six," she says. "The dressing room is on your right, if you still need to get ready. If not, please head over to the green room. It's on your left. Please be on standby after team number five leaves to perform."

I look to my right, where a crowd's already formed at the dressing room door. Thank God Lana had the brilliant idea to get us ready before we left.

Once we're in the green room, Lana leans back against the wall and is immediately engrossed in texting Tiffany. I settle down onto the couch with my bag, in between two Korean girls I recognize from practice. I think I actually know one of them from back when my parents used to make me go to Korean school. But they both give me wary looks before scooting farther away from me, whispering between themselves.

I try not to let that bother me. Instead, I close my eyes and sit back, trying to relax. My heart is already starting to beat faster than usual, and now I feel even crappier than I did before.

The room is full of nervous energy, and understandably so. Although we technically performed for a studio audience during the main auditions, this just isn't the same. We had months to prepare for those performances, and we didn't have to depend on another person to do well like we have to for this round.

The people who aren't warming up their voices and running through scales are on their phones, furiously texting or scrolling through Instagram. Many of them smile, and a quick glance at the other girls on the couch tells me that their friends and families are sending them encouraging messages. Besides Henry's, I don't have any other messages. Mom went back to passive-aggressively ignoring me again after the premiere last week, and Dad's in Seattle this weekend on an important business trip.

I didn't tell any of my friends about this performance since I knew they'd be just as nervous about it as I am. And I didn't want them screaming about it when I can barely handle myself. We'd already agreed to FaceTime after every episode, so I figured having their support when this episode airs a few weeks from now would be enough.

But now, I kind of regret being secretive. Even though it's mostly my own fault that my phone is silent, I can't help but feel lonely that no one's texting me well-wishes.

Instead of dwelling on how sad I'm feeling, I watch the TV as I run through some vocal exercises. The chairs and couches in the room are set up around it so we can watch what's happening onstage while we wait for our own turns. Currently, Mindy—the SpongeBob T-shirt girl—and Isabel are singing their rendition of Blackpink's "Kill This Love." Mindy can't be more than ten, but she has more swag than I can ever dream of having, and Isabel raps flawlessly in Korean. They're both so good that I can practically see fire emojis around them. When they reach the chorus, the audience sings along, shouting, "LET'S KILL THIS LOVE!" Before they even finish, the judges stop them and shower the two with praise.

Mindy and Isabel are a tough act to follow, and a guy in the duo after them totally freezes while singing a BTS song. Bora doesn't even give him a moment to recover before she slams her hand down on the big red reject button in the middle of the judges' table.

"NEXT!" she yells.

The guy bursts into tears, while his partner looks like she wants to murder him. Davey Kim, who's back to emcee this episode, tries to console the two as he escorts them offstage.

I wince. Man, things are getting brutal.

So far, no one has thought to incorporate dance into their performances. Even Mindy and Isabel focused more on the rap and vocals, only bouncing up and down occasionally to the beat. I smile. This means that Lana and I will stick out, and *not* in a bad way.

When team number four leaves for the stage, Lana comes to stand next to me. She raises her eyebrows at the gap between the girls and me on the couch.

What the heck? she mouths at me.

I shake my head, not wanting to start drama.

Lana just shrugs and plops down right between us. The other girls yell and jump up. They look annoyed but don't say anything when Lana flat-out ignores them. I laugh. Lana is the *best*.

When it's finally our turn, we head over to where the stage manager stands at the very edge of backstage.

"On my cue," she says.

"Next up, we have Lana Min and Skye Shin!" yells Davey Kim.

"Okay," the stage manager hisses. "Go. They'll start your music shortly."

As Lana and I walk onto the stage, I think about all the articles I saw on Mom's phone. *The Korean Adele.* I'm still not sure how I feel about that nickname, especially since I first heard it from my mom. But honestly? I don't want to be compared to anyone, period. I want everyone to know *my* name.

I take a quick glance around the audience, ever thankful that, unlike the guy who was just eliminated, I don't have stage fright. At first, I think I'm seeing things, but then I realize that some people are holding up signs with my face on them, like I've seen people do for K-pop stars at concerts. A lot of them have super-nice messages in Korean and English, like GO, GO, SKYE! and WE LOVE OUR QUEEN SKYE. I pretty much avoided social media altogether after the premiere, so I didn't really know the full scale of people watching the show until now.

This much love after the first episode alone . . . I try not to let it overwhelm me and instead think back to what Henry said about me being "worth all the hype." His words make me smile, and I'm still grinning when our music starts.

On our cue, Lana and I stomp across the stage in perfect unison, like we're going down the catwalk. Lana did our makeup so we'd look fierce like Beyoncé, and we're both wearing curve-hugging black dresses and high heels. I look and feel like a goddess, especially when people start screaming our names.

In the twenty seconds before we start singing, we move along to the beat, following the choreography that I made for the song. The audience goes *wild*. We're delivering fierce girl power, and the crowd is all for it.

My voice is lower, so I come in to harmonize with Lana. But just because I harmonize doesn't mean I'm outshined by her. To make things fair, Lana and I divided the song into parts so we each get moments where we can show off our voices. As we sing, we rotate between staring out at the crowd, at the cameras, and then at each other.

Lana's mouth quirks into a slight grin when our eyes meet.

It doesn't take long for me to lose myself in the rhythm and powerful vocals of "Crazy in Love." When it gets to my solo part, I really let go, letting the music pour out of my mouth like a flood. People scream, and they keep on cheering as Lana takes over and sings her part.

We then go back to singing together, our voices joining forces as we walk hand in hand down the stage. The cheers just get louder and louder so that by the time we finish, I can barely hear the music.

After the song comes to an end. Lana and I smile at each other before slowly dropping our hands back to our sides.

"There you have it, Lana Min and Skye Shin!" Davey announces, running across the stage.

We walk back to center stage as the judges finish scribbling down their notes.

Mr. Park goes first, and he claps loudly before saying, "*Brava*, ladies. You both did a really good job, and especially Ms. Skye Shin. You really are the Korean Adele. Or maybe even the Korean Beyoncé? I'm assuming the dance elements were your idea."

I nod, and he gives me a pleased smile. "Thinking like a girl group member already. Well done."

Next is Bora. She's actually smiling, something I've never seen her do before. But she's looking at Lana, not me.

"You girls really killed it out there," she says. "Amazing job."

When she turns to look at me, though, her smile immediately drops.

Oh boy, here it comes, I think.

"Miss Shin," she says, "you really are the Korean Adele. I agree with Mr. Park about that. But Adele is in her thirties, while you are a teenage girl. There simply isn't room in the industry for someone like you. You could have a great career if you were just a bit . . . thinner. You're still young enough that losing weight should be easy for you. Why don't you try a bit harder?"

Lana squeezes my hand tight. With my other hand, I lift the mic to my mouth and say, "Bora, like I told you before, I've tried my entire life to lose weight. I didn't always want to, but I was forced to by my mom. I've been on really extreme diets when I was a kid, before I realized that I'm perfectly fine the way I am. So, no, I will not 'try a bit harder' to lose weight, because that shouldn't matter in terms of my musical career."

I expect to be met with silence like last time, but today, the audience explodes into loud cheers. Some people even boo Bora.

Bora's face reddens, so slightly that I almost think it's a trick of the light. When she doesn't say anything in response, I know I've embarrassed her. Admittedly, I'm not sure if this is a good thing. On one hand, I'm proud of myself for standing up to her again, but I'm also not sure if this is the smartest thing to do to a judge.

Gary glances at Bora with a nervous smile before turning to face us.

"Both of you really killed it today," he says. "Good job."

And that's that. We go backstage, where Tiffany is waiting for us.

Almost immediately, Tiffany pulls Lana into a tight hug.

"You were amazing," she says, nuzzling her on the shoulder. She then meets my eyes and releases Lana to give me a hug as well. "*You* were awesome too."

"Thanks," I say, unable to keep the tension from my voice. I can't help it. Like she always does, Bora's puts me on edge.

Lana notices and gives me a quick nudge. "Hey. Don't worry about Bora, okay? She's just one out of three judges. Plus, think about all the kids you'll inspire around the world when this episode airs! For all we know, you might change someone's life by standing up for yourself like that."

I nod, feeling somewhat better. Even though I have no idea what the reality will be, it's easier to believe that Lana's right.

Chapter Twenty-Three

BY THE TIME THE VOCAL ROUND IS OVER, BACK-stage is a flurry of singers leaving the venue as dancers come in. I only have fifteen minutes to change and retouch my makeup, so I pull Lana and Tiffany into another quick hug.

"Good luck!" Lana says.

"Thanks! Good luck, Tiffany!"

"You too!"

I grab my bag from the green room and head over to the dressing room. It's pretty easy to find, since that's where people are entering and exiting the most. When I actually get to the doorway, my jaw drops. The room is even busier than backstage, with people yelling and even crying as they get ready. Everyone is scrambling to get into their outfits and do their makeup, pushing and tripping on other people in the process. It's pure chaos.

A girl's hair even catches on fire, causing everyone to scream.

I close the door. *Looks like I'm changing in the restroom.*

Thanks to years of choir and dance performances, I get ready pretty quickly in the restroom. Since the choreography for the dance portion requires a lot more movement and flexibility, I slip into my blue dancing dress and a clean pair of beige Bandelettes thigh bands.

I can't do my makeup as well as Lana did it for me, but I retouch it as best as I can.

After I'm done changing, I find Henry waiting for me at the edge of the stage. He's only wearing a gray tank and black sweatpants, but he might as well be on the cover of *GQ*. He looks that ridiculously good. The tank is tight enough to show that his abs are no joke.

I freeze, remembering the glimpse I had of them a few weeks ago.

He chuckles. "Hey, eyes up here."

"You're enjoying this, aren't you?" I grumble at him.

"Yup. I wouldn't be a model if I didn't."

I try to give him a light shove, but he dodges away with a grin.

At that moment, the stage manager walks in. "All right, we're going to start rolling the cameras soon. Bobby Lim and Cassie Chang, since you guys are up first, please stay here on standby. Henry Cho and Skye Shin, you two are up next, so please stay here, too. I'm going to have to ask the rest of you to either go to the green room or back to the dressing room if you're not ready yet, since it's not safe for everyone to be out here. The third couple should come out on standby when Skye and Henry go onstage."

I almost groan out loud. Because I was so busy this week, I didn't get the chance to check the list of who's going when. Now, I really regret not checking. Out of all people, why do we have to go after *Bobby Lim*?

Everyone else leaves. The stage manager is quiet, listening intently to her earpiece. She isn't doing anything interesting, so I chance a glance at Bobby and Cassie. They're both dressed in fancy matching outfits, and Bobby's shirt looks like it's made from the same material as Cassie's dress. They look like they could appear on *So You Think You Can Dance*. It makes me wonder if Henry and I should have gotten our outfits professionally made too.

That's when I notice the way Cassie's standing, with her legs crossed tightly together like she's trying to take up as little space as possible. She's also fidgeting, and she keeps adjusting the straps of her plunging V-neck dress. It makes me wonder if Bobby even consulted her before choosing their outfits.

"What are you staring at?" Cassie suddenly says. The venom in her voice makes me take a step back.

"Your dress—it looks really nice," I manage to say. I don't blame Cassie for being mad at me, but I don't want us to stay enemies.

She blinks, but quickly recovers enough to scowl at me.

"Thanks." She doesn't sound any less angry, but at least she stops fidgeting.

"Is *that* what you're wearing onstage?" Bobby asks me then. "God, I'm so glad I didn't end up with you."

Anger floods into me. I see red for a hot second.

"We're in a K-pop competition," I say through gritted teeth. "Not ballroom. So I highly doubt the judges will care if we're all dressed up or not."

Yeah, my usual blue dance dress is kind of old, but it's pretty enough. Most important, it's very flexible and stretchy, perfect for high kicks and splits. I could have asked Mom for a new dance dress, but I doubt she would have bought me one. If I pressed her, she'd probably make some snide comment about how it doesn't matter what I wear because I look bad in everything. Or about how "hard" it is to find decent clothes for me because of my size.

Yeah, no. I don't need that kind of extra negativity in my life. I'd rather wear an old dress.

"She looks fine," Henry says. "If anyone's underdressed, it's me."

Bobby turns to Henry. "I hope you're not regretting the switch, Cho. Because it's definitely too late now!"

He laughs, and Cassie stares at the floor, like she's embarrassed to be standing next to him. I'm about to give Bobby a piece of my mind when Henry says breezily, "No, I'm not. In fact, being Skye's partner is the best thing to have happened to me in this entire competition."

Bobby stammers for a second before saying, "Let's see if you still feel the same way when you're both eliminated."

Henry's totally sweet answer doesn't escape me, but by that point, I'm so mad that I don't care about much else.

"Are you really that insecure of your chances that you can't just leave us alone?" I blurt out. "If you're so convinced that you guys will win and we'll get eliminated, then go prove it. Blow us out of the water."

Bobby looks like he's about to respond, but at that moment, the stage manager clears her throat.

"Bobby and Cassie?" she says. "They're ready for you. Please head to the stage."

As they leave, Bobby pushes up the tip of his nose with one index finger.

Oh no he didn't.

"You're such a child!" I'm so fired up that I start after them, but Henry gently pulls me back.

"Hey," he says. "*Hey*. He's not worth it."

"I know, but we really shouldn't let him go around doing stuff like that. You saw Cassie, right? She looked miserable! Who knows what kind of crap he put her through over the past few weeks? And he just thinks it's okay to walk in here and say stuff like that to my face, to make that pig face at me—"

Henry places his hands on my shoulders and leans down so we're eye to eye. Our noses almost touch. In the quiet moment between us, I realize I'm crying. I've always been an angry crier, and today's no exception.

"Skye," he says gently. "We're better than him. *You're* better than him. Like you said, he's just acting like that because he feels inferior. You're entirely valid in being angry at him, of course. Heck, I'm *this* close to going after him myself. But we have to focus. Let's show everyone that we're better."

And then, finally, the fear I've been keeping trapped beneath all my layers of anger sticks its ugly head out. "But what if he's right? What if we don't make it past this round?"

Henry reassuringly squeezes my shoulder. "Come on, of course we will. We're amazing. *You're* amazing. I believe in us."

I take a deep breath and then let it all out. My heart is still beating quickly, but it's kind of impossible to stay on edge when Henry's so close to me, his large, dreamy brown eyes staring calmly into mine.

Someone coughs. I look up, expecting to see the stage manager. But she's nowhere in sight, and instead, there's a small crowd of cameras gathered around us, recording everything. Great. I was so preoccupied with my emotions that I didn't even notice that they were there. Were they there this entire time? It scares me that I have absolutely no idea.

I sigh, accepting my fate. Guess my mini breakdown is going to be on the show.

Henry looks up too, and if he's surprised by all the people watching us, he doesn't show it. Suspicion flares inside my head. Did Henry know about all the cameras? Was everything he said just for the show?

The stage manager walks in then, pushing through the crowd with a look of annoyance on her face.

"All right," she says. "Skye and Henry, please proceed to the stage."

"Ready?" Henry asks.

"Yup."

As we walk onstage, I push away all other thoughts from my head. I feel weirdly nervous and confident at the same time. But even though my heart feels like it's about to burst out of my chest, I know we're as ready as we'll ever be.

Chapter Twenty-Four

AS SOON AS WE STEP ONSTAGE, THE ENTIRE AUDI-torium explodes with screams and cheers. I hear "Skye!" a few times, but most of the voices, predictably enough, scream Henry's name.

"Wow," Henry says with a laugh that's barely audible with all the noise. For a second, I see a flash of tension on his face before he hides it under his professional smile. He gives the audience a quick wave, and the shrieking reaches a feverish pitch.

We stand on our taped-on marks, our eyes staring at the floor beneath our feet. It's something both of us decided to do when we were rehearsing, since it not only makes for a more dramatic beginning but also keeps us from being distracted by the audience. It seemed like a silly precaution when we were alone in Henry's private studio, but now, in the middle of all the screaming, I'm really glad we thought of this in advance.

The stage lights shine hot and bright down on me, and their

heat makes me feel like I'm slowly burning up. My heart beats superfast. Henry is motionless beside me, and I resist the urge to look up to see how he's doing.

There's a commotion backstage, and all of a sudden, Davey Kim comes running out onto the stage. "Sorry, everyone," he says, addressing the audience. He's all sweaty and flustered, but he speaks with a cheerful calm. I can see why he was hired to be the emcee. "There seems to be an issue with the main camera. We'll continue with our scheduled performances shortly."

The audience boos and makes other sounds of disappointment. Personally, I'm not sure how I feel about the delay. Part of me is relieved, but another part of me just wants to get everything over with already.

"You doing all right?" Henry asks quietly after Davey leaves the stage.

By now, the crowd must be resigned to waiting, because the noise level drops to a dim roar that's quiet enough for us to clearly hear each other.

"Yeah," I say. "I mean, the delay sucks, but I guess it can't be helped."

I chance a glance up at him. His eyes are still on the ground, and despite how hard he's trying to hide it, I can see from the way he's frozen stiff that he's *really* nervous. At first, I think I'm imagining it, but nope, he's really shaking from head to toe.

"Hey, are *you* okay?" I ask him. He's usually so calm that

it's scary to see him like this.

"Yeah. Sorry. Just stage fright."

"Ah." I think back to how he was also visibly nervous before the first elimination round. Curiosity gets the best of me, and before I can stop myself, I ask, "You're so good with cameras and people, though. How do you have stage fright?"

He shrugs. "Photo shoots and interviews . . . all of that is different from being onstage like this. I'm not a K-pop star. And I'm not a stage actor."

"True. But if you have such bad stage fright, how did you audition for this show? *Why* did you?"

"Pure determination and adrenaline. And the only reason I auditioned for the competition was because . . ." He winces. "You're going to think I'm really shallow."

"Try me."

"My ex. I was trying to prove a point to my ex."

I resist the urge to eye-roll. "Melinda? Is that why you guys had that fight on the first day of practice?"

He narrows his eyes, and I immediately regret bringing it up.

"No. That's not why," Henry says softly. "Well, I guess it's kind of related, because it all boils down to her being an unkind person. I auditioned because she told me I was nothing but a pretty boy that got lucky."

I don't say anything, since this is exactly what Lana and I said the first day we saw Henry at auditions. Now I know that's not true, because I know how hard Henry works to maintain his modeling career and how busy he is.

"So," I start. "Sorry if this is the wrong time to bring it up, but . . . Melinda and I had a little . . . 'chat' two weeks ago. And she said you guys were just on a break."

Henry groans. "Oh no, I'm so sorry you had to deal with her. But no, we're done. Definitely. *She* dumped me, and I don't do take-backs. After we broke up, I was really depressed. But then I found out about this competition and went, fine, I'll prove to her that I'm good for something. I'm not just a pretty face. Honestly, I don't care if I win or not. I just want to last longer than her in this competition."

I can't help but laugh. Despite our differences, Henry and I auditioned for *You're My Shining Star* for the same reason. We both wanted to prove to someone that we're more than our appearance.

"What's so funny?" Henry asks, looking slightly hurt.

I explain, and he laughs. "Honestly, you have a far nobler cause," he says. "I'm just being petty."

"Petty or not, I need your help to make it to the next round, okay? I know you're nervous, but just do what we did in practice and you'll be fine. You can creepily stare into my eyes for the entire performance if that helps."

"I'm not *that* bad," Henry replies. "Honestly, by the time we start dancing, I'll shake most of it off. It's the waiting that always gets to me."

Davey comes out again, grinning widely.

"They're finally ready," he says. "Thank you for waiting, everyone."

The audience roars in approval and excitement. He gives the crowd a quick bow before getting off the stage.

Henry tenses up again, and I give his hand a reassuring squeeze.

"We can do this," I tell him.

He squeezes my hand back just as the music starts.

We burst into action, spinning and moving around with the beat. Everything from the music to the audience is so loud that if it weren't for the earpiece in my ear, I probably couldn't hear the music. It's pretty overwhelming, but I still push on.

My body takes over, and as I'm dancing, I'm only vaguely aware of the crowd and the cameras flitting across the stage around us. I've run through the choreography so many times that I barely register the way my body moves. Instead, I focus on being onstage with Henry. And I focus on the small smile that appears on Henry's lips as he eases into the dance.

I've never been a couple-dance kind of person. I always thought that dancing with another person would tie me down. Limit me somehow. But dancing with Henry isn't like that. Maybe it's because I'm so at ease with him, but dancing with Henry is just as freeing as dancing by myself.

The spotlight flashes bright as it moves across the stage, casting shadows behind our dancing bodies. Henry drops me into a spontaneous dip as the camera zooms in close, and the crowd explodes into hoots and screams.

"Nice," I whisper into his ear before he twirls me out.

He doesn't have time to reply, but he smirks in a way that

says, "Told you I'd be fine."

And then, it's over. The camera does a final pan across the stage before swerving to the cheering audience.

Henry and I smile, for the audiences, yeah, but also for each other. We did it. We made it through the entire routine without a single mistake. I see the ecstatic joy I'm feeling reflected in Henry's eyes.

As we're staring at each other, something in Henry's expression shifts. He takes a step back and blinks like he's confused. I'm about to ask him what's wrong when Davey walks over to the front of the stage.

"What an astounding performance from Henry and Skye!" he says, gesturing at us in a grand flourish.

The roar of the audience is so loud that the judges have to wait before they can give us their evaluations. Everyone's enthusiasm makes my heart flutter, and I'm about to turn back around to smile at Henry when I see Bora whispering something into Mr. Park's ear. Mr. Park immediately whispers back, and Gary shoots both of them a confused look.

Uh-oh, I think. *This can't be good.*

Everyone slowly stops clapping when they realize the judges aren't showering us with praise. There's a tense moment of silence, and the room grows so quiet you could hear a pin drop.

"Okaaay," Gary says at last, still looking perplexed. I guess he couldn't hear what the other two judges were whispering about. "I'll go first. Henry and Skye, you two totally blew it out of the water. Even though everyone was assigned the same choreography, you guys somehow managed to make your rendition so unique and personal that everything was fresh and heart-stopping. Fantastic job."

There are some cheers from the audience, although it's obvious from the anticipation in everyone's faces that they're all waiting to hear from the other two judges.

Bora and Mr. Park stare at each other. Dread starts piling up inside of me like heavy weights, slowly suffocating me in a way that makes me want to scream, *Just say it!*

Finally, Bora leans forward to speak into the mic.

"I'm sorry, Miss Shin," she says. "But Mr. Park and I have chosen to eliminate you from the dance portion of *You're My Shining Star.*"

Chapter Twenty-Five

"WHAT?" HENRY CRIES OUT, AND HE'S NOT THE only person in the room voicing his disbelief. Gasps and confused murmurs in both Korean and English fill the audience. Even Gary says into his mic, "You have *got* to be kidding me! Park, are you actually okay with this?"

At Gary's protest, more voices join in the complaints, until I can't hear anything but angry voices. But instead of rejecting what Bora said, Mr. Park just remains still in his seat, staring at me with a pensive look on his face.

Meanwhile, I'm speechless. Even though I'd been dreading it, nothing could have prepared me for the gut punch of finding out I've been eliminated for real. Instead of being comforting, the crowd's complaints only makes the pressure inside my chest worse, because I can't help but think of all the people who wrote on social media that I'm an inspiration. I can't help but think of the countless other people who'll see me eliminated when this episode airs.

You still have the vocal portion of the competition. You're not completely eliminated yet.

I try to think positively, but I know it's different. No one ever doubted my ability to sing just because of the way I look. No one told me I couldn't sing because I'm fat.

"I thought you guys were eliminating people by group," says Henry. He sounds really angry, and some part of me dully registers how sweet he's being by standing up for me like this.

"We are," Bora says with a glance back at the still-silent Mr. Park. "In most cases. But Miss Shin has proven herself to be . . . problematic and unprofessional. Perhaps in an American competition, a contestant like her would be tolerated, but not here. Mr. Park and I have agreed that in the Korean music industry, such unprofessionalism would not be acceptable, and especially not in the world of dance."

As she finishes talking, an unmistakably triumphant smile flashes on her face. And then, I know. She's making all this up. All so she can say that she's won, and I've lost.

I feel sick. All my life, Mom's been telling me that I can't dance. Not because I'm not a good enough dancer but because of what I look like. It was painful enough to grow up with that, but it's ten times more hurtful to see someone trying so hard to get me eliminated just because they think my size isn't "professional."

I know I should say something, I know I should fight back and be strong for the people in the audience and for everyone who'll eventually see this episode at home. But what can I say?

If I defend myself, Bora will use it against me somehow. And I'm so tired of always having to fight.

My lip quivers, but I don't cry. I'm *not* going to let Bora see me break down onstage.

"Are you just going to keep sitting there and let her talk for you, Park?" Gary asks. "Jesus, I thought you were better than this."

Mr. Park slowly sits up, as if breaking out of some deep train of thought. "Please calm down, Gary. Perhaps you are too American to understand our decision, but I'm afraid this is a decision that Miss Jang and I have both made."

The producer then stares directly at me, and he actually looks sad as he says, "I apologize, Miss Shin. But I do wish you luck on the other half of the competition. Like I've said multiple times, you are clearly talented, and it'd be such a shame to completely lose you so early."

I can't tell if Mr. Park means his words as a threat or as an encouragement. Maybe they're a little bit of both. But the message is clear. *Don't get yourself eliminated for both.*

And I can't help it. Even though I know I'll be letting thousands of viewers down, I worked way too hard to completely let go of my chances at this competition now.

I clench my fists and bow first at Mr. Park and then at Gary, who still looks like he's about to walk out of the room. I skip Bora, because, duh.

"Thank you. I'll see you at our next practice."

Mr. Park gives me a firm nod.

Davey walks over to usher us offstage. Henry puts up a fight at first, but sadly falls limp when he sees that I'm not resisting. I don't meet his eyes. I can't. Not after I didn't say anything to defend myself.

Once we're backstage, Imani and Tiffany pounce on us, much to the chagrin of the stage manager. I can tell from her annoyed expression that they're not supposed to be out here.

"I can't believe the judges just did that!" Tiffany exclaims.

"Oh my gosh, Skye," says Imani. "Are you okay?"

By then, I'm barely holding it together. But somehow, I manage, mostly because of the cameras that have gathered around us. They already caught me in one compromised situation today. I don't want to let them witness another one.

"Excuse me," the stage manager says before I can think of what to say. "Please only stay here if you haven't performed yet. Everyone else has to leave."

"I'm gonna go," I say. "I'll talk to you guys later."

"Wait." Henry grabs my arm before I can turn around. "Let me go with you. I'll give you a ride back home."

It only hits me then that I don't have a ride back home without Lana or Tiffany. That's how out of it I am.

"Okay," I say. "Thanks."

I follow Henry out to the parking lot, where Portia and Steve are waiting in the SUV. As soon as we're in the privacy of the back seat, Henry places a hand on my shoulder and asks, "Hey, you want to talk about what happened? Or, I don't know, do you want to grab a bite to eat before we drop you off? You didn't have time to eat between the two rounds, right? You must be starving."

As if on cue, my stomach growls, and I only then remember that I haven't eaten anything since this morning. But I don't feel like eating.

Maybe Bora's right. The thought comes into my head before I can stop it. *Maybe I should try to lose weight again.*

Tears well up in my eyes as I think about the years I spent hating myself and my body. Entire days and even weeks went by when I barely ate anything, until I didn't even feel hungry anymore. I did lose a few pounds, but it was only a few compared to the crushing amounts of emotional pain I felt. No matter how much I worked out and no matter how little I ate, it was never enough. Do I really want to go back to living like that? Is there even hope for me in this industry *without* it? Sure, Bora is just one person. But there are probably countless like-minded people in the business. After all, she managed to get Mr. Park on her side.

I wonder if I should just give up now.

"Hey," Henry tries again. "Let's go to In-N-Out. Or, I don't know, anywhere else you want. You don't look well. You should eat something. I'm pretty hungry too."

And that's all it takes for me to completely lose it. Ugly sobs force their way out of my chest. I'm so ashamed that I almost let Bora think I wasn't good enough, that I almost let her win. I think about the posters I saw in the audience today, about all the posts on social media, and about what Lana said about me being an inspiration to the people watching me on TV. I feel like a big phony, and today, I feel like I let all those people down.

Without hesitation, Henry pulls me tight into his arms.

His grip is firm but gentle, and his body heat is so comforting that part of me wishes I could stay in his arms forever. But I get ahold of myself and pull away. When I do, large, wet puddles of snot and tears stain the gray fabric of his tank top. I'm so embarrassed that I cry even harder.

"Sorry," I say in between my sobs. "I made a mess of your shirt."

"No, no," says Henry. "Don't apologize. It's just a shirt. I may be a model, but I'm not *that* superficial."

He tries to smile at me, but his eyes are still so sad, even with his lopsided grin. This makes me cry more.

"Are you sure you don't want me to just sue all of them?" Henry asks. "Because this is thinly veiled discrimination. There was this guy in auditions who literally called Mr. Park an 'old man' and he *still* got in. Our family lawyer would have a field day with their 'professionalism' argument."

I cringe, thinking about how my mom would react if this turned into an entire lawsuit. She'd probably never speak to me again. And it's not like I want to ruin the entire competition, either, not when it's such an important opportunity for so many people. Besides, at the end of the day, I'm still in this competition through the singing category.

I still have a chance to win on my own terms.

I explain my reasoning to Henry, and he grimly replies with, "Fair."

"I appreciate it, though. Really."

He sighs. "Okay, then, what now?"

"Let's go to In-N-Out," I say. "What happened with Bora sucks, but I can't let her stop me from eating good food and living my life. I'll worry about everything else tomorrow, but for now, I need a break."

"Okay," replies Henry. "Animal-style fries today, competition tomorrow. You're going to knock everyone out of the vocals competition. I'm totally Team Skye, by the way."

I snort, but my insides feel all warm and fuzzy.

I only then realize how close Henry is to me now. Our noses almost touch, and his body heat again feels so good against my skin.

I'm about to kiss Henry when Steve clears his throat loudly from the front and says, "Excuse me. So, which In-N-Out are we going to?"

It's the first time I've heard Steve talk, but his voice isn't much of a surprise. He even *sounds* like the Rock.

Henry and I fall back against the back seat and laugh.

Chapter Twenty-Six

AT VOCAL PRACTICE THE FOLLOWING SATURDAY, our group is much smaller. Including me, ten people were eliminated from both vocals and dance, leaving the top ten for each category. Tiffany was eliminated from the dance category after me, so my only consolation is the fact that Imani and Lana made it to the next round while Bobby and Cassie did not.

The next challenge turns out to be a "versus battle," where each person will be mentored by one of the judges and then be pitted against another contestant in the next elimination round.

I expect Gary to "adopt" me, but he backs out, saying there's nothing he'd be able to teach me that I don't already know. Mr. Park chooses me without hesitation and makes me practice with a vengeance, pushing me into singing songs in styles I've never sung before, having me improvise and switch keys, and assigning me set practice times to follow at home.

"This is how hard you'll have to work once you become a

trainee," he tells me and the rest of his mentees. "If you can't handle this now, this path is not for you."

He seems to be training me *extra* hard, though, and by the end of the first week, I'm close to losing my voice. I'm wondering if he's trying to get me to drop out of the competition when I realize he's doing the opposite. As he pushes me, his expression isn't malicious at all, but determined and benevolent. It's like he's trying to get me to be the best vocalist I can be to make up for the fact that he eliminated me from the dance part of the competition.

Besides nearly losing my voice, everything is now admittedly a lot easier. Without having to worry about the dance part of the competition, I have more time to do homework and hang out with my friends from school. Although I stopped watching *You're My Shining Star* after that first episode, Clarissa and Rebecca give me the play-by-play every Saturday night. And I have to admit, even though all the antics on the show are things I've witnessed myself in real life, it's ten times more hilarious to see my friends react to them during our weekly FaceTime sessions like my life is some dramatic sitcom.

"OMG, I almost died during that moment between Melinda and Henry!" Clarissa exclaims. "That tension!"

"Skye!" Rebecca yells. "You did *not* just pick one of Lee Hi's songs for your first song. That ambition, though!"

"You and Henry are totally going to date," Clarissa says with a resigned sigh. "I can already see it. He only had eyes for you during the auditions!"

I don't respond to that last one. Even though Henry and I don't really have an excuse to interact with each other anymore, we've been FaceTiming almost every day since the second elimination round, switching to text when my voice can't handle it. Neither of us have tried to DTR, but I like the way things are now.

Or at least, I think I do, until Henry stops replying to my texts again and I'm left with nothing but questions. In the end, though, I just assume that work caught up to him. After all, it's not like we're dating. He's not obligated to always answer my texts.

In what seems like almost no time at all, it's Halloween. Rather than doing something scary for the holiday, though, Tiffany has a better idea. She texts Lana and me in our group chat.

TIFFANY LEE: Hey Skye, with the third elimination round coming up next week, Lana's been pretty stressed and anxious. And I know you probably are too. Wanna come to the Korean spa with us?

Lana jumps in.

LANA MIN: OMG YAS! Let's get rid of all that toxic stress and treat ourselves to a spa day!!!

And I have to admit, it sounds like a really nice idea. In theory.

But my heart still starts pounding, even more than it ever does onstage. Performances in front of thousands of people,

231

I can handle. But a trip to the Korean spa? Nope. No way. The thing about Korean spas is that everyone is naked, or at least, they are in the bathing area sectioned off for each gender. Sure, you can always skip washing up and change directly into the spa uniform instead, but doing that is kind of a waste of money, since most of the expense comes from running the baths. And not bathing before going into the sauna rooms when everyone else is clean also sounds too gross and rude for me to even think about.

Although I don't have problems with my naked body, I have way too many bad memories of my mom comparing me to every other girl in the Korean spa.

"Look how slim that girl's waist is!" she'd say. "And that other girl's thighs! Haneul, look how beautiful everyone is. Don't you want to be beautiful?"

Yeah, it got old pretty fast. Although I doubt Lana and Tiffany would be mean enough to make comments like that about my body, I can't help but feel uneasy. I've never even gone to the Korean spa with my school friends, and I've known them for years.

ME: Sorry, I'm not much of a spa person. You guys should go without me!

TIFFANY LEE: Oh, come on. It'll be fun! AND you can invite Henry.

I can almost see Tiffany raising her eyebrows right now.

LANA MIN: Yeah!!! DEFINITELY invite Henry.

I laugh to myself as I reply.

Henry's definitely not a spa person.

Of course, I don't know him well enough to know that for sure, but there's zero privacy in a Korean spa. He'd probably be lucky if no one secretly took a photo of him naked and posted it online. It sounds like a celebrity's worst nightmare.

LANA MIN: You can still ask? Please? Tiffany and I go to the spa together all the time, so it won't be as fun if you guys don't come.

I send multiple upside-down-smiley-face emojis.

ME: Fine. But if Henry doesn't want to come, I'm not going either.

I say this only because I'm sure that Henry would never say yes. He hasn't responded to me for several days now. He probably won't even reply to my text.

Much to my horror, Henry responds back only a few seconds later with, **Sure. Sounds fun. Which spa?**

I've never felt so betrayed by Henry. Why can't he be too busy to respond when I really need him to be?

When I don't reply for more than an hour, I get a text from Tiffany.

Well?

ME: . . .

TIFFANY LEE: . . . ???

ME: He said yes.

LANA MIN: YAY! Coming to pick you up in a bit!

I sigh and start getting my stuff ready for the spa.

Hopefully it won't be as bad as I think it'll be.

~

Lana drives us to the spa, which is on the outskirts of Korea-town. It's a Saturday in an unusually chilly October, so I'm not really surprised that the parking lot is nearly full, even though it's Halloween. We barely manage to find a space, and it takes me a while to spot Henry's car toward the back of the lot. I can't tell if there's anyone in it, so I shoot him a text.

Hey, are you inside?

HENRY CHO: Nah, still in the car. Can you come here for a sec?

We walk over to the SUV. Even when we're right next to it, Henry doesn't come out. I'm wondering if I was wrong about it being Henry's when I get another text.

HENRY CHO: Um . . . you didn't tell me you were coming with friends.

Shoot, I think, feeling instantly guilty. Heat flares up in my cheeks, and I hope Henry can't see me blush from behind the SUV's tinted windows. Sorry! I text back. Wait, did you think this was a date or something?

Henry types something. And then stops. I wait for him to continue. He doesn't. As more time passes, my cheeks get hotter.

"What's wrong?" Lana asks then. "Why isn't he coming out? Why are you blushing?"

I start to show Lana my phone when I get a series of rapid-fire texts from Henry.

Wait!

Don't show her the phone. Too embarrassing.

I'm coming out.

234

I'm fumbling in my efforts to hide my phone from Lana when the SUV's back door opens, revealing Henry and his dog, Snowball.

"Oh my gosh!" I scream. "It's Snowball!"

At the sound of her name, Snowball jumps out of the car. She's so big that she knocks me over, and I'm a giggling, screaming mess as she licks my face. Lana and Tiffany kneel down to pet her, and soon, Snowball's bouncing up and down as she tries to lick all of our faces.

"I know how much of a Snowball fan you are," Henry says. "So I brought her. She isn't going to the spa with us, unfortunately, for obvious reasons."

By then, I've calmed down enough to notice that Henry's wearing a "disguise" again, although I'm not sure how much a hoodie and glasses will help him when he needs to change— *and strip*—in the locker room.

"Hi, Skye!" Portia says from the passenger seat. Steve gives me a friendly wave.

Introductions aren't as awkward as I thought they would be. After Snowball settles back inside the car, Tiffany and Henry just nod at each other while Lana says, "So *you're* Henry Cho. You know, I thought you'd be a total jerk. But you brought your dog here for Skye . . . so I guess you're all right in my book."

"Well," Henry says, "I'm glad I have your approval now."

He laughs, but it's the same fake laugh he gave everyone on the first day of the competition. His eyes are guarded as he looks from Tiffany to Lana, and by now, I know him well enough to know he must be feeling really uncomfortable. Again, I feel guilty for forgetting to tell Henry that it wasn't going to be just the two of us.

"Oh, so," he continues, "I guess this is as good a time as any to tell you guys that I've never been to a Korean spa before."

"You've *never* been to a jjimjilbang?" Lana asks.

"Nope." He grimaces. "My family's always been too well known in Korea to go to public places like this. I always wanted to go, though. The ones in Korean dramas look really fun."

"Er . . . are you sure that you want to come inside with us?" Lana asks. "It's a Saturday, so it'll probably be really crowded."

Henry glances at me before responding, "I'll be fine. I checked the spa website, and people aren't allowed to take pictures in the locker rooms or the bathing areas. Plus, I'll have Steve with me."

As if on cue, Steve opens the driver's door and steps out. He's not wearing his usual suit, just a normal black shirt and a pair of sweatpants. Even in casual clothes, though, Steve is so tall and built that he looks intimidating.

"Whoa," says Lana. "He's like twice my size."

Steve gives us a sheepish grin.

"Is Portia coming?" I ask.

"I'm fine, sweetie!" Portia says from inside the car. "I have a lot of work to catch up on, so I'll just stay here with Snowball. Thanks for asking, though!"

"You guys go ahead," Henry says. "Steve and I will check

in together afterwards. Don't want to attract too much attention."

"All right," I say. "See you."

The lobby is pretty crowded with people either lounging about on the sofas or waiting to be checked in to the spa. There are cute jack-o'-lanterns and other Halloween decorations everywhere, but no one is in costume as far as I can tell. Practically everyone is Korean, and as we line up at the front counter, a few people turn around to stare at us. At first, I think they're staring because Henry changed his mind and followed us inside. But when I look back, he's nowhere in sight.

"My treat, guys!" Lana announces. Before either Tiffany or I can protest, Lana tells the lady at the counter, "Entry for three people, please."

At the sound of her voice, even *more* people turn around to stare at us. Some even take out their phones.

"Um, guys," I whisper. "People are staring at us. And taking pictures."

Chapter Twenty-Seven

LANA GLANCES AWAY FROM THE COUNTER TO look behind us. She, however, doesn't seem that disturbed. She even smiles *sweetly* and makes a victory sign with her fingers. "Oh," she says. "I think they recognize us from *You're My Shining Star.*"

"Right." I want to slap myself on the forehead. *Duh.* Even though episodes have been airing every Saturday night for three weeks, I've never really felt "famous." Not a lot of people at school watch the show, and nothing major ever really happened besides that one awkward moment in the bathroom after I got tagged on Henry's Instagram.

But Dad did mention that his friends occasionally ask about me, and Mom stopped talking to me after the first episode aired. I guess I should have known that even though I'm still a nobody to people at school, I'm a someone to viewers of the show.

And now, everyone at this spa—well, at least, all the

women—is going to see me naked.

I'm still not sure how I feel about even Lana and Tiffany seeing me without any clothes on. It's not that I feel uncomfortable in my body or wish my body was different. But I've never stripped in front of my friends before. I'm not sure how they'll react. Lana and Tiffany are even skinnier than my friends at school. And if anyone says anything about my weight . . . well, I'm not sure if I'll be able to forgive them.

The employee hands us our spa uniforms and locker key bracelets, and I'm feeling super self-conscious as we walk into the women's locker room. Like I expected, everyone, from really old grandmothers with bent backs to little kids holding hands with their moms, is naked. And almost all the girls around my age are skinny and tiny like Tiffany and Lana.

See, Haneul? I hear Mom's voice in my head. *Those girls are so beautiful! If only you tried a bit harder . . .*

My stomach starts churning, and I almost run right out of the locker room. But Lana and Tiffany look really happy and excited, or at least, they do until Lana sees my expression.

"What's wrong?" she asks, placing a hand on my shoulder.

I shake my head. I don't want to ruin everyone's fun.

I'm better than this, I think over and over again as I follow Tiffany and Lana to our lockers. But when they begin taking off their clothes, my stomach feels like it's flipping around in circles.

It's a total hetero misconception that queer girls shouldn't be in locker rooms with other girls. Sure, I'm attracted to girls, but that doesn't mean that I'm a pervert. The only thing I think when Lana and Tiffany take off their clothes is, *Wow, they're so pretty.*

Unlike me. The thought escapes before I can stop it. *No, I tell myself. No, your body is perfect just the way it is. The fact that you grew up hearing your mom say it's not doesn't make it true.*

Someone coughs. I'm mortified when I realize I have my eyes squeezed shut. I barely stop myself from groaning out loud. It probably looks like I'm embarrassed to see Lana and Tiffany without their clothes on. Or worse, like I'm perverted in some weird way. I slowly, reluctantly open my eyes to see that the two of them, still very naked, are staring at me with concerned expressions.

"Are you okay, Skye?" Lana asks. "And don't just nod your head. I *know* something's bothering you."

I blink, and suddenly I'm crying. A rush of embarrassment hits me, but no matter how hard I try to stop, I can't. What starts as just a little drop or two in the corners of my eyes becomes a huge, uncontrollable flood.

"Oh, Skye!" Lana reaches over to me, but I instinctively back away. I hate crying, especially in front of other people. I'm so mortified that all this is happening. "What's wrong?"

It's only then that I realize I'm the only one still wearing clothes in the locker room. If it weren't for me holding everyone up, we could have gone into the baths by now. It takes all of my energy to stop myself from crying even harder.

"Oh my gosh," I say, wiping away my tears. "Sorry, I'm keeping you guys waiting. I'll take off my clothes right away."

"Well, normally, I love it when girls say that," Tiffany quips. Lana elbows her in the ribs, and Tiffany continues, "But really, there's no rush. Is there something wrong? You're crying. Don't pretend things are okay when they're not. It only makes things worse."

I hesitate, unsure how to even begin to explain what's going through my head. But since it's unlikely that Lana and Tiffany are just going to let this one go, I slowly say, "It's been a long time since I've been to a Korean spa."

"How come?" Lana asks gently.

I take a deep breath. It's hard to believe I'm actually telling anyone about this. It's one of the few things that I never dared to mention even to my school counselor, since Dr. Franklin probably wouldn't get the concept of a Korean spa in the first place. I'd be lucky if he didn't spend most of the time asking, *But why is everyone naked?*

"Every time my mom and I went . . . ." I finally say. "Well, she's not really *abusive*, like she doesn't hit me or anything, but she'd always comment on how everyone's skinnier than me, and her comments about my body just added up. Like, I'm okay with my body. Most of the time. But she always made me feel like I'm not good enough. And because of that, I'm always afraid of meeting new people, period, since I'm scared they'll be jerks like her."

"Aw, Skye," says Lana. She gives me a big hug. I would have

never thought someone that small could squeeze so hard. "Well, I mean, that's another type of abuse, you know? Emotional. It obviously hurt you enough that it still bothers you today."

"I guess."

Although Mom's and my relationship for sure isn't smooth, I never thought of it as *abusive*. There are so many forms of Asian-parent tough love, where parents say and do mean things only because they want the best for us. Is all of that "tough love" abusive? What distinguishes tough-love parenting from abuse? After all, Mom did say she's afraid of what other people might say about me. Even though she *is* mostly afraid that people might think she's a bad parent, isn't the fact that she's worried about me a good thing?

Even as I think all this, the sick feeling in my stomach after hearing Lana's words tells me some part of me knows she's right.

"If you don't feel comfortable stripping and going into the water with us, that's totally fine," Lana adds as she pulls away. "You can just join us upstairs for the saunas."

It's tempting, but I know that if I chicken out now, I'll never get over this.

"It's okay," I say. "Just give me a moment and I'll come join you guys."

Tiffany puts a hand on my shoulder. "Are you sure?"

I give her a small nod. "I'm sure."

After Tiffany and Lana leave, I slowly reach down to my dress and lift it over my head. I stare at my own reflection in the mirror beside my locker.

"You are beautiful," I whisper to myself. "Don't let anyone, not even yourself, tell you any different."

I take a deep breath and let myself have the time I need to process things. It's quiet in our corner of the locker room, and now, without Lana and Tiffany, I can finally gather my thoughts and feelings about being here without any outside influences.

Am I really comfortable with all this? I ask myself. *Or am I being forced to do something I don't want to do?*

Slowly but steadily, I decide I want to be here. Sure, going to the Korean spa seemed like a horrible idea at first, but maybe I really do owe it to myself to have a fun time at the spa with my friends. I've worked so hard for the last couple of months. Don't I deserve a spa day as much as a thin person?

Part of me also wants to replace all those bad memories of being here with Mom with happy ones. Even though that's probably not *exactly* how people's brains work, I figure it's better than just having negative memories rolling around in my brain all the time.

Hopefully it'll be fun, I think.

When I finally come out, Lana tackles me into a big hug.

"Yay, let's go!" she exclaims. "Spa time!"

Tiffany, who's apparently the designated towel person, waves our three white bath towels enthusiastically.

And that's it. Neither Lana nor Tiffany mention what happened earlier again.

The bathhouse part of the spa is built like one of the traditional bathhouses in Korea, with waters of various temperatures and scents. Some waters have herbal health benefits—there's even a green tea bath—while others are just regular water. After a quick shower, we jump into each one, giggling and thoroughly enjoying ourselves.

All the while, we laugh and talk about the competition, our schools, our friends, basically anything and everything.

"Now that I'm out of the competition, the entirety of my hopes and dreams lies with you, Lana," jokes Tiffany.

"Wow, so much pressure!" Lana says. "What about Skye? She's still in this too."

"Fine," Tiffany concedes. "You too, Skye. Seriously, if neither of you win, I'm going to give Park Tae-Suk a good talking-to."

"I'm honestly looking forward to the day that happens," I say. "Can you get Bora while you're at it?"

"Oh, believe me. Bora's been on my list from Day One."

We all laugh, and bit by bit, I find myself loosening up in the gentle, therapeutic heat of the water. By the time we leave the bathing area, I feel so at ease that I don't even care about the women who stare at us as we walk by.

"Let's go up to the jjimjilbang level," says Tiffany. "Hopefully Henry is still alive."

It's only then that I remember we left Henry and Steve to

fend for themselves in the men's section of the spa.

"Oh, shoot." I quickly open my locker and fish out my phone to find that I have four texts from Henry.

Okay, so, I didn't get ambushed in the men's locker room. That's always good.

And I didn't see anyone trying to take pics of me! God bless the strict spa rules.

. . . I think no one knows who I am here? Can I just stay here all day? This is amazing. None of these ahjussis and screaming kids care about me.

NEVER MIND.

The texts stop there. I scroll and scroll, as if that'll somehow make more text messages from Henry pop up. But nope. Nothing. I have no idea if he ever made it out of the men's locker room.

Lana glances at my phone.

"What the . . ." she says. "Is he okay?"

"I'm not sure, honestly."

I tap out a quick message to Henry.

Hey, sorry. Are you okay? We're about to get dressed and head up to the jjimjilbang level now.

Henry doesn't respond. With each passing second, my heart beats faster and faster until I get this sudden, irrational urge to run to the opposite side of the building and burst into the men's locker room, all in the name of saving him. I feel really bad, since I'm the reason why he came here in the first place.

But then, I get a new message.

HENRY CHO: Um, so, I tried going out to the jjimjilbang level but then got ambushed by a bunch of people . . . turns out they were just waiting for me to exit the locker room so they could take pics. I'm fine. Steve is here with me.

"Wait," says Tiffany. "Where did everyone go?"

The women's locker room, which had been pretty full before we went out into the spa area, is now almost empty. Besides us three, there are only a few old ladies and little kids with their moms walking around.

"Oh no," I say. "Henry!"

Chapter Twenty-Eight

IN A MAD RUSH, THE THREE OF US DRY OFF AND pull on our spa uniforms before running up the stairs to the sauna level. When we get to the third floor, we can barely squeeze past the crowd to exit the staircase.

"Move it, people!" Tiffany yells. "Let us through! I'm pretty sure crowding the stairs like this is a fire hazard! It's illegal!"

"Where is he?" Lana asks, looking around. "I don't see him."

I pull out my phone to text him again. Hey, we're on the sauna level. Where are you??

Suddenly, Lana says, "I have a pretty good idea where he might be. Look!"

She points at the crowd ahead of us. Everyone has their backs to us, circling around something—or someone.

"Excuse me!" Tiffany shouts, aggressively pushing her way through. The bodies don't part easily, but Tiffany uses her hands and elbows to shove away everyone who doesn't budge. Lana follows closely after her, apologizing to everyone who shoots us dirty looks. They make such a cute team that I can't help but grin as I follow them.

Halfway through the crowd, I catch sight of Steve. He's standing in front of a door with his arms crossed, looking resolutely ahead like a bouncer at an exclusive nightclub. Except, unlike a bouncer, he isn't letting anyone through, no matter what they say to him. A few girls try to talk to him, but he ignores them. He stands absolutely still, like a stone giant. I'm not even sure he's blinking.

When he sees us, though, Steve breaks into a huge smile.

"Skye!" he says, giving me an enthusiastic wave. "Henry's inside. He's been waiting for you."

Steve lets the three of us in and immediately closes the door after us. A few people yell and curse at us, but their voices become muffled the instant the door shuts. We're in a dimly lit space, so it takes a while for my eyes to adjust. When they do, though, I notice three things: 1) we're in a private massage room, 2) Henry's receiving a massage on one of the beds, and 3) he's *shirtless.*

Okay, so maybe it wasn't exactly in that order. Probably the reverse.

When he hears us enter, Henry briefly glances up, lifting his head from the circular headrest. The old lady giving him a back rub pauses for a second to give us a sharp look before continuing her work.

"Oh, hey," he says. "You guys came."

His voice sounds very mellowed out, probably the most

relaxed I've ever heard him.

"Seriously?" says Tiffany. "You're getting a massage, *right now*?"

Henry slowly gets up from the bed and thanks the old lady in Korean while handing her a few twenties. The lady nods and moves to stand in the back of the room.

"Sorry," he says. "This was kind of an accident. I was just looking for a place to hide until the people outside calmed down. I ducked in here, which turned out to be a massage room. I felt bad for using it as my hideout, so I asked for a massage."

Even though I'm vaguely aware of what Henry is saying, most of it goes out the other ear because I'm so freakin' distracted by the fact that I'm face-to-face with a *shirtless Henry Cho*. Even though it's not the first time I'm seeing him without a shirt, it's the first time I've seen him shirtless so . . . directly. I try not to look down from his face. I really do. But his bare chest is pretty hard to ignore. And so are his shoulders.

God, he has such wide, beautiful shoulders, I think, just as Lana catches my eye and grins.

"Okay," she whispers. "I'm gay and I still think he's hot, in an aesthetically appealing kind of way. Dang, no wonder this guy's a model."

Henry smirks, like he heard what Lana said. I wouldn't be surprised. Lana's whisper was closer in volume to a normal person's shout than an actual whisper. I blush crimson.

Tiffany, though, is unfazed.

"Put a freakin' shirt on!" she yells at him, throwing a towel at his face. "Our Skye is still really innocent!"

Henry catches it with a laugh. "Okay, okay. *But* this isn't the first time Skye's seen me shirtless."

He raises his eyebrows at me, and Lana and Tiffany gasp simultaneously.

"Skye!" Lana "whispers." "I thought you said nothing's going on between the two of you!"

Henry grabs his spa shirt off one of the counters and casually puts it on, as if he can't tell that I'm giving him total murder eyes right now.

"It was only one other time!" I try to explain myself. "And he was injured, so he was getting treated—I just happened to look—I mean, I didn't . . ."

When I finally trail off, everyone laughs. Even I end up laughing at my failed attempts to talk.

Without Henry's shirtless chest in front of me, I can finally think about other things. But even though my brain starts functioning normally again, I have to clear my throat a few times before I can form actually coherent sentences.

"So," I finally say, addressing Henry. "Are you going to have to stay in here the entire time we're at the spa?"

He shrugs. "I mean, I could probably move to a different area if you guys want to check out somewhere else. Is there a particular sauna room you want to try?" All of a sudden, he glances past me and adds, "Really subtle, guys. Really subtle."

I look back to see Lana and Tiffany freeze midtiptoe. Tiffany keeps her back turned toward us, while Lana turns around to give us a wave. "You two have fun! Tiffany and I are going to go room hopping."

I can't tell if they're leaving so they can enjoy the spa together, or if they're trying to set me and Henry up. Knowing them, it's probably both.

When we make eye contact, Lana giggles. Yup, definitely both.

"All right," I say reluctantly. "I'll catch you guys later?"

"Yeah!" Lana says. "Just text me when you're ready to go."

After they leave, I look back to see that Henry's *still* staring at me.

"So?" he asks.

"Huh?"

"You never answered my question."

"What question?"

Henry reaches over to feel my forehead. "Are you okay?" he says, with concern that'd actually be convincing if it weren't for his lopsided grin. "Your face is so red. I asked you which sauna room you wanted to check out first."

I swat his hand away, trying to ignore the fact that my face is burning hot *again*. "Hush! Let's check out the Himalayan salt room. That's a childhood favorite of mine."

Henry chuckles. "Okay."

Steve does a pretty impressive job of shielding both Henry and me as we move to the Himalayan salt room. As we pass, people call our names. I look up instinctively the first few times, before I finally manage to get myself to stop. It's obvious they're only calling us so they'll have better photos.

Fortunately, the room is empty, since everyone is outside trying to get a glimpse of Henry. Steve stands guard at the door so we can slip inside.

The sauna looks exactly the way you'd imagine a Himalayan salt room to look, with pink salt blocks covering the entire space from floor to ceiling. Everything smells pleasantly clean, and I slowly breathe in the smell of the salts.

The temperature indicator outside the sauna showed that it's 102 degrees inside, but it feels even warmer with Henry by my side. I've only been to saunas with my mom before, and most of those occasions were filled with her complaining away about something or someone. With only Henry and me here, the silence in the room is palpable.

Sweat slowly beads and drips down my face. I look down to see that gross stains have begun to form on my shirt underneath my armpits. Feeling self-conscious, I fold my arms against my chest. In the dim, steamy space, I can see just enough to make out Henry's face.

When our eyes meet, he smiles and holds out a towel.

"Hey," he says. "Do you know how to make those lamb towel hats that people always wear in Korean dramas?"

Although I've seen them on TV plenty of times, I never actually learned how to make one because Mom probably would have said they looked foolish. When I explain this to Henry, he frowns and says, "Here. I'll make one for you. Or try to, at least. I looked up how on my way here."

With quick, deft hands, Henry folds the towel in half and then does it again, until the towel is long and thin. He then carefully rolls up each side, so both ends are curled up like cute little ram horns.

"Here," he says. "Try this on."

It takes some adjusting to make the towel completely cover my hair, but when I'm done, Henry's face lights up into one of the brightest smiles I've ever seen on him.

"You look really cute," he says. "I kind of want to take a picture of you right now." He sees my expression and rushes on to say, "Not to post on Instagram or anything. But just to . . . capture this moment. The lighting is too dim for a decent photo, though."

Henry thinks I look cute? The compliment makes my heart skip a beat, but I don't let my face show it. In middle school, a couple of boys called me cute and then laughed at me when I looked pleased. Henry looks genuine enough, but he probably just means I look cute at this specific moment in time. I think I look cute on most days, but I doubt anyone who dated someone as flawless as Melinda would go for someone like me.

That's when I remember how he'd suddenly stopped responding to my texts for several days before today. Part of me wonders if I should just leave it, but at the same time, I know it's going to bother me later if I don't ask Henry about it now. The fact that this isn't the first time he's ghosted me for a mysterious reason doesn't help, either.

"Why did you suddenly stop responding to my texts? I thought you were sick of me or something. And then I was really surprised when you texted me back today."

Henry's easy grin drops from his face. He doesn't even meet my eyes. "I . . . I guess I sort of panicked," he says.

"Wait, why?"

He shrugs. I can see that he's trying really hard to act casual.

"It's been a while since I've been this close with someone. Not just physically but . . . everything else."

"What, because of the whole no-friends thing?"

"Sort of." His voice sounds strained and weird. It's so different from its usual honey-like smoothness that it's almost funny.

"But weren't you close with the people you've dated?"

I think back to all those Instagram stories with Melinda. They *looked* pretty intimate in them, with so much kissing and hand-holding that it grossed me out sometimes.

"Not really. When celebrities date . . . it's not always because of some emotional connection. Far from it. A lot of it is superficial. For example . . ." Henry exhales sharply. "You were there when Melinda and I had a huge fight, right?"

I nod, holding my breath. I still feel bad about intruding on their private moment, even though the cameras were also there.

"Melinda and I should never have gotten together." Henry cringes at the thought. "When we first became a thing, I had really low self-esteem. I was new to the industry, was new to modeling and all that, and, well, I guess I thought I was lucky that she even liked me, even though I knew she only liked me because I looked like a K-pop star."

"Ew, what?"

"Yeah . . . she called me oppa and stuff. It was weird. But anyway, when we broke up, she basically told me that I was good for nothing because I just *looked* like a K-pop star but had no talent to support that. And then she went ahead and auditioned for this competition herself! The fight on the first day was because I was trying to get her to not participate in the competition. I knew she was only auditioning because she was fetishizing our culture."

I think back to the awkward kimchi moment I had with Melinda and shudder.

"But you still protected her in the end," I say.

"Well, yeah. She may be a jerk, but she didn't deserve to be featured on TV like that. Anyway, you and I aren't like that. I—"

Steve pushes open the door and yells in a very dad-like voice, "It's time to come outside! You shouldn't stay in one room for so long. It's not good for you."

On our way out, I glance at Henry, expecting him to finish speaking. But he doesn't.

And because I'm too busy looking at him, I almost run into Tiffany and Lana, who are standing right next to the door. Lana giggles when she sees my lamb towel hat.

"Oh my gosh," she says. "Skye, that lamb hat is so cute. Did you make it yourself?"

"No, Henry did."

Her giggles intensify.

Even Tiffany looks like she's trying hard not to smile. She wiggles her eyebrows at us.

"Lucky you two had some alone time, huh?"

I turn around to look at Henry, expecting him to look proud of himself. But he's back to smiling that fake smile of his again.

"I can make one for you," Tiffany says to Lana as we head to our next sauna room.

Lana beams and squeezes Tiffany's hand almost imperceptibly. The small gesture makes me so happy and sad, all at once. Lana and Tiffany are such a cute couple, and it makes me sad that they can't express their affection in Korean public places like a heterosexual couple can. Normally, I'm not a huge fan of PDA, but queer PDA happens so rarely that I wish it was more common.

Steve does his best to keep people away, but even then, it takes us a few minutes to find another empty sauna room. Now that the surprise factor of Henry's presence has worn off, a lot of people have gone back to doing what they were doing before he arrived.

The second room we go into is covered with red clay bricks that feel pleasantly hot under my feet. As soon as we're settled down on the mats inside, Tiffany starts making a towel hat for Lana. Lana giggles, and then sets her towel on the ground as well, and before I know what's happening, they're both making towel hats for each other.

"They're so cute together," I say. It's only after the words leave my mouth that I remember who I'm talking to.

Oh shoot. Henry doesn't know about Lana and Tiffany being a couple. Panic and fear fills my head, but he just nods and says, "Yeah."

I glance at his face, looking for any signs of a negative reaction. He appears mostly amused, although there's something else in his expression that I can't place. Regret? Sadness? Whatever it is makes my heart ache, even though I have no idea what he's thinking about.

"Can we get patbingsu after this?" Henry asks all of a sudden, completely throwing me off.

"What?"

"Patbingsu. Korean shaved ice."

"I *know* what patbingsu is. I was just surprised. Wait, have you never had patbingsu, either?"

"Nope. I always see people in K-dramas get patbingsu at Korean spas, and I've wanted to try it too."

That catches Tiffany's and Lana's attention. Tiffany groans.

"Is there *anything* that you've tried before?" she asks.

"I've had overpriced French food," Henry replies. "And some of the best pasta around. My family doesn't really eat Korean food. And if they do, it's always very traditional and extravagant jeong-sik. The really gourmet stuff that kings used to eat."

"Rich-people problems," Tiffany mutters, rolling her eyes.

"Tell me about it," Henry groans.

"Let's all share one big patbingsu!" exclaims Lana.

We all laugh, because she's so happy and excited that her voice comes out in a squeak.

"Yeah!" I reply. "I'm down."

I look at Henry, and we both smile.

Chapter Twenty-Nine

AFTER THE SUGARY PATBINGSU, TIFFANY AND Lana pass out in a food coma on the heated spa floors, so Henry offers to give me a ride home.

I'm still feeling a bit buzzy from all the chocolate and condensed milk, so I don't notice that he's been quiet for most of the car ride until he clears his throat.

"So . . . Lana and Tiffany. They're a couple, right? Like, they're dating each other?"

I glance up at the front of the car. Steve is listening to some comedy podcast at high volume, and both he and Portia are laughing along to the jokes. I doubt that they can hear us above the noise.

"Yeah, they are."

I must look really nervous, because Henry holds his hands out in front of him. "Don't get me wrong. I have nothing against them. It's just that . . . well, remember what Lana said about how she thought I was a jerk?"

"I'm pretty sure she was just kidding," I quickly say. This entire conversation is making me uncomfortable, like we're talking about something that I'm not supposed to know about.

"Nope. Lana probably already told you, but some of her friends went to my old school. I actually remember seeing her in a lot of my friends' posts before we met today . . . back when we still followed each other on social media. And Harvard-Westlake is pretty small. So, she's probably warned you about me. Am I right?"

I suck at lying, so I nod and say, "Yeah . . . but this was before we got to know each other."

Henry laughs, but it comes out all sharp and bitter. "It's fine. The rumors are true. Like I said before, I really don't have any friends anymore. And it's all my fault."

"What happened?"

Wordlessly, Henry stares at me for a moment, like he's debating whether or not he can trust me.

"One of the guys at Harvard-Westlake," he says at last. "He was my boyfriend."

I'm still processing his words when Henry adds, "I mean, I'm bi. I like girls, too. But at that time, I had a boyfriend."

Henry's bi, I think. *Like me.* I have this sudden urge to high-five him, like I just found out that we're both members of some exclusive club. But it doesn't really seem appropriate right now, so I keep quiet and listen.

"When I signed my modeling contract, my parents suddenly launched themselves into my life. They'd left me alone for the most part ever since I started going to Harvard-Westlake. I was alone in the States, they were back in Korea . . . it was really nice. But then, I became a 'celebrity' like them. I guess it's understandable, since the Korean press found out about my modeling contract and went running with it. I had so many interviews and features online and on print, it was embarrassing. And suddenly, my parents wanted to be in control of *everything*. Even my personal life."

"Oh no," I say. It hurts me how much I can see where this is going.

"Things kind of exploded when they found out I had a boyfriend. They said I'd never make it big in Korea if everyone found out I wasn't straight. I told them I was bi, that I liked both guys and girls, but that didn't matter. They just said, 'Well then, find yourself a nice girlfriend instead. Girls won't develop crushes on you if they know you have a boyfriend. It won't help your image at all.'"

"Henry. I'm so sorry."

"No," he says. Everything comes out in a quiet rush, like he can't stop now that he's started telling me everything. "You have nothing to be sorry about. And I don't deserve the sympathy, either. I was extremely naive. I wanted to get my parents off my back, so I lied to them. I told them that I broke up with my boyfriend. It was fine for a while, but then, we got caught. Some girl took a picture of us kissing. My parents went berserk. They paid off the person who took the photo of us so she wouldn't post it online. And then, they offered my boyfriend an outrageous amount of money so he'd break up with me."

"*What?*" I'm so mad that my voice comes out in a loud yell.

Both Portia and Steve glance back at us. Portia lowers the volume of the podcast and asks, "Is everything okay?"

"Yeah," I say. "Sorry."

Henry waits until Portia turns up the podcast again before continuing. "It was a threat disguised as a bribe. My boyfriend, of course, completely lost it. And he had every right to. His parents found out, and they transferred him out of the school. Both our parents kept everything hush-hush, so our friends never learned about the details. But they knew something really bad happened, and that it was my fault. All of my friends were also friends with him, so. Yeah, I lost all my friends. That's why I have no friends left."

Henry's story makes me feel really sad. It's a painful reminder of why I can't date girls.

"Lana and Tiffany . . ." I say. "Apparently they were both kicked out of their houses."

Henry sighs.

"They're okay now, though. They live together and, well, you saw them. They're really cute. And happy."

"That's good. I'm glad for them."

"Let's not be douchey homophobic parents, yeah?"

Henry raises his eyebrows. "Whoa, don't you think it's too early to be talking about kids?"

I lightly punch him in the arm. "You know what I mean. We're, like . . . the future of Koreans and Korean Americans, you know? We have to be better than our parents' generation."

"Yup, definitely."

I wait a few seconds before saying, "I'm bi too."

He sits up immediately, a smile tentatively spreading across his face. "Wait, you are? That's awesome."

And that's that. Henry accepts me without a moment of hesitation. And I accept him, too.

"I guess that makes us . . . what, bi squared?"

"Bi squared," he says with a smile. "I like it."

Chapter Thirty

THE NEXT ROUND OF THE COMPETITION IS BRUtal. Things really get ugly as people butt heads onstage, doing their best to win against each other. Since there are only ten people total in the vocals portion for this round, we all huddle up around the TV in the green room as we wait for our turn to perform.

By some cruel twist of fate—or, more likely, the cruel whims of the judges—Mindy, mentored by Gary, and Isabel, mentored by Mr. Park, end up facing each other onstage, even though they were partners in the previous round. Isabel wins against Mindy with a powerful song-and-rap combo that blows Mindy's cute but otherwise unremarkable rendition of a Mamamoo song out of the water. When the judges select Isabel as the winner, Mindy runs from the stage crying.

Lana, mentored by Mr. Park, is up next. Before she leaves, she gives my hand a tight squeeze.

"Good luck," I tell her as she goes out the door.

I anxiously watch the TV as she goes up against Kevin Byun, a Korean American guy mentored by Gary who sounds impossibly more angelic than she does. *This isn't good!* I think, even more so when Lana gets too nervous and overshoots a high note. I've never heard Lana make a pitch mistake before, but I guess that's just how much pressure she's under during her performance.

When she gets eliminated, Lana looks so sad I want to run to the stage and give her a hug. But since I can't right now, I send her a text filled with hearts and what I hope are words of encouragement instead. I'll have to catch up with her later.

A bunch of other drama happens, like when one of the singers admits to spying on the other contestant and choosing a song from the same artist so he could one-up his rival. We all expect the judges to disqualify him right away, but instead, the judges eliminate the *other* contestant, saying that the spying guy was, in Mr. Park's words, "indeed better than the other individual." A fight breaks out between the two guys and security has to escort them offstage.

Finally, we're down to the last four people who haven't performed yet. It oddly feels like an "and then there were none" moment, as if we're all getting picked off one by one. Sweat forms on my forehead, and I clench and unclench my fists to relieve some tension.

Aside from me, there's Melinda and two other people who I only know the faces of. Melinda doesn't even look at me, or at any of the other competitors in the room. Instead, she resolutely stares ahead like she's way above us. Appearance-wise, she definitely is on another level than anyone else. Her blond hair is curled in perfect ringlets, her skin is clear and *actually* dewy, and her eyes are rimmed with just the right amount of smoky eyeliner. I wouldn't be surprised if she'd had her makeup professionally done.

I'm back to watching people perform on TV again when I get a text.

HENRY CHO: How are you holding up? Is it time for you to go yet?

ME: Not yet. Trying not to let my nerves get to me. How about you?

HENRY CHO: Just left for the venue rn. Dance performances start right after you guys finish.

My heart aches a little bit at the mention of dance. But I still try to be encouraging as I reply to Henry.

Good luck! Lmk how it goes.

HENRY CHO: Will do. Good luck to you, too.

He sends me a picture of Snowball eating a dog popsicle, and I stifle a giggle.

ME: SO CUTE.

HENRY CHO: Looking at these pics makes me realize how much I spoil this dog. 😑

ME: She deserves it!!!!

I smile to myself until, out of the corner of my eye, I spot Melinda scowling at me from across the room. Her face is full of accusations, as if she knows I'm texting Henry. I try to ignore her the best I can. I really don't want any drama today.

But of course, at that moment, since this is *that* type of show, the stage manager walks into the room and says, "Skye and Melinda, you two are up. Please come stand by backstage."

Why am I even surprised?

I suppress a groan as I follow Melinda out of the green room. It's clear from the pairings today that the show producers did everything they could to make things as "dramatic" as possible. I'm honestly disappointed in myself for not expecting this.

If looks could electrocute people, Melinda would have fried me a hundred times over by the time we get onstage. I try to shake it off as best I can. I've already been eliminated from one part of the competition. I really can't afford to be distracted now.

"Ladies," Davey says after we reach our marks. "Here's how this round will proceed. First, we will ask Melinda to sing. Then Skye. The judges will give evaluations for both of you after Skye finishes. The winner of this round will move on to become one of the top five vocalists for the final round of *You're My Shining Star.*"

Unlike the other times I've stood onstage, the studio audience is completely silent, waiting in hushed anticipation as Melinda gets ready to sing. The moment the opening notes of her accompaniment begin to play, though, everybody—including me—gasps.

She's singing "No One," by Lee Hi, the artist I covered in the first round.

Oh no she didn't! I can't stop my jaw from dropping in disbelief, even with one camera trained on me to capture my reaction. Although it's not as bad as singing a song by the same artist I'm singing today, it's still pretty bad, and the audience's reaction confirms it. For the first few lines, they remain completely silent.

I have to give it to her, though. Melinda's Korean pronunciation is excellent, and she's serving every bit of the sultriness that this song deserves. Swaying her hips back and forth to the beat, she's soon got the audience captured in the spell of her fairylike soprano voice as she sings about being lonely at night. All the while, she looks straight at the camera with sexy confidence, like a teenage Victoria's Secret model.

By the time Melinda reaches the chorus, everyone cheers for her, and a few guys at the front even *drool* as they watch her sing. I try not to grimace too noticeably on camera. Melinda's song choice, the audience's reactions . . . it's all a bit too much.

I have to win against Melinda, I think. *I have to.*

But even as I try to focus, my vision starts blurring under the hot stage lights.

". . . Skye?"

At the sound of my name, I jerk back to attention. Melinda's finished singing, and the judges, the audience, the cameras, *everyone*, is staring at me. I want to scream. How could I have let myself be so overwhelmed?

"It's your turn," Mr. Park says in a slightly annoyed tone.

268

He's probably thinking about how I'm bringing shame on him as his mentee.

"Right." I nod, indicating that I'm ready to start.

"Next up is Skye Shin!" Davey announces.

The opening flute notes of Chungha's "Gotta Go" start playing, and I let out a quick breath before I come in. I can't pull off wispy fairy magic like Melinda can, but sexy confidence? I can do sexy confidence.

Snapping my fingers to the beat, I come in at my cue, trying my best to convey the wistfulness of having to leave the love of your life at midnight. I sing, letting the music take over me so I'm completely lost in it by the time I hit the chorus.

Chungha is such a dance-focused artist, so I can't help but break into some of the choreography as I sing the song, rocking my hips back and forth and waving my arms around my body. Bora raises her eyebrows, but Mr. Park watches me with a proud look in his eyes.

By the time I hit the bridge, the audience is roaring, and I spot a bunch of people dancing along with me in the audience. When I hit the high note toward the end of the song, I let my voice ring out in the theater to thunderous applause.

"There you have it, folks!" Davey says. "Melinda and Skye, two ladies of wondrous talent. Who will be asked to stay and who will be sent home?"

Mr. Park picks up the mic first.

"Miss Shin," Mr. Park says with a twinkle in his eyes. "Well done. You made me proud today, no matter the result."

Gary looks at Melinda, and then me.

"Wow," he says. "This is a really hard choice to make. Melinda, you did an amazing job. This round was definitely not easy for you, with the language barrier and everything. And your rendition of Lee Hi's song was so well done. You took all my tips and suggestions to heart." He then turns to me. "Skye, you were phenomenal as usual. The emotion, the high notes, the sexiness. It was all there. This is going to be a really hard decision for me to make."

He pauses, and in that moment, my heart feels like it's about to collapse. Bora's definitely not going to vote for me, so without Gary's vote, I'm doomed. I close my eyes, praying to whoever's out there that he'll vote for me.

"Gah," Gary says, sitting back in his seat. He waves at Davey. "Come back to me. I still need some time to process."

When it's her turn, Bora doesn't even look at me. "Melinda, you were fantastic. You are truly talented."

She then, of course, votes without hesitation for Melinda. My heartbeat grows louder and louder, and my ears are ringing by the time Gary picks up his mic again.

"Okay," he says. "I think I've made my decision."

"The anticipation is killing us!" Davey exclaims, and the audience roars in agreement. "Who will Gary vote for? Melinda or Skye?"

I know Davey's only amping up the suspense because that's his job, but at this moment, I want to hit him. As even more seconds pass, my legs start shaking, and I feel like I'm about to collapse onto the ground.

"Melinda," Gary says.

My stomach drops.

"I am so proud of you. You've come so far."

Melinda smiles.

But then Gary turns to look at me.

"But Skye, you were the superior singer tonight. I don't think I can ever listen to the original song again without thinking of your version of it."

Cheers erupt from the audience. Melinda starts screaming angrily, and she rushes forward like she's about to attack me. Luckily, Davey steps in between us and holds up my arm.

"Congratulations, Skye!" he says. "You are the fourth member of the final five."

He then turns to the cameras and says, "Remember: the final performance will be broadcast live and you—yes, you—will have the chance to vote for your favorite competitor to win *You're My Shining Star*! December fifth, six p.m. PST, and December sixth, eleven a.m. KST, right here on SBC. Please tune in to vote for your fave!"

We're then escorted offstage, with Melinda cursing at me the entire time. But I don't care, because at that moment, I spot Henry waiting for me backstage.

"You did it!" he says. "You knocked Melinda out of this competition."

My heart's still pounding from the judges' evaluations, and the huge smile on Henry's face only makes it beat faster. Before

I realize what's happening, he wraps his arms around me in a big hug that makes me melt.

The cameras are all around us, but in this moment, I couldn't care less.

"Yeah," I reply. "Congrats, she's gone."

He laughs. "I'm the one who should be congratulating you. I'm so proud of you."

"All dancers should remain in the green room!" the stage manager yells then, with a pointed look at Henry.

He lets go of me and says, "Hey, listen. Let's hang out soon. I'll text you, okay? There's somewhere I really want to take you."

"Okay," I reply, trying to keep it cool despite the blush burning on my face. "I'm looking forward to it."

Henry gives me his genuine lopsided grin before leaving backstage.

Chapter Thirty-One

COMPARED TO HOW JAM-PACKED THE LAST month was, the weeks leading up to Thanksgiving break crawl on by. In my new moments of free time, I find myself checking social media. Before, I occasionally saw a post or tweet because my school friends linked me to them. But this is the first time since the premiere that I let myself fully immerse in Twitter and Instagram.

When Clarissa learns I've lifted my self-imposed social media ban, she shows me the #QueenSkyeFanClub hashtag, with which so many other plus-size girls from all over the world have posted personal messages about how *I* inspire them. I really want to reply to everyone and tell them how much they mean to me, but Rebecca stops me.

"It's better not to engage," she warns. "They're not your friends. At best, they're fans. And fans can turn nasty at any second."

"Yeah," Clarissa chimes in. "Think about how quickly people cancel celebrities on social media. It's a real thing!"

My friends' advice, as always, makes a lot of sense. So, for the time being, I don't reply to any of the tweets or mentions on Instagram.

All the attention is bizarre and makes me feel so grateful, but I also feel incredibly guilty because no one—not even my school friends—knows that I got eliminated from dance after my performance with Henry. Not yet, anyway. That episode premieres tomorrow night.

I can't stop thinking about what it'll look like when I get eliminated—even if it's just from one category—after standing up against Bora. I'm worried that I might become another "lesson" to fat girls who might be too afraid to stand up for themselves.

I lie in bed and find myself scrolling through Instagram, looking at posts from people who are still in the dance portion of the competition. Henry's last post was of him lying on the floor of his rented studio, looking flawless as ever, with the caption "brief respite after a long day." Imani's was of her stretching at a barre with some of her ballet friends. I finally stop.

It's embarrassingly late by the time I close Instagram. Luckily, it's a Friday night, so it sucks less than it would if it were a school night. But still, I have practice tomorrow morning, so I could use the rest.

I'm about to go to sleep when I notice I have unread notifications. The most recent one is from Henry, who sent me a funny dog meme several hours ago.

It's been so long since he sent the meme that I don't know how to respond. I type "LOLLLLL," then delete it and write something less cringey. Before I can hit Send, though, a speech bubble with three dots appears.

HENRY CHO: You still up?

I bolt up into a sitting position and stare at the text, feeling kind of embarrassed that Henry saw me struggle with a response. I take a few quick breaths before replying.

Yeah, couldn't sleep. They're broadcasting the episode with our dance performance tomorrow.

HENRY CHO: I know.

There's a pause, and the three dots fade in and out again like Henry's trying to figure out what to say. My heart is about to burst from the anticipation when finally, I get another text.

HENRY CHO: Do you want to go up to the Griffith Observatory tonight?

For a long beat, I think I've misread the text. The Griffith Observatory is a little north of Hollywood, up on a hill near the Hollywood sign. Back when Dad lived at home, he used to take me hiking up to the observatory every month or so for father-daughter bonding time. On those Sunday mornings, Dad and I used to talk about anything and everything. It was one of my favorite things to do as a kid, but the last time I went up there was *years* ago, right before Dad moved to NorCal.

And now, Henry wants to spontaneously go there. At three a.m.

Uh, I'm sure it's closed by now, I reply. And I live pretty far from LA.

HENRY CHO: I can pick you up. And the park around the observatory is open 24 hours. We just have to hike up there, but it's not that bad. I'll bring Snowball.

It's the last line that wins me over. Or so I tell myself.

I just want to see Snowball, I think over and over again. I try to keep it casual as I reply.

Cool! Text me when you're here.

Henry sends back a smiley face and a thumbs-up.

I rush back and forth in my room, doing my best not to make any noise. It's chilly during the nights now—or at least as chilly as it gets in LA—so I change into a warm but cute pink sweatshirt and a comfy pair of sweatpants.

Dad is back home for the weekend, and his snores echo through the hallway as I sneak downstairs and out the back door. Three a.m. is like the only time in LA when there's little or no traffic, so Henry gets to my house in less than an hour.

I was expecting him to show up in the SUV, but instead, he shows up in a sky-blue vintage convertible. He's wearing a navy-blue leather jacket, and the outfit combined with the car makes him look like he's from a fifties movie. Snowball's sitting in the back seat, and in the dim twilight of the street-lights, the two of them in the convertible look like something out of my dreams.

"Are you for real?" I whisper when he stops in front of our house. Mom's a pretty light sleeper, so I don't want to wake her up. "Man, you really pull out all the stops when you're trying to impress a girl."

"It's good to see you, too," he whispers back with a grin. "It's been a while."

Henry leans over to open the passenger door. Snowball tackles me as soon as I'm seated and licks me all over my face. I hug her tight. Her white, fluffy fur is so soft and thick. I nestle my face against her as we pull onto the highway.

"The Suburban is Steve's and I didn't want to wake him or Portia this early in the morning. This is my actual car," Henry explains. "It's the first thing I bought when I signed my modeling contract. I only drive it late at night or early on weekend mornings when there's no traffic, though. Getting stuck in LA traffic in a convertible is hell on earth."

"Understandable."

We go up the 5, which is pretty deserted at this hour. It's cold enough that I'm glad I thought to wear a sweatshirt as Henry's convertible speeds down the highway in the quiet of the night. It never snows in SoCal, but winter temperatures get down to forty degrees, and snow is visible on the peaks of the San Gabriel Mountains surrounding LA. The moon is out, and I can see the stars in the cloudless night sky.

Henry's silent for the entire drive to the observatory, although he does turn on some Korean hip-hop and puts the volume on low. The music and the engine create a soft hum, and soon I find myself dozing off.

"Hey, we're here."

I wake up to find that Henry's parked in a forested area. There are a few cars parked near us, despite the fact that it's so late. Henry gets two flashlights from the back seat.

"Take one," he says. "We're going to need them to see during the hike up."

We get out of the car and turn on the flashlights. Snowball jumps out too, and she rushes ahead of us as we slowly make our way up the hill.

"She always likes to go up ahead and wait for me at the top," Henry explains. "Let's hope she doesn't show up with a dead rabbit or something."

"If she does, chances are, we won't be able to see it."

Other than the area lit by our flashlights, everything is pitch-dark. I can't even see my own legs when I look down.

"Why does it feel like we're about to bury a dead body?" I ask as we continue hiking.

Henry laughs. "The view is worth it, I promise. I always come up here late at night when I need a quiet space to think or relax. Here, take my hand."

Before I know what's happening, Henry's leading me up the trail with his hand securely around mine. It's nice and warm, and I'm glad that it's too dark for him to see me blush.

I have no grasp on how long it takes for us to go up the hill because of the darkness. It feels like forever, especially since I have to be careful not to trip on the rocks in our path. But soon enough, I see a faint golden glow of the observatory up ahead. And I hear the jingle of Snowball's tags.

"We probably only have a minute left now," Henry says. "Snowball! Come here!"

The jingling grows louder, and without warning, I get a face full of dog slobber.

"Gross! Snowball!" I laugh and shine my flashlight down on her. She's thankfully rabbit-free and looks up at me with what can only be described as a dog smile.

It kind of reminds me of Henry's grin.

"You're lucky you're cute," I tell her, petting her head.

"Skye, look up."

I glance up, and the sight before me takes my breath away.

Bathed in golden light, the Griffith Observatory sits on top of the hill, just a few feet away from us. The observatory's white walls and gray domes look pretty plain during the day, but now, lit up against the dark night sky, the building looks like it could be anything from a mystical temple to an alien spaceship about to take flight.

But the observatory isn't the *only* beautiful thing we can see from up here. Behind the building is a stunning view of the Los Angeles skyline. LA isn't an attractive city; it's sprawling and messy, with the occasional searchlight and flashes of passing helicopters. But even though I know the city is really a mess, from up here in the hills, the gold and white lights of the skyscrapers and the buildings around them are stunning.

"So, is the view worth it?" Henry asks. "I figured you could use a distraction from everything."

"Yeah, it is," I say softly.

The combination of the gorgeous view and Henry's thoughtfulness makes my breath catch.

"Thanks," I continue. "You're always so nice to me."

"I mean . . . you deserve the best. You're Queen Skye."

Seeing "Queen Skye" on people's signs made me smile, but hearing Henry say it right to my face makes me full-on blush.

"Oh, stop it," I say.

"No, really. I still remember seeing you on that stage when you first auditioned . . . you were so *amazing*. I bet you changed the lives of countless people that day, and you're continuing to inspire them by sticking it out in this competition."

"Aw, Henry."

He looks down at me, and the sudden intensity of his eyes takes my breath away like the observatory had just a few minutes ago. I've always thought Henry was hot, but now, with the LA skyline behind him and the white gold lights of the observatory shining on his face, he's glowing like an angel. It's ridiculous how someone can be this attractive.

I'm so busy staring at Henry that I don't realize he's staring at me too, until he looks away. That's when I realize that he's *blushing*. Henry Cho, the professional model. Blushing!

"What is it?"

"Sorry," he says. "You're just . . . so beautiful."

Every day, I try my hardest to fight against the stereotype that fat kids have low self-esteem. Sure, I feel bad from time to time because of what Mom or other people say, and I did hate how I looked when I was younger. But nowadays, I never really think I'm ugly. I'm cute, and sometimes even beautiful, depending on what I'm going for on a given day. And I know it.

But even though I *know* I'm beautiful and cute, the fact that Henry thinks I'm beautiful still makes me really happy. Because I've always thought he looked beautiful too.

"Skye," he says, slowly and deliberately.

"Yeah?"

"I've been trying to say this for a while now, but I think I'm finally ready."

"Ready for what?"

I'm so full of anticipation for what he might say that I'm almost afraid to breathe.

"I like you."

The moment he says the words, I realize this is something I've known all along. Although it *is* kind of hard to believe that someone like Henry Cho would like a total nobody like me, it's not like he was being subtle about the looks he's given me ever since we met. Nor was he subtle about making grand gestures, like driving all the way down to Orange County and back again just to show me this view.

And just like some part of me has always known he likes me, some part of me has known how I feel about him for a long time.

"I like you too," I say.

Henry closes his eyes with relief. That small gesture is so endearing. I've heard horror stories of how hot guys at our school are extremely stuck-up and just automatically assume that everyone likes them. Henry is more attractive and famous than all of them combined. Yet the fact that he was still scared that I didn't like him back makes him so adorable that I want to kiss him, right here, right now.

"Can I kiss you?" I blurt out before I can stop myself.

Henry startles, but then slowly smiles. "Yeah, of course. Thanks for asking."

He leans in, and our lips touch. Once, twice, until soon, we're full-on kissing each other. Henry's lips are soft and warm against mine, and all the while, I think, *I can't believe this is really happening.*

Chapter Thirty-Two

WHEN WE FINALLY STOP, HENRY'S FLUSHED, LIKE he'd been blushing the entire time we've been kissing.

I playfully slap him on the arm. "Why are you so cute?"

He blushes harder. I think about how he was so cocky when I was eyeing him in his tight shirt. That Henry couldn't be more different from the bashful one in front of me now.

"I don't get it," I say. "You weren't this shy before. What changed?"

Avoiding my gaze, he looks at the ground instead. "I mean, it's different. I'm used to people thinking I'm hot. If that weren't the case, I wouldn't be able to make a living. But this . . . isn't the same. Emotions and feelings are really overwhelming for me sometimes."

"Well, I do think you're really hot," I admit. "But honestly, that just made me want to *not* like you even more. I thought you were a conceited jerk."

"Well, I'm glad it wasn't enough to completely stop you."

"Yeah, whatever," I say, rolling my eyes.

He snickers.

By then, it's starting to turn light out, and in the pink and blue of the sunrise, I see the faint outline of the Hollywood sign on the hill next to us.

"Wow," I say. "I didn't know the sign doesn't light up at night. Why hasn't anyone thought of putting lights on the Hollywood sign?"

"Apparently it's a safety hazard," Henry explains. "The sign used to light up, but then it caused this life-threatening traffic jam a while back and trapped everyone in the canyon."

"Of course traffic would be the reason. Why am I not surprised?"

"Hashtag LA problems."

"Exactly."

A strong breeze suddenly blows into us, sending chills down my spine. I shiver. "Okay, I don't care what everyone says about LA people being wusses. Fifty degrees is still cold. I really should have worn something warmer."

"Here." Henry shrugs off his leather jacket and drapes it over my shoulders. "I don't get cold easily. It gets a *lot* colder in Korea."

When we're back in Henry's car, I say, "So."

"So?"

"Are we a thing now?"

"Only if you want us to be."

"I do."

Henry leans in for another kiss, but my phone rings. I check the screen to see that it's Mom. Of course it is.

I pick up.

"Haneul, why aren't you home?"

Hearing her voice is kind of jarring, since I can't even remember the last time she talked to me.

I hurriedly fish for the best lie I can think of. "Lana had to run errands in LA, so she picked me up really early today. Sorry I forgot to tell you. I was in a rush to get ready."

"I see," she says. "The competition is almost over, isn't it? You should hurry up and finish so you can focus on your classes."

"Hurry up and finish . . ." I repeat slowly. It's amazing how few words it takes for me to wish Mom wasn't speaking to me again. "Are you saying I should get eliminated on purpose?"

"Well, aren't you tired of being on TV every week? You're not—"

I hang up. *Not today, Satan. Not today.*

I try to pretend like nothing's wrong, but Henry still asks, "Are you okay?"

I sigh. "It's fine. My mom's being a jerk as usual."

"She still doesn't support you?"

"Nope. She just told me I should drop out of the competition because she's sick of seeing me on TV."

Henry narrows his eyes. "She sounds a lot like my parents before I got my modeling contract."

"Ugh, sorry you have to deal with it too."

"It's fine. They're back in Korea, and I'm here."

We stop to get breakfast at a diner, and then Henry drives me to the studio.

"Have fun at rehearsal today," he says before he leaves.

"Thanks."

I don't think much about the fact that Henry just dropped me off until I enter the building and find everyone—the other four remaining contestants, the staff members, *and* the camera crew—staring at me. They must have seen Henry and me through the windows.

And of course, the cameras are already recording my every move.

"Did Henry Cho just drop you off?" Isabel asks. "Are you guys a thing now?"

The whispers spread. At first, I'm really daunted by the attention, and then I figure: *Why the heck not?* I have nothing to hide. Plus, thanks to the rumors, everyone and their mom already thinks we're going out anyway.

So, I shrug and say, "Yup. It's official now."

Everyone—well, everyone besides the girls who're glaring at me like I ran over their dogs—bursts into cheers. I lose count of the number of people who tell me congratulations. Their level of enthusiasm is actually kind of hilarious.

Thankfully, people lose interest in me as soon as Mr. Park and Gary get us started with this final practice. The challenge for the final round is straightforward: just perform the song that best showcases your abilities. No teams, no versus battles, no partners. Even still, everyone's too nervous about the final round being filmed *live* to socialize much.

When I'm alone in my practice room, I wish we were required to do something ridiculous, because just practicing alone without Lana to pop her head in or hang out with during breaks is really boring. I'm grateful for having made it this far, but I can't shake off my loneliness. In an attempt to get over it, I focus completely on my music for the next few hours. It's a cover of a song by a Korean girl group, but slowed down a bit so it sounds less peppy and more expressive. I'm hoping the judges—well, Mr. Park and Gary—and the viewers voting during the live show will give me extra brownie points for being creative.

As I'm running through the song again and again, I think about all the plus-size girls around the world who said I inspired them. It makes me happy and honored, but it also makes me want to try even harder, especially since I know what's to come in the episode that's dropping tonight.

Hopefully I'll make everyone proud in the end, I think. *Hopefully they'll keep watching after tonight's episode.*

Later, I'm back home, trying to work on my homework and making a point to *not* watch *You're My Shining Star*, when my phone rings. I cringe, hoping it's not Mom—who's not home from work yet—or my friends. I don't think I'm ready to deal with any of their reactions yet. But it's not either of them. Instead, it's Dad.

I pick up immediately.

"Hey, what's up?" I say.

"Skye! Skye! Did you hear?"

"About what?"

"Try Googling your name," he says.

"What?"

I'm still trying to process the fact that Dad told me to Google myself when I see the results.

Korean Adele Is Also an Amazing Dancer

Who Is This New Wonder Girl?

Skye Shin: Korea's Next K-Pop Superstar

My name appears in a lot of major Korean online news sites, and clips of me dancing with Henry are all over social media. But instead of just saying "girl dancing with Henry," the captions say my name, over and over again.

I go on Twitter. Someone's mentioned me in a tweet: What the hell? @newskye16 got eliminated? I call BS.

I expand the thread to look at the replies.

She was the best dancer in the competition! someone else says. I bet they just eliminated her because she's fat.

Wtf isn't that discrimination? That's illegal, isn't it?

The thread's getting more and more likes by the second. And it's already somehow hit a thousand likes. I check the time. It's been less than an hour since the episode aired.

I close the app on my phone and take a deep breath. Although I have no idea if a social media outcry will do anything, I'm so glad and thankful that these people are all in my corner.

"Are you still there?" Dad says, and I remember that he's still on the line.

"Yeah."

"People are getting angry that you got eliminated. Do you think that'll change anything?"

Since I really have no idea, I just say, "I don't know, Dad. Maybe."

"Whatever happens, I'm so proud of you," he says. "You're inspiring so many people! My little Skye, making a real change in this world. At just sixteen, too! I can't even imagine what you'll accomplish as an adult."

"Jeez, talk about pressure."

Dad laughs. I can almost see him wink. "I meant it in a good way. So proud."

"Thanks, Dad."

There's a lot of background noise where Dad is. I hear an announcement, someone paging a passenger for a Southwest Airlines flight.

"Are you headed back to NorCal?" I ask, feeling kind of sad like I always do whenever I don't get to spend much time with Dad on the weekends that he's home. That's one thing I really hate about this competition. Since I'm always so busy practicing and catching up on homework, I rarely get to see Dad when he's in town anymore.

"Yup," he replies. "I *would* stay until tomorrow, but we're working on a big project right now. Probably need to go into the office on Sunday."

"Ugh, gross, I'm so sorry," I say.

Dad laughs. "It's okay. I'm used to it. And besides, it's not like I have anyone waiting for me at home."

There's an awkward silence filled with nothing but airport noises, and I realize Dad never meant to say that last part out loud. I try to change the subject.

"Do you . . ." I trail off, trying to reel in the terror instantly builds up in my chest. "Do you know if Mom saw me getting eliminated from the dance competition?"

Dad doesn't respond for a few more seconds, and in the meantime, an announcement blares from the intercom. It's very faint, but I can hear the word "boarding."

"She told me she's really busy today," he says at last. His line becomes staticky, and I hear the rustle of people moving about, like Dad and the other passengers are getting on the plane. "But knowing her, she probably found time to watch it at some point. I already texted her to say she should be nice to you, but she hasn't responded yet."

I sigh. "Thanks for trying."

"No problem. I have to go now. Plane's going to depart soon. Talk to you when I land, and good luck."

"Okay, thanks, Appa. Have a safe flight."

We hang up, and in a tight ball of anxiety, I wait for Mom to come home.

Chapter Thirty-Three

MOM HAS A FIELD DAY ABOUT THE FACT THAT I was eliminated from the dance portion of the competition. She starts talking my ears off as soon as I get home, and she's still going on and on when we sit down for dinner.

"Well, it's for the best, Haneul," she says at last. "Singing really was your one true talent, and I'm so glad that you're still in the competition for it now."

I wish she could understand that I love singing and dancing equally. That even if I do only win this competition for vocals, I want to be the type of K-pop star who can sing *and* dance really well, so I can show everyone that big bodies aren't something to be afraid of. I grew up thinking someone my size could never dance. And I don't want the other kids watching at home to think that too.

All this is running through my head as I try—and fail—to keep eating my dinner.

Mom notices that I've stopped eating and says, "Why don't

you have an appetite? I made your favorite, beef soondubu. Did you finally start a diet?"

And that's when I decide that enough is enough. I may not be able to do anything about Bora disqualifying me from the dance part of the competition, but I can change what goes on in my own home.

"No, Mom," I say. Since I know she'll only dismiss me if I start to get emotional, I keep my voice flat and even. I sound strange and stiff to my own ears. "I lost my appetite because of the incredibly rude comments you made about my weight."

"Honey, I only want the best for you. When you're a parent yourself, you'll look back and feel grateful that I cared so much about you."

"Grateful? Mom, there is no way I'll ever be grateful for the things you've said to me throughout the years."

I think back to the Korean spa day, about how I burst into tears in front of Lana and Tiffany because Mom's words made me painfully self-conscious. Why can't my own mom, the person who claims that she loves and cares about me the most, see how much she's hurting me?

That's another type of abuse, Lana said that day. And the more I reflect on it, the more I realize she's right.

"All these years, you've told me that I'm not skinny or pretty enough. It's made me hate myself for most of my life. I've finally managed to love and accept myself, so why can't you just support me?'

"Support you? Haneul. Look at you. It's great that you

accept yourself, but no amount of accepting yourself is going to change how you really look. It's not going to change what people see when they look at you."

"Mom, there's nothing wrong with being fat. Just because you felt the need to change yourself because you were so afraid of other people doesn't mean I have to!"

Mom freezes. When she speaks again, her voice comes out in a whisper.

"Shin Haneul. What are you talking about?"

"Sally showed me the photos. I know what you looked like in middle school. You were fat, like me."

At the word "fat," Mom flinches back like I slapped her.

"I know you were bullied a lot when you were a kid," I continue when she doesn't say anything in response. "And I get that that made you afraid of how I look. But I am perfectly healthy and happy in my own skin. So please stop trying to change me."

Mom looks pained, but she otherwise doesn't react to anything I say. She doesn't insult me further, but she doesn't say she accepts me, either. Her silence speaks volumes.

By now, I'm crying like a baby. But instead of feeling like I'm breaking into pieces, I'm strangely calm inside. Crying doesn't feel like an act of defeat this time. It's more of a release. Because everything that happened in the last three months has been more than enough for me to stop caring about what other people think about me. And that includes Mom.

Instead of tearing me apart, her refusal to accept me sparks an idea in my head.

Despite my tears, my voice comes out strong and firm as I say, "I may have gotten disqualified from the dance portion of the competition, but I'll still prove to you that you're wrong. I'm going to make the entire world see that I'm beautiful and powerful just the way I am, and you're going to have to watch."

Mom's still staring at me openmouthed when I leave the room.

Later that night, I search YouTube for clips of Lana's and my performance. Although the *You're My Shining Star* channel just uploaded the video two hours ago, it already has two thousand views and counting. After watching it a few times, I find the clip of Henry and me dancing. This one was uploaded around the same time but has three times as many views.

The end of the second one is too painful to watch, so I always make sure to stop before that point in the video as I rewatch Henry's and my performance a few more times.

Then, I form a group text with Henry, Lana, and Tiffany.

Hey guys, I type. I need your help.

Chapter Thirty-Four

"I CAN'T WAIT TO SEE THE LOOK ON BORA'S FACE," Lana says on our way to the performance venue in downtown LA.

We're all sitting in Henry's Suburban, slowly creeping our way up Figueroa as we head toward the final round of *You're My Shining Star.* Unlike in the last few rounds, today's call time is in the late afternoon, and traffic is terrible. Luckily, we left early enough to not have to be in a huge rush.

"Do you guys really think this will work?" I ask. I try not to show it, but the nervousness creeps into my voice.

"It better," Tiffany says. "We worked way too hard for this."

"I think they'll probably be too busy to notice," Henry says. "Or at least, they won't bother. If they *do* make a big deal about it, I'll call Steve."

Steve holds up a victory sign from where he sits in the driver's seat. "Don't worry, Skye. I can think of a good distraction or two. I have a few tricks up my sleeve from my days as a bouncer in Vegas."

From the front seat, Portia giggles. I can't even imagine what sort of wild distraction Steve has in mind, so I just laugh along.

"Thanks, Steve," I say. "Thanks, everyone."

Everyone says some variation of "No problem," and I feel like the luckiest girl ever to have them all by my side.

Just then, I get a text.

REBECCA NGUYEN: Clarissa and I are on our way to the theater! So, so excited to see you perform!

I smile and reply back with several heart emojis.

Every final contestant received two guest tickets to give to family or friends. Dad's in Seattle again for a business trip, and I didn't even bother asking Mom. My school friends were an easy choice.

It was a risky decision, but in the end, I switched my song choice to a girl-power anthem by Ailee, my favorite Korean singer. People call Ailee the Korean Beyoncé (she was definitely the Korean Beyoncé *years* before anyone called *me* that), because of her fierceness and unbelievable vocal skills. She's exactly who I want to channel in my last performance of the competition.

Luckily, the dance that goes along with the song is pretty easy while still being really flashy. In other words, it's perfect for the plan that my friends and I have been working on for most of Thanksgiving break.

When we get to the concert venue, it's exactly like Henry

said. This is the only performance of the competition that's going to be broadcast live on TV, so things are ten times crazier than they usually are. Backstage, people are so busy running around to get ready that no one even gives us a second look. Henry gets a few glances, but they're fleeting at most. Most people ignore him, too.

The stage manager does a double take and glares at my friends when she sees that I'm not alone, but she doesn't shoo them away. Instead, sounding very frazzled, she says to me, "You're due to be onstage in two hours. Go to the dressing room for hair and makeup."

"I'll see you guys later," I say, waving at my friends.

"Good luck!" Lana winks and gives me an enthusiastic wave.

I take one last look at my friends before I hop into the dressing room. The three of them are on their phones with their backs against the walls, just chilling. Since they're staying still and minding their own business, everyone soon forgets that they're even there.

I'm so nervous that I barely register all the pulling and pushing as the hair and makeup ladies get me ready for the stage. Professional hair and makeup are apparently a perk that the remaining contestants and I get as members of the final five.

Since I'm trying to channel strong women like Beyoncé and Ailee, I ask for fierce eyeliner and bold, red lipstick, both things Mom always said I should avoid. I also change into a gold-sequined dress that hugs my curves and screams "Queen!" It not only makes me look and feel good but also catches the eye in a way that would be Mom's worst nightmare.

This whole night, in fact, is probably going to be her worst nightmare. But it's going to be for her own good. I really hope she watches the show tonight.

When I return backstage, Lana and Tiffany whistle.

"Wow, Skye!" Lana cries out. She takes my hand and twirls me around. "Look at those sequins! And those curves! You're glowing, baby!"

Henry stays quiet, and I'm almost hurt by his lack of a response when I notice that his mouth is slightly open. He's *actually* gaping at me, like guys do in the movies. He doesn't even blink, so I'm getting a little concerned when he snaps out of it and finally says, "You look amazing, Skye. I mean, you always look amazing, but . . . wow."

Tiffany gives Henry a playful shove. "Stop drooling and get out of the way, lover boy."

Henry lets Lana and Tiffany pass, but when I come near him, he gently grabs my arms and pulls me into a hug. And then we're kissing, not full-blown making out, but enough to leave me breathless.

"You're gonna get glitter all over you!" I exclaim when we finally stop.

He smirks. "Do I look like I care? That kiss was totally worth it."

I laugh. "Priorities, I guess."

"Exactly. Good luck tonight, Skye. And no matter what the outcome is . . . I'm so proud of you. I have no doubt that you're going to wow everyone. They are *not* ready for you."

"Aw, thanks."

I give him a peck on the cheek, and he blushes.

Henry then gives me some space so I can warm up before going onstage. Time seems to pass way too quickly, and in almost no time at all, the stage manager hisses, "Skye! Go onstage in five . . . four . . ."

I glance over at Henry, and he gives me a reassuring smile. I prepare to walk onstage, with Lana and Tiffany standing slightly behind me. They still look like they're busy on their phones, and not like they're about to come onstage with me.

Which, of course, is *exactly* what they're about to do.

"Three . . . two . . . one. Go!"

When I go onstage, I'm overwhelmed by a loud rush of noise and light. The competition committee really stepped up the game with this last round, and it looks like they have five times more lights than they usually do. They also hired a live band.

The crowd goes wild when they see me, and I hear chants of "Queen Skye! Queen Skye!"

"Hey! You can't go out there!"

There's some commotion behind me, but Henry blocks the stagehands so Lana and Tiffany can stumble out onstage to join me. The audience gasps in confusion. But it's too late for anyone to do anything because at that moment, the trumpet players blast out the opening of my song. It worked!

Lana and Tiffany immediately jump into action, dancing in sync behind me as I move across the stage. I don't have to glance back to know how awesome they look. We've been dancing together almost every day of this week in Henry's practice room.

I start singing, and people gasp at the sheer power of my voice. All the worries and anxieties of the past few weeks drop from my shoulders as I dance along with Lana and Tiffany, all while never singing a wrong note.

The live band gets really into it, and I break away from Tiffany and Lana to groove with them. The entire time, I'm smiling at the camera and also at the judges, who stare at me with obvious shock in their eyes.

Bora looks visibly pissed. She's angrily whispering in the ear of one of the staff members, but he only shakes his head.

Good, I think. I hope he told her that she can't stop me.

Meanwhile, the crowd is going wild. They even sing along with the oohs and aahs in the chorus as I belt out the notes, and everyone's bobbing up and down to the music. When it's time for the instrumental solo, Lana, Tiffany, and I dance in formation. And the crowd only gets louder.

I break away from my friends again to go back-to-back with one of the trumpet players. I match each of his soaring notes with notes of my own.

The song is essentially a breakup song, but it's also about showing the world that you don't need anyone and don't care about what haters do or think. And that's exactly what I'm going for. Looking directly at Bora, I puncture through my last high note, letting my vibrato take over my voice.

The auditorium practically shakes with all of the noise the audience is making. Bora and Mr. Park try to calm everyone down, but they're relentless, screaming and chanting, "Queen Skye! Queen Skye!" over and over again.

Davey comes out onto the stage and waves his hands at the crowd. "Whoa, whoa, whoa! Settle down, everyone. It's time to hear the judges' comments!"

Even then, it takes a few more minutes for everyone to be quiet.

"Well," Mr. Park says with a cough when we can finally make out what he's saying. "You certainly know how to throw a surprise, Miss Shin."

"Tell me about it," says Gary. "What an awesome turn of events."

"On the contrary," Bora cuts in. "I would not say it's 'awesome.' Not in the slightest. Miss Shin, you just broke the rules. You selfishly gave yourself an unfair advantage over everyone else. You deserve to be disqualified."

Several people boo, although I'm not sure if they're booing at me or at Bora.

"What, like the way I was disqualified from the dance portion for some rule that didn't even exist?" I snap back at her. "First, I wasn't 'professional' enough for you. Now you have to make up another rule to disqualify me here, too?"

There are some oohs from the audience, and this time, it's clear whose side everyone is on. Bora's lips curl.

"You can disqualify me again, Bora," I continue. "But I just want everyone to know that there are no official rules saying contestants aren't allowed to refute judges when they make unfair, discriminatory comments. And there aren't any rules saying that contestants can't bring in backup dancers or dance while singing during their performances. I checked. There *are*, however, rules against bullying."

Bora narrows her eyes. "What are you implying?"

"Man, she got you good," Gary says with a laugh. "Come on, Bora. Look at them!" He gestures at not just me, but also at Tiffany and Lana, who are still trying to catch their breath. "This probably took them a whole lot of extra work. And that level of dedication is amazing."

Mr. Park, who's been silently watching us the entire time, finally speaks up again. "So, tell me, Miss Shin. What made you decide to step up the game like this? Was there any special reason? You must have had one, because this could not have been easy. You weren't even officially given the time to practice the dance. And my records indicate that this isn't the song you originally said you would perform."

I smile at the camera as I respond. "I just wanted to make my last performance here in LA a memorable one."

I'm careful not to say last performance, period, since I'm not ruling out the chance that I'll be able to perform in Korea.

"I see. Well, congratulations. You definitely succeeded in making it memorable."

Davey jumps in. "If Skye is your favorite to win, let us know on social media with the hashtag 'QueenSkye'! And if you haven't already, please remember to vote, vote, vote for your favorite member of the final five before polls close at the end of the last performance. Give it up for Skye Shin!"

The crowd roars again, and Lana, Tiffany, and I all rush off the stage with large, beaming smiles on our faces.

Backstage, I run right into Henry's arms.

"You were amazing," he says. "Look."

He shows me his phone, which is playing the official live-stream of the competition. Multiple new messages appear in the comments every second. Although there are still a few pig emojis and mean messages here and there, most people say I was fantastic and deserve to win. The broadcast switches to the scoreboard. It live-updates with the number of people who've texted to vote for me from all across the world. I have the most points out of all the competitors so far.

He switches over to Twitter and Instagram, where already, people have started posting screenshots and videos of me. And that's not all. There are also countless posts by fat girls saying things like, "She's my shero! #QueenSkye" and "#QueenSkye inspired me to love myself!"

My heart feels so full that I start to cry. It's one thing to see people post things weeks after the fact, but it's a whole other experience to see people all over the world reacting just minutes after I performed.

"You did it," Henry says gently. "I'm so proud of you."

"The results aren't finalized yet. Congratulate me later!"

"Okay, I'll congratulate you now *and* later."

Since they aren't announcing the winners until the end of the night, I hang out in the green room with the other finalists, watching the dancers on TV. Everyone's too anxious about their own performances to talk much, and I'm honestly grateful for the silence. My heart is racing from the nervous anticipation of finding out not just how I'll do but also how everyone else will do as well. I can't even look at my phone anymore.

The only two people still in the competition I'm really invested in are Henry and Imani, and they both do amazing. Henry delivers a killer cover of Stray Kids' "District 9" that makes me so happy, especially since he actually looks like he's having a blast onstage.

But the real star of the show is Imani, who blows everyone out of the water with her rendition of ACE's "Cactus." The choreography for "Cactus" is complex, requiring several changes in tempo and precise break-dancing moves that the dancer has to rapidly execute while traveling across the stage. Imani does all that *and* flawlessly conveys the emotion in the lyrics, bringing a few people to tears. She's a ten, while everyone else is a five.

The audience gives her a standing ovation, and I feel so much pride for how amazing she is. People always discredit girl dancers in K-pop, saying that they can only do easier choreographies, but Imani is a testament to how girls can dance better than even the original boy band members.

And then finally, it's time for the results. We're all escorted back onstage, and all the dancers stand in one group while I stand in another group with the singers. I share looks with both Henry and Imani, and we silently wish each other luck.

Henry turns out to be right. At a whopping *one hundred* points ahead of everyone else, I win the vocal portion of *You're My Shining Star.* And like I thought she would, Imani wins the dance portion.

Imani and I give each other a big hug as the auditorium erupts with applause. Happy tears stream down from both our eyes as we stand side by side onstage with our crowns. Glittery, star-shaped balloons drop down from the sky, and for a brief moment, I'm surrounded by light.

Everyone in the auditorium cheers for us, even Mr. Park. Bora, however, is nowhere to be seen.

"I heard she got fired for bullying you," Imani whispers in my ear. "And for trying to influence another judge."

Before I can even dwell on that, the cameras surround us, and Davey pushes the mic into my face.

"You first, Skye," he says. "Some words of reflection on your win?"

I stare out at the flashing lights of the cameras and cell phones and say, "This is for middle school Skye, who was told by other people that she wasn't capable of following her dreams. This is also for all the other girls out there who are told every day that they can't do something just because of what they look like. If I can do this, then you can achieve your dreams too."

Davey claps, and then moves on to Imani.

"This is for all the Black girls out there who love K-pop," she says. "So much of the fandom—and even some of the stars—hate us, instead of thinking about how much we contribute to the community. Well, it's time for a change, and I'm going to try my best to make it happen. I'll make you proud. Just watch me."

The audience cheers as Davey hands each of us a trophy and a white envelope.

"Skye Shin and Imani Stevens," he says. "Congratulations on winning *You're My Shining Star*. Inside your envelopes, you will find a plane ticket to South Korea, where you'll have the chance to enter PTS Entertainment as two of their trainees in June of next year."

By then, I'm crying so much that I can barely read what's on the ticket. But I'm beyond caring right now.

I look out into the cameras, hoping Mom is watching back home.

Chapter Thirty-Five

DAD FACETIMES ME AS SOON AS I'M BACKSTAGE. The connection is really bad, so I can barely make out what he's saying. And I just see random flashes of Dad and his very confused-looking coworkers. From what I can tell, they're out for dinner. But I guess that didn't stop Dad from keeping tabs on the final round of the competition.

The audio sounds a bit like this: "AHHHHH! Skye . . . so proud . . . here's Tim . . . and Jacob . . . AHHHHHHH!"

I never knew Dad's voice could go that high, but I guess I had to get it from somewhere.

As soon as I hang up, Lana and Tiffany rush over to give me a big hug. I'm a sobbing mess as I say, "I couldn't have done any of this without you guys. Thank you so much."

"You deserve *everything*!" Lana says. "Thanks for giving Tiffany and me a final moment to shine. It was so fun."

"Definitely a good way to spend our last night in LA," adds Tiffany.

"You guys are leaving tomorrow?" I feel a sudden wave of sadness as I realize the full implications of this competition ending. I'll see Imani again in Korea, and I'll hang out with Henry here in LA, but when will I see Lana and Tiffany again?

"Aw, don't be sad!" Lana says. "Not on your big day, at least. NorCal really isn't that far from LA. You should visit us in the Bay Area when you have the chance! You can just stay with your dad, right?"

I nod and hug them even more tightly, making promises to see them again.

Clarissa and Rebecca ambush me the moment I exit backstage, crying and cheering.

"OH MY GOD!" exclaims Rebecca, while Clarissa screams, *"Queen!"*

Clarissa gets so excited that she almost whacks me with the bouquet of pink flowers that she and Rebecca brought me. I laugh, my body shaking from both relief and whatever's left of my adrenaline from performing onstage.

We're in a tight group hug when someone clears his throat behind us. I don't even have to look to know who it is. My friends' wide-eyed expressions say it all.

"Hey," Henry says. "It's nice to meet you. I'm Henry Cho."

I always thought Clarissa would scream and completely lose it when she finally met Henry, but what actually happens is a bit more concerning. She just stands there, her face white as a sheet. Rebecca's not faring any better, but she manages to snap out of it and say, "Sorry you lost. I thought you were really great, though."

Henry shrugs good-naturedly. "Imani was way, way better. She totally deserves it. And I had fun, which is more than I could have ever expected from all of this."

My friends look puzzled, but I know exactly what he means. And I'm really happy for him. Henry came into this competition because he was angry at someone but came out of it truly enjoying himself.

Henry's eyes focus on me then, and his gaze softens. He approaches me, and I let go of my friends so Henry can wrap me in a big hug.

"Hey, you," he whispers. "Congratulations. See? I knew you'd win."

It's only when I see my friends' shocked reactions over Henry's shoulder that I realize I forgot to tell them a very important detail.

"Oops." I let go of Henry and give my friends a nervous smile. "Um, yeah, so . . . surprise! You guys were right. Henry and I are dating now . . . for real. It's not just for the show."

"Skye!" Clarissa yells, at the same time Rebecca asks, "Since when?"

And then, I can't help it. I laugh until tears come out of my eyes.

The house is quiet when I walk through the front door. The lights are out, so I have no way of knowing if anyone's even home. Which is weird, since it's past ten. Mom's usually home by now.

"Mom?" I call out. It occurs to me that she might not respond, even if she's home. She went back to giving me the silent treatment after our fight at the dinner table.

Of course, I knew I couldn't expect the same kind of recognition that Dad gave me earlier from Mom, but still, I expected . . . *something*.

In the end, I find Mom out in the garden, tending to the bushes. I don't question why she's gardening when it's pitch-dark and cold. It's pretty obvious from the timing that she's trying to avoid me.

At first, I think she didn't hear me approach. But then she says, "So, you did it."

Her voice is strangely flat, and for a second, I wonder if I should turn back and hope she goes back to ignoring me again. A cold shoulder is better than whatever bitter words she might have for me after my win.

"Y-yeah," I say, and I hate how my voice breaks. But I can't help it. I'm all tensed up around her, unsure what to expect next.

"I saw your performance. You did a great job."

"Thanks."

I don't let my guard down. I'm still waiting for a "but."

But that dress was very unflattering on you.

But you didn't have to dance.

But your friends were prettier than you.

My mind is swimming with so many "buts" that by the time she actually continues talking, I don't catch what she says.

"Wait, sorry, what did you say?"

"I said, 'Congratulations on the win.' You were far better than anyone else in that competition. Honestly, some of the others had zero talent. I questioned the judging calls on that show sometimes."

"Wait," I say again. I know I'm probably just asking for it now, but I can't help but prolong this moment. "You liked my performance?"

"Yes. I thought it was very . . . innovative. That Bora gave you such a hard time, but Gary was right. You're the one that took the initiative to bring in your friends and include dance choreography."

"And you liked my dancing?"

Mom stills. I know I've pushed my luck too far. All my walls come back up again.

"You're a good dancer, Haneul," she says finally. Her voice is tense, like she's trying extra hard to keep a neutral tone. "You always have been. Besides, you did what you promised you would do. You showed me and everyone else in the world that you could win this. And here we are now. Congratulations. Your dad and I both voted for you."

"Thanks."

Whenever I pictured this moment, I always imagined a big, shameful look on my mom's face, counterbalanced by my own smug grin. But instead of feeling smug, I still feel pretty sad.

And Mom looks anything but ashamed. She actually looks kind of proud of me, in her own restrained kind of way.

Everything still feels surreal, like I'm not really awake. And this conversation seems more fake than me winning the competition.

"I do admit that I was very hard on you," Mom continues when I don't say anything else. "I always wanted perfection from you, I admit that. And you're right, part of that has to do with my own upbringing and the things I experienced as a child. Your dad and I actually had a long conversation on the phone about this before you came home."

I half expect her to apologize for all the cruel things she's said to me in the last couple of years. But she resumes gardening like I'm not there.

I'm about to go back inside when she asks, "So, when is your flight to Korea?"

"Not until summer. I think they're trying to be considerate of students like me."

"Good. Now you can focus on school. But you know, if the training goes well, you might have to stay in Korea long-term. You know that, right? Then, you'll probably have to be homeschooled or transfer to one of the high schools near the company as you continue your training."

My heart beats faster just thinking about it. Living in Korea long-term is something I never even thought of in my wildest dreams. But it's a new adventure I'm ready for. "I know."

She looks back at me again. There aren't tears in her eyes

like there are in mine, but her expression softens a tiny bit.

"Like I told you before, I *am* proud of you," she says. "I'm sorry if I ever sounded like I was otherwise."

Part of me knows she's only saying all of this now because I won, but I just decide to take it as it is. Maybe I didn't need her approval, after all. I know my worth, now more than ever. If this is all I'm ever going to get from her, then so be it.

"Thanks," I say again.

I don't say, "Thanks for believing in me," or "Thanks for always being there for me," because we both know those words would just be lies. That's not the kind of relationship I have with Mom. It's time that I finally accepted it.

Chapter Thirty-Six

THE NEXT MORNING, HENRY SURPRISES ME BY showing up at my house.

"We're going to Santa Monica."

"What, really? But it's still really cold out."

I don't mention it, but even the slightest mention of the beach brings back painful memories of Mom telling me I should have gotten a "summer body" before I went down to the beach.

He rolls his eyes. "It's sixty degrees. In non-SoCal measures, it's perfectly good weather. Besides, it's not like we're going into the water. It'll be fun, I promise."

Traffic to Santa Monica is so bad that by the time we get there, it's past noon and I've caught up on all my friends' Instagram stories. Rebecca and Clarissa are having brunch in Malibu (#tfti), Imani is at Big Bear celebrating with her family, and Lana and Tiffany are driving back up to NorCal, blasting old-school Korean hip-hop with the car windows down.

Seeing that my friends are having a good day is enough to make me happy, or at least it is until the cars come to a total standstill. We're just blocks away from the beach. The road is basically one long parking lot.

"Let's go to the beach, he said," I grumble. "It'll be fun, he said."

"Don't be ridiculous," Henry laughs. "Come on, we can walk from here. Maybe ten minutes max?"

After saying goodbye to Steve and Portia, we walk the remainder of the way. Like Henry said, it only takes ten minutes to reach our destination.

Santa Monica is as LA as a beach can get. Under the cloudless blue sky, the pier itself is crowded with people fishing, taking pictures, or going into the shops and restaurants. Musicians busk with their guitars and drums, while food carts sell hot dogs and other snacks. And towering over everything is the Ferris wheel, painted in bright red and yellow tones to match the rest of the rides.

In the midst of the hustle and bustle, seagulls fly closely overhead. They occasionally land right in front of us with expressions demanding food, even though Henry and I aren't eating anything.

"So," I say. "We're here. What do you want to do?"

"Let's go up in the Ferris wheel," he says. "I heard the view is amazing. Come on, my treat."

"That's like the most clichéd thing to do here, but okay."

I, of course, don't tell Henry about the many times I've fantasized about riding the Ferris wheel on a date. It'd just be too embarrassing.

When we reach it, I expect Henry to go ahead and get our tickets. But instead, he motions me over.

"Here, let's take a picture together. Just to have something to remember this day by."

I'm about to lean in closer when a girl exclaims, "Look! It's Skye Shin and Henry Cho!"

She and her two friends approach us. At first, I think they're all going to ask Henry for his autograph, but then, they hold out their pens and their Santa Monica brochures to *me*.

"Can you please sign this?" says the first girl. "You're such a big inspiration to me. I've struggled for such a long time to love my body and . . . well, seeing you on *You're My Shining Star* totally changed my life."

"Same," says one of the girl's friends. "I was bullied so much in school, and after a while the haters really got to me, you know? I don't know anything about K-pop but I saw those clips of you standing up to that judge on Twitter. You're *amazing*."

The girls circled around me are of varying sizes and shapes. From skinny to fat, they're all so beautiful.

"Sure," I say. "I'd be happy to give you guys my autograph."

Henry, meanwhile, seems pretty content with being in the back. He snaps a few photos of me signing the girls' pamphlets.

"Queen Skye in action," he says with a proud grin.

After the girls leave, Henry switches his phone to selfie mode so he can take a picture of the two of us.

"Actually," I say. "Here, let me."

Seeing the girls gave me an idea. I get out my phone and snap a picture of us.

"I'm going to post this," I say. "And you can repost it to your Instagram. Or Portia can, whatever."

Henry blinks. "Are you sure?"

"Yup," I say. "It's time I stopped hiding from everyone on social media."

Henry's mouth widens into his full lopsided grin. He looks like a little kid who woke up to find a Christmas tree full of presents.

"Let's take *all* the cute pics!" he yells.

I have to laugh at his enthusiasm. "God," I say. "No wonder you have so many followers on Instagram."

By the time we're done taking pictures around the pier—with occasional breaks to sign stuff for people who recognize us from *You're My Shining Star*—the sun is setting on the horizon.

"Okay," Henry says. "*Now* let's go up on the Ferris wheel."

Even in the reddish-orange glow of the setting sun, the neon pink and blue lights of the ride shine bright against the darkening sky. It looks like something out of a fairy-tale book. While Henry gets our tickets, I take a quick picture of it. Then, I post all the good photos of us, the Ferris wheel, and the pier to my Instagram, tagging Henry in the post.

When we're sitting across from each other on the ride, Henry sheepishly says, "I know you said this is one of the most clichéd things to do here on a date, but I've always wanted to come up here with someone I care about."

"Okay, but same."

He laughs. "Good. Then I'm not the only one crossing off a bucket list item today."

Henry leans over to kiss me, and soon we're making out as the wheel slowly takes us higher in the air.

When our car reaches the very top, Henry pulls away with a smile. "Look outside. You're going to love the view."

Now that the sun's gone down, the entire pier is lit with all sorts of bright lights. They look tiny, like neon-colored fairy lights. But everything is still really pretty.

It's too dark to see the ocean around us, but I can hear the gentle whisper of the waves below us. And the cool ocean breeze feels so nice that I close my eyes.

"I honestly can't believe any of this is real," I say.

Henry gently grabs my hand. "It's real. And it's all thanks to you. You worked really hard, you got yourself through the competition, and you inspired so many people. You're amazing, Skye."

"You know that's probably the billionth time you've called me amazing, right?"

"I can't help it." He's closer now, his face inches away from mine. "It's true."

And then we're kissing again, gently and softly at first, but then long and hard, until we have to stop to catch our breath.

I tell him the words I couldn't say to Mom. "Thanks for believing in me for all this time."

"Of course. I'm going to keep believing in you. Because you're—"

I laugh. "Amazing, I know."

He lightly taps my nose. "No. This time, I was going to say fabulous."

I let out a laugh. "Really?"

"Just kidding. I was actually going to say you're an extremely hard worker. You work harder than anyone I know."

We snuggle against each other until the Ferris wheel car descends back to the ground.

"I'm honestly really worried about what'll happen in Korea," I say as we get out. "What if hard work's not enough? There are probably so many people out there who think like Bora."

"Well," Henry says in an incredible impression of Steve that makes me giggle, "I can always call them and give them a good talking—"

I laugh and lightly smack his arm. "Stop it, that was so good it was actually kind of scary. I eventually figured out what to do with this competition, so I guess I can figure it out in Korea, too."

"There you go. If it makes you feel any better, when I first started modeling, I had no idea if things were going to work out for me, either. Sometimes you just have to take that leap of faith."

"Okay, thanks."

Henry holds out his hand, and I take it.

We slowly walk down the brightly lit pier in comfortable silence while little kids rush up and down it, nearly running into us. It feels like I'm living out a scene in a Korean drama.

"Besides," Henry finally says when we reach the end, "you'll have me there with you for moral support."

"Wait, what?"

He holds up his phone. On the screen is a round-trip ticket to Korea.

"You didn't!"

He shrugs. "I have family there, remember? I can just crash with them over the summer while you're there."

"I thought you hated your family. Actually, don't go. Your parents sound terrible."

Panic flashes across my mind as I think about what they did to Henry.

His eyes get a faraway look, but then he squeezes my hand tighter. "Yeah . . . but seeing how you stood up against Bora made me realize something. And hearing about you and your mom."

I spent a good part of last night giving Henry the play-by-play on what happened with Mom after the final round.

"Realize what?" I ask.

"I can't just keep running away. They're my family, so I have to deal with them sooner or later. They probably won't ever accept me for who I am, but I can try my best on my end so that when it's time to let go, I can make peace with myself and say that I tried."

I pull him into a hug.

"If you're sure," I say.

"I'm sure."

We only stop walking when we reach the edge of the beach. The sounds of voices and laughter are faint now, nearly swallowed up by the soft roar of waves crashing onto the shore.

"When's the last time you visited Korea?" Henry asks, looking out at the Pacific Ocean.

"I haven't been since I was little. Once I hit puberty, my mom became too ashamed of my size to take me to see our family."

It's something I haven't told anyone, and the rawness of my voice makes Henry squeeze my hand tight.

"I'm sorry."

"It is what it is. But for what it's worth, my mom seems oddly excited for me to go there now. She's even insisting on traveling back with me. Probably because she has something to brag about."

"Probably."

"But you know what? Yesterday, I realized that I don't really care about what she thinks anymore. My mom is who she is. But I can still change myself and what sort of impact I have on other people. So I'm going to try to become stronger as a person and keep having a positive impact on people, like I have here."

"I have complete faith that you will."

We look out at the ocean for a bit longer, until it becomes too chilly for comfort.

I check to see if Henry's looking in my direction. He's not.

"Still think it isn't cold?"

I kick the water so it splashes onto his leg. I don't stick around long enough to see his reaction, but I hear him curse as I run.

"Are you kidding me! Why, you little—"

He starts chasing me, and soon, we're both laughing as we run across the sand, headed back toward the lights of the pier. Henry's a faster runner than I thought he'd be, and he catches up with me in almost no time at all.

"Got you!"

We crash into a pile on the sand. Henry somehow ends up on top of me, and although it's too dark for me to clearly see his face, I'm pretty sure he's blushing. And that's all it takes for me to kiss him, again and again.

When we stop, Henry gets up and gently pulls me up with him. Most of the sand falls off my body when I stand, though some of it sticks to my skin. But I don't care. The kisses were worth it.

Henry texts Portia, and we're walking back to the parking lot when I remember the pictures I posted right before we rode the Ferris wheel.

"Wait, let me check Instagram."

Henry groans. "You're becoming one of us."

But he lets me check it anyway. My post already has five hundred likes and counting, with strangers leaving comments like they did on Henry's. I recently took my Instagram off private mode, and my account has been exploding with new followers ever since.

I scroll through the comments, which are mostly nice. But there are still some pig emojis and other disgusting comments.

But unlike before, the comments don't really make me sad. Sure, they still hurt—I'd be lying if I said they didn't. But the pain is nothing compared to the bone-crushing shame I felt the first time I saw similar comments on Henry's Instagram.

"Sorry, Skye," Henry says. "I shouldn't have suggested taking photos—"

"No," I cut in. "I'm fat. People think it means I should hate myself, and when I don't, it makes them uncomfortable. But this is just another part of who I am, and I'm *happy* with who I am."

Henry smiles, like he finally understands what I'm getting at.

"You're living your best life," he says. "They're not."

"Exactly."

And then, in front of the fairy-tale lights of the Santa Monica pier, I pull Henry in for another kiss.

Acknowledgments

Writing this book was one of the hardest things I've ever done, and I couldn't have done it without the amazing people in my life.

First and foremost, I'd like to thank my parents. Thank you for not batting an eye when fourth-grade me first said I wanted to be a writer, but also thank you for advising me to pursue other, more practical career paths (lol). In the end, all my eclectic experiences made me into the writer I am today. We've had a long journey together with many ups and downs, and I am grateful for your support today.

Second, I would like to thank my friends, who were so supportive from the moment I started writing this book. Aneeqah, I've already told you countless times about how vital our writing dates were to my process. Thank you for pushing me to be a better writer (as well as a more outgoing one, as my "unofficial publicist"). Thank you also to Brianna Lei, Anita Chen, Francesca Flores, Rebecca Kuang, Becca Mix, Katie Zhao,

Anusha Naeem, Andrew Su, and everyone else who read early versions of this book. Your encouragement and feedback were vital to this book in more ways than I can say. Thank you also to the #magicsprintingsquad, for giving me the family I always wanted in publishing. Here's hoping we have many more retreats.

It takes an entire team to make a story into a real, physical book, and I'm so grateful for the people who were involved in the process of making mine. A huge thank-you goes to my agent, Penny Moore, who read through several of my manuscripts and went bravely to battle with each one until we found not one, but two (!) that stuck. Thank you for not giving up on me, for always being there for me, and for being enthusiastic about all my zany projects. And thank you to Mabel Hsu, my editor, who called this book her "dream project." Thank you always for your sharp eye and wise insight. Here's to both of our dreams coming true. Thank you also to Molly Fehr, Amy Ryan, Michael Frost, and Tanya Murray Frost for giving *I'll Be the One* the perfect cover and design, and to Nicole Moreno, Gweneth Morton, Kristin Eckhardt, Aubrey Churchward, Sabrina Abballe, and Tanu Srivastava for providing additional support.

Although I have tangentially related experiences that informed the writing of this book, I am not a K-pop star, nor am I plus-size. A special thanks to Dong-geun "Donny" Han, for sitting down with me in your studio one summer night in

Seoul to give me insight on your K-pop competition and industry experiences. Thank you also to Sophia Carter-Kahn and April K. Quioh, the cocreators of the *She's All Fat* podcast, for their discussions on the plus-size experience and the importance of radical self-love. I can never recommend their funny, brilliant, and super-important podcast enough. Additionally, I would like to thank Sarah Taphom and Min Trindade for their insight.

I'd like to also give a special shout-out to the many artists whose music is the underlying heartbeat of this book. This book wouldn't have existed without the K-pop dance rabbit hole I fell into during one of the darkest periods of my life. Dance and K-pop got me through that time, and pop music in general fueled me for the countless hours that I worked on this book. It'd be impossible to list all the artists I listened (and danced!) to during the writing of this book, but I want to especially thank the queens of pop who came together to form Skye's character, namely: CLC, Lee Hi, Ariana Grande, Heize, Sunmi, Blackpink, Momoland, Lady Gaga, Beyoncé, Dua Lipa, Chungha, Yeseo, Sia, and Ailee. You gave Skye her confidence and her voice, as well as a passion for the stage that was so tangible that I could feel it as if it were my own.

Lastly, thank you to my grandfathers, both of whom I lost during the time I worked on this book. Thank you for always encouraging me to read and write since I was a little kid, and thank you for your love of storytelling, which in turn gave rise to mine. Even though I was unable to write my books fast enough for you to read them, I know you're watching over me from wherever you are now. I'm eternally grateful for all the summers we spent together, and for the shared memories and laughs. 사랑해요.